Love's Taming

The Love's Series

By
Maryann Jordan

Love's Taming
Copyright © 2014 Maryann Jordan
Print Edition

This book is a work of fiction. Names, characters, places, and incidents either are products of the author's imagination or are used fictitiously. Any resemblance to actual persons, living or dead, events, or locales is entirely coincidental.

Cover Design by: Kari Ayasha, Cover to Cover Designs
covertocoverdesigns.com

Cover Photography: Mandy Hollis, MHPhotography
Cover Models: Steven Preston and Mandy Hollis
Editor: Shannon Brandee Eversoll

ISBN 978-0-9916522-7-3

Dedication

This book is dedicated to a group of fellow indie authors who have joined with me, whose sole purpose is to support each other, rally behind each other, nudge each other along, and most importantly...become my friends. We share suggestions, promote each other's work selflessly, and have immense respect for our diverse talents.

The laughter we share lasts long beyond our sales. To MJ Nightingale, Andrea Michelle, Andie M. Long, EJ Shortall, V.L. Brock, Jen Andrews, Sandee Love, A.D. Ellis, M.L. Steinbrunn: you all have my devotion, my heart, and my love. The IEZ ladies absolutely rock!

Acknowledgements

First and foremost, I have to thank my husband, Michael. Always believing in me and wanting me to pursue my dreams, this book would not be possible without his support. To my daughters, MaryBeth and Nicole, I taught you to follow your dreams and now it is time for me to take my own advice. You two are my inspiration. Also, special thanks goes to my daughter, MaryBeth, who is a veterinarian and gave technical assistance to the story.

My best friend, Tammie, who for eighteen years has been with me through thick and thin. You've filled the role of confidant, supporter, and sister.

My dear friend, Myckel Anne, who keeps me on track, keeps me grounded, and most of all – keeps my secrets. Thank you for not only being my proofreader, but my friend.

Going from blogger to author has allowed me to have the friendship and advice of several wonderful authors who always answered my questions, helped me over rough spots, and cheered me on. To Kristine Raymond, you gave me the green light when I wondered if I was crazy and you never let me give up. MJ Nightingale and Andrea Michelle – you two have made a huge impact on my life. EJ Shorthall, Victoria Brock,

Jen Andrews, Andrea Long, A.d. Ellis, ML Steinbrunn, Sandee Love, thank you from the bottom of my heart.

My beta readers kept me sane, cheered me on, found all my silly errors, and often helped me understand my characters through their eyes. A huge thank you to Denise VanPlew, Sandi Laubhan, Barbara Martoncik, Tera Northcutt, Kayla McCoy, Vanessa Spradling, Jennifer Alumbaugh, Anna Mychals, Danielle Petersen, Amber Vaughn, Shannon Brandee, Leeann Wright, and Tracey Markin for being my beta girls who love alphas!

Shannon Brandee Eversoll as my editor and Myckel Anne Phillips as my proofreader gave their time and talents to making Love's Taming as well written as it can be.

My street team, The Ladies of Fairfield, you all are amazing! You volunteer your time to promote my books and I cannot thank you enough! I hope you will stay with me, because I have lots more stories inside, just waiting to be written!

My Personal Assistants Amber Vaughn and Barbara Martoncik are the two women that keep me going when I feel overwhelmed and I am so grateful for not only their assistance, but their friendship.

This is the fourth book cover that Kari Ayasha from Cover to Cover Designs has created for me and her talent is evident in every detail. Thank you for working with me. This cover utilizes the amazing talents of Mandy Hollis (photographer from MHPhotography) and model Steven Preston. I thank all of them for capturing my idea and making it a reality.

As the owner of the blog, Lost in Romance Books, I know the selflessness of bloggers. We promote indie authors on our own time because we believe fully in the indie author community. I want to thank the many bloggers that I have served with, and who are assisting in promoting my series.

Most importantly, thank you readers. You allow me into your home for a few hours as you disappear into my characters and you support me as I follow my indie author dreams.

Author Information

Maryann Jordan

I am an avid reader of romance novels, often joking that I cut my teeth on the old bodice rippers. I have been reading and reviewing for years. In 2013, I created the blog, Lost in Romance Books to promote and showcase indie authors. In 2014, I finally gave in to the characters in my head, screaming for their story to be told. From these musings, my first novel, Emma's Home, The Fairfield Series Book 1 was born.

I am a high school counselor having worked in education for thirty years. I live in Virginia, having also lived in four states and two foreign countries. I have been married to a wonderfully patient man for thirty two years and am the mother to two adult daughters. When writing, my dog or one of my four cats can generally be found in the same room if not on my lap.

Please take time to leave a review of this book (on Goodreads). Reviews are the lifeline for indie authors.

Feel free to contact me, especially if you enjoyed my book. I love to hear from readers!

Facebook:
http://www.facebook.com/authormaryannjordan

Facebook:
http://www.facebook.com/lostinromancebooks

Booktropolous:
https://booktropoloussocial.com/index.php?do=/profile-1765/

Email:
authormaryannjordan@gmail.com

Email:
lostinromancebooks@gmail.com

Blog:
http://www.lostinromancebooks.com

Chapter 1

THE ILLUMINATION FROM the dim street lights provided little guidance, but perfect cover for the man slipping through the darkness. Staying close to the shadows next to the brick buildings, he carried his heavy load, watching carefully around for signs of life in the alley he dodged into. He knew his destination. He'd been watching her for weeks, knowing that at some point the time would be right. It hadn't been hard – watching her. She was beautiful, but her skills were what he needed. *Yeah, keep telling yourself that. She's fuckin' gorgeous.* His mind drifted to watching her in the neighborhood. Nice. Sweet. Wholesome. Clean. *Not for you, man. Not where you've gone and what you've seen. Fuck!* Rubbing his hand over his face, feeling the rough stubble of his unshaven face, he locked those thoughts down. *It's a job. Just do your fuckin' job.* Looking down at the bundle in his arms, he wondered how long he would have to wait before making his next move. I've got to get her when she's alone. Knowing her routine, it wouldn't be hard to do that. *Jesus, a woman alone, keeping the same routine.* In another world, he would have protected her. Made sure she was safe. Now, she was just a mark. A mark with skills he needed. Shifting his weight so that he was more comfortable, he crouched down, waiting. He'd done a lot of that in the past two years. Just waiting.

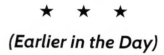

(Earlier in the Day)

THE RADIO ALARM belted out the latest country music at six-thirty a.m. jerking Annie Donavan awake. Slapping her hand on the snooze button she rolled over, keeping her eyes tightly shut. *Just ten more minutes.* A soft pad touched her face; first her forehead, then her closed eyelid. Then a wet nose sniffed her ear. Opening her eyes, she grumbled, "Go away, Boo," while reaching out her hand to stroke the large tabby cat's fur. Letting her hand fall back to the bed, she attempted to snooze once again. In what seemed just seconds the alarm was playing again, only this time when she opened her eyes she was presented with an up close view of a cat butt. *Great. Just what I want to see first thing in the morning.*

Pushing the cat to the side, she turned off the radio while swinging her legs over the side of the bed. Boo quickly came back, rubbing his whole body against hers. Two more cats wandered in the bedroom, circling her legs while meowing in unison.

"I know. I know guys," she acknowledged, heading into the kitchen to feed her menagerie. Putting the coffee on to brew, she walked back to the tiny bathroom. Staring critically into the mirror at her sleepy image, she shook her head. Her long, coppery hair was untamed and curling around her face. Pulling the mane into a messy bun, she quickly washed her face and applied simple makeup.

Changing out of her pink drawstring pajama bottoms and matching pink camisole, she stood at her minuscule closet pretending to wonder what to wear. *Hmmm, should I wear the pencil skirt and sex-kitten heels? How about the low-cut blouse and tight pants. Or maybe a kick-ass pair of boots. Yeah. Right.* Her closet held none of those items and she smirked as she dressed in clean scrubs, pulling her lab coat off of the hanger. Her cats had finished their breakfast and were lying on the living area rug cleaning their faces by the time she walked back into her kitchen.

Pouring milk into her bowl of cereal, she walked into the living area, sitting on the sofa to eat. Her thoughts were already on her day, as they were each morning. *First thing, surgery. Two spays, one neuter, one dental. Jesus, I hope Mrs. Rosini remembers to not feed her dog before bringing him in. After surgery, seven known appointments, not including walk-ins.*

Finishing her cereal, she allowed her eyes to roam around her small apartment as the morning's sunlight began to filter through the blinds. All three cats moved over to the old, dark green rug trying to find a place in the barely-there sunspot. The rug covered the wooden floors which were not in bad shape, but worn from many years of tenants. The tan sofa Annie sat on was as worn as the floors, but it was clean, and since it came with the apartment she couldn't quibble about a free couch. Two chairs faced her, both bought on Craig's List, along with the coffee table in between.

The living area was just that. One room. A small table and two chairs sat near the kitchen, but since it was covered with her laptop and papers, it hardly qualified as a dining area. The tiny kitchen held serviceable, although outdated appliances, as well as a few cabinets.

She had painted the walls in a soft cream color, desperate to make the apartment appear bigger than it really was. Family pictures adorned the walls, as well as some throw pillows, gave the room splashes of color. *Well, it's mine and it's home,* she thought as she pushed herself off of the sofa.

"All right, guys. Time for momma to head out. I've got to get donuts for the gang, so I'll see you later," she said with affection to the three cats. All three raised their heads, large eyes staring at her, but with the sunspot-coma coming on none of them moved.

This is my life. Talking to my cats. She wondered if she would eventually be found mummified in this old apartment, littered with cat food cans outside of the door. Shaking her head as she washed her cereal bowl and left it in the sink, she pushed back the morbid thoughts. *I'm young. I'm a professional. I own my own veterinary practice. I'm successful.* Unfortunately, those thoughts were crowded with others, less positive. *I'm single with no social life in the foreseeable future. No fiancé to plan a future with. No boyfriend to hang out with on weekends. No friend-with-benefits, therefore giving my battery boyfriend all my business. Hell, no one-night stands. I live in a tiny-ass apartment because it's all I can afford while I pay off vet school loans. I work from sun-up to beyond sun-down. And...I talk to cats. Yep, I'm a real winner.*

Looking at the clock one more time, Annie realized she needed to hustle to get the donuts before opening the clinic. Grabbing her keys and purse, she locked the door behind her and jogged down the stairs.

"Annie!" came the familiar call as she walked briskly down the street toward the bakery.

Looking across the street, she smiled and waved. "Mr. Machelli – good morning."

"Your turn to get the goodies?" he called as he continued to sweep the sidewalk in front of his butcher shop. "Give Mrs. Greenwald my greetings."

She smiled in return. Mrs. Greenwald owned the bakery down the street and had been a widow for over two years. It was a well-known fact in the neighborhood that Mr. Machelli was interested, but he always said he didn't want to move too quickly in a courtship. She thought that secretly he was just afraid that Mrs. Greenwald would turn him down if he asked her out. Knowing her, he might just be right in playing it safe. She could be a fire-cracker and no one knew what would come out of her mouth.

Waving her response, she continued into the bakery. Hit with the smells of homemade breads and pastries, her stomach rumbled as she pushed her way through the crowd up to the counter. Mrs. Greenwald came from the back waving a bag of pastries in her hand. "You're late. You're never late. Why are you late?" she huffed while shoving the bag into Annie's hand. "Here. Take this too. You're too skinny," she added while handing Annie an enormous loaf of bread.

Knowing that no answer was expected, she took the offerings, smiling her thanks. "By the way, Mrs. Greenwald. Mr. Machelli sends his usual morning greetings," she said with a wink.

"Bah! That man moves too slow for me. One day, I will find a man who loves my food and won't waste time asking me out!"

Laughing, Annie quickly paid the young man at the counter, then jogged back down the block to her clinic. As she approached, her eyes caught the sign hanging above the door.

Cranston and Donavan Veterinary Clinic

Her mind drifted back to Dr. Cranston and her interview when he had been looking for a young vet to mentor. He asked her the normal questions about her experience and background, then he sat behind his old wooden desk piled high with records and peered at her silently. His silence began to make her nervous, but she held his gaze. Finally, he asked her one more question.

"What would you be if you couldn't be a veterinarian?"

She didn't hesitate, answering him in a clear voice. "Nothing."

At his raised eyebrows, she continued, "Dr. Cranston, being a veterinarian is all I've ever wanted to be. It's not what I do. It's who I am. If it were taken from me, it would take my reason for getting up each morning. I've never considered another job, another career. It's everything to me."

A slow smile crept across his face as he stood and leaned over his desk with his hand held out. "Good answer, Dr. Donavan. Welcome to my practice."

Annie's mind drifted over to him and the two years he mentored her as a young vet. One day, she had come to work and a new sign was being hung over the door. Instead of just Cranston's Veterinary Clinic, her name was now proudly displayed. She didn't realize it at the time, but he knew. The cancer was eating away at him and in the end he gave his most-valuable possession to the woman that he often said he considered his daughter. When he died six months later, she was stunned to find that he left the entire practice, including the apartment above the clinic, to her.

The sign still had his name on it, swinging proudly above the door. She simply could not stand the idea of having a new sign with just her name. Somehow it seemed disloyal.

Pushing open the door to the clinic, she was greeted with exuberance.

"Finally! I thought I was going to have to send out the cavalry for the fucking pastries!"

Leon reached over the counter, grabbing the bag from her hand and popped a donut into his mouth before she could react.

"Leon! Do you treat Shirley this way when she brings you donuts?" Annie asked, glaring at him.

"Doc, my woman greets me at the door with her bodacious booty, and when I give her the business, I never have to wait on my donuts."

Annie threw her hand up in his face, laughing as she walked toward the back. "Too much information. I do not need that image in my mind."

"Well, doc, if you were getting some of the business yourself it wouldn't seem like too much information!"

"I don't have time to get anyone to give me the business."

"What about that nice doctor over at the emergency vet clinic? He was interested," Leon added, following her through the hall toward the back of the clinic.

Annie's nose wrinkled as she thought about her date with Dr. Ketchum several months ago. She could tell he was interested, but between his schedule and hers there hadn't been time for more dates. "Leon, I told you. We didn't have enough time to see if there could have been interest."

"Girl, when the sparks are flyin' you don't need time

to figure that out. It's either there or it isn't."

"I think Shirley has been reading her romance novels to you at night," Annie laughed. "Anyway, I just don't have time in my life for a man right now."

"If you don't make time, doc, it'll pass you by. Be spontaneous. Be daring, doc. Damn, learn to have time for some fun!"

Leon winked as she walked by, then handed the bag to Suzanne as she came toward the reception area.

Annie turned and looked at her two employees. Suzanne was taller than she, with her long black hair pulled away from her face in a tight ponytail and blue eyes that belied her Irish heritage. Drop dead gorgeous, Annie knew Suzanne had men panting after her, but she rarely dated and no long term boyfriends were on the horizon. Annie wondered if anyone would ever take that title. Whereas she wished she had time for a man, she knew that Suzanne avoided the dating scene. But for whatever reason, she never asked, and Suzanne never talked about it. Suzanne was a vet tech student, a hard worker who also served as her receptionist, and Annie valued her friendship as well as her skills in the clinic.

Tall, dark, with ebony skin and gorgeous eyes, Leon was her vet tech and assistant when needed. Shirley, his long-time girlfriend, was not-so-patiently waiting on him to pop the question so she could plan their wedding. Annie feared that Leon was waiting until his salary increased and guiltily, she had no idea when she would be able to pay Leon or Suzanne more. Leon may joke about Shirley, but the honest truth was that he would do anything for her...and she for him.

One day, maybe for me. After I build the business. After I pay the bills. After I...yeah right. Looks like crazy cat lady may be my only title after all.

Taking a deep breath, she turned and walked toward the back surgical area, calling out, "Okay, folks, let's get ready for the day."

Suzanne and Leon watched Annie's back as she left the reception area then turned their eyes to each other.

"Lordy, I wish that woman could find herself some fun. And a man. Hell, fun with a man," Leon exclaimed loudly. As usual whatever came into his mind, came out of his mouth.

Suzanne, quieter, just nodded before adding, "But she doesn't need just any man and fun. She needs the right man and fun."

"Can't argue with that, but if she doesn't ever go out, how is she going to meet the right man? It's not like Mr. Right is going to drop into her clinic out of nowhere."

Shrugging, Suzanne finished her pastry as she headed to the reception area as the door opened and their first customer came in.

"Mrs. Rosini! How nice to see you and Zoey. Now please tell me you did not give Zoey any treats this morning!"

Chapter 2

THE LAST CLIENT was checking out with Leon, so Annie went around gathering the trash.

"Dr. Donavan, I told you I'd get the trash," Suzanne called from the back room. "I've just got to finish sweeping out the exam rooms."

Smiling, Annie knew that Suzanne would do everything if she could. Hardworking, diligent, caring…and worked cheap. *Thank goodness for that.* Veterinary school loans and then taking over the small animal practice in downtown Richland was taking a toll on her finances. Yelling back she answered, "It's okay. I've got it." Pulling her long hair back up in a messy bun, she grabbed the last of the trash and piled it near the back alley door.

Popping around the corner Suzanne looked at Annie with irritation. "Dr. Donavan you should have waited. You work too hard as it is."

Annie looked at her young vet tech with affection. Suzanne had only been working for her for about six months, but the two of them had become friends. Physically, they could not have been more opposite in height and coloring. *Oh, to be twenty and gorgeous,*

Annie thought, feeling much older than her twenty-eight years. Petite, with her ginger hair and green eyes, she sometimes felt frumpy next to the young beauty.

"And how many times do I have to tell you to call me Annie?"

Laughing, Suzanne admitted, "I know, but I call you Dr. Donavan all during the day in front of clients. It's hard to switch."

"Well, we're finished here. Hopefully, as soon as you finish your vet tech program in a couple of months, I can pay both of you to be techs and hire someone else to be the receptionist. Then neither of you will have to pull double duty." Looking around to make sure everything was done for the evening, Annie put her arm around Suzanne and steered her toward the front door. "Leon, are you ready? I'll have you watch Suzanne get in her car tonight, and I'll toss the trash out. See you guys on Monday morning."

Waving goodbye, Suzanne and Leon headed out of the door and Annie watched as they drove off. Looking around the neighborhood for a moment, Annie sighed. *Fresh air. Green grass. Room for a dog to run.* That had been her ideal setting when she graduated from vet school, but jobs were not as plentiful as she had hoped. When Dr. Cranston was looking for a young doctor to help with his inner-city practice that came with a small apartment over it, she jumped at the chance to start paying off the loans.

The old neighborhood, filled with tall brick dwellings, a few homeless people shuffling down the street, and some rough looking characters driving by in a car had her shutting and locking the front door securely. *One day maybe. A vet clinic in the country.*

Annie headed towards the back door, grabbing the trash bags on her way out. Stepping into the alley, she tossed the bags into the dumpster behind her building.

The alley was quiet, almost eerily so. Turning to go back inside, a large body was standing right in front of her. Screaming, she jumped back stumbling over her feet. A hand snapped out of the darkness, grabbing her arm. Heart pounding, chest heaving, she stared up at the tall figure in front of her. *Oh Jesus. I'm going to be murdered. I'm going to be raped. I'm going to be...*

"Doctor. Are you all right?" a deep voice resonated from the shadowed figure.

All right? Do murderers ask if you are all right? Still in shock, Annie just stared at the man.

"Doctor. Are. You. All. Right?" He enunciated each word as though she did not understand him the first time.

"Y...yes," she answered tentatively, slowly finding her voice.

"I need your help." Stepping from the shadows into the dim light, she saw his features instead of just a shape. *Oh my, he's big.* Her fear at an all-time high, she looked into his shadowed face. Broad shoulders that tapered to a slimmer waist, he was wearing a dark, opened jacket that allowed her to see his tattooed chest.

Twisting as he knelt down, she noticed his large thighs in old, faded, slightly torn blue jeans. He picked up a large blanketed object from behind the dumpster.

Annie heard a whimper, her fear immediately replaced by concern. Stepping forward she pulled the blanket back slightly seeing the face of a German shepherd. Its eyes were closed and its nose was warm. "What did you do to it?" she asked sharply placing her hands on its head.

Sucking in a quick breath, the man growled, "What makes you think I did this? I'm here for help, doc."

Pulling her lips in, she looked back at his face, but it was still too much in the shadows for her to see clearly.

"What happened?"

"I found him like this when I got home. I think he musta' eaten somethin' he shouldn't. Been throwin' up. Don't know what's wrong, but I know he needs help. I don't want him to die."

Hesitating for just a moment trying to decide if she should trust the stranger, she knew she couldn't let the dog suffer. Skirting around him, she called out as she walked back in the office, "Come on. Bring him in."

The man followed quickly as though afraid she would change her mind and she shut the door behind him. Walking to the first exam room, she directed him to lay the dog on the table. Pulling back the blanket she began to assess the dog, her focus entirely on the patient in front of her.

While her attention was on the dog, the man was

able to see the vet up close in the bright light of the examination room. Rubbing his hand over his beard, he couldn't help but stare at the beauty leaning over the table. Her hair was the most unusual color. Not red. Not blond. Under the florescent lights, it glistened like copper. She was short, much shorter than his six feet, two inches. And tiny. Her small hands were moving over the large animal assessing its condition. As his dog made a snap in pain, he found himself jumping forward to protect her if needed.

Startled by the sudden movement of the stranger, she looked up quickly. Her eyes met his and for the first time, she could see his face clearly in the light. His hair and beard were dark, long, and shaggy framing a face that was both rugged and handsome all at the same time. But his eyes were what captured her attention. Unusually dark, almost black. Staring. Unblinking. At her.

Sucking her lips in again, she glanced at the door, calculating. *If he comes after me can I get to the door? Can I shut it on him if I have to? Damn, I can't lock it from the other side.*

His eyes cut over to the door following the path that hers had taken and he stepped back raising his hands. "I'm not gonna hurt you, I swear. I just wanna help my dog."

Blushing, she mumbled an apology as she leaned back over her patient.

Shaking his head, he growled, "Don't apologize,

doc. You got a right to be cautious. Makes you smart. You're a woman alone who just let in a stranger. But I swear, I got no other reason to be here except for him."

Annie spared another glance at the rough man filling up all of the space in the room, then patted the dog. "I need to get x-rays to see what's going on. I can work up a fee payment for you first." As the words came out of her mouth, she knew he couldn't afford to pay for a vet. *Another charity case. Jesus, I must be an idiot. I'll never pay all my bills.*

"No need, doc. I can pay."

Unable to hide her surprise, she looked up at the man, wide-eyed.

Drawing himself up to his full height, towering over her, he cocked his eyebrow. "I can pay. Up front. In cash."

Her mouth snapped shut as she turned back to the dog. "Fine," she bit out. *Great. I've just insulted Mr. Scary.*

Grasping the blanket around the dog, she started to pick him up when she was gently shouldered out of the way and the stranger scooped up his dog. "Where to?"

Quickly moving out of the room she led him to the back surgical area where she had her digital x-ray equipment. After settling the dog in position on the table, she began. The radiographs appeared on the computer screen next to the table completely capturing her attention.

"There is definitely something in the intestines," she

said leaning in closer to observe the pictures.

He watched her carefully, waiting to see if recognition would flash across her face. It didn't. Instead, he noticed her brow furrow as she squinted in concentration.

"I don't know what he swallowed but we have to do surgery. Those objects won't pass the way they are." Leaning in closer to the x-rays, she tried to figure out what they were. Shaking her head, "I just can't tell what he ate. Do you have kids? Is it a kid toy?"

"No," came the short reply. The voice was right behind her as he had silently moved to see the picture closely.

"Look mister. I'm trying to help but here's the problem. Your dog has a foreign object in his intestines and he needs surgery. I can't do it alone and my tech isn't here. You can take him to Emergi-Vet which is a twenty-four hour service. It's about fifteen minutes away."

"No," came the same short reply.

Putting her hands on her hips, looking almost straight up into his eyes, she huffed and blew her bangs up in the air. "Can you say anything without growling 'no'?"

He looked down at her flushed, beautiful face, focusing on her large green eyes, porcelain complexion, and cupid bow mouth. *Perfection. Good. Clean. Beautiful. How long has it been since I've been around someone like this. Two years? Jesus, seems like fuckin' forever.*

"Well? What's it going to be?" she said trying to read his facial expression but coming up empty.

Jarred out of his perusal of her, he blinked. "Not takin' him anywhere else. You do the surgery."

"Look mister, I just told you, I can't. My vet tech is gone and I can't do the surgery and run the anesthesia myself. You have to take him somewhere else." Turning, she continued, "I'll call ahead and let them know you're coming. I know they're more expensive, but I'll put in a good word and see what I can do."

Before she could take a step, her arm was caught in his grasp. Firm, but not painful. Pulled back around to face him her anger won out over her fear. "Take your hands off of me."

He slowly let go of her arm, keeping his eyes directed onto her. "Sorry, doc. But Sarge needs surgery now and I want you to do it. I'll help. You tell me what to do and I'll do it."

Sarge was whimpering on the table and Annie ran back over. *What are you doing? The dog could die if you try this without Suzanne or Leon. But if the man won't take him somewhere else he's going to die anyway.*

As though reading her thoughts he spoke, this time more softly. "Doc, I'm not here to cause trouble. I just trust you and my dog needs you. Please."

It was the last word that came out of his mouth that caused her to reconsider. It was soft. Pleading. His need speaking.

Sighing deeply, Annie hung her head. "Mister, this

is probably going to be a huge mistake. Sarge could die under my hand if we don't do this right. But, if you're refusing other treatment, then we can try."

"That's all I ask, doc. I trust you," his voice carried across the room, this time less gravelly.

Nodding to the sink on the side, she ordered, "Go scrub in." Looking at his open jacket which had seen better days, she added, "And ditch the jacket. Scrubs are in the cabinet over there," she said pointing to a corner closet.

Turning away, she went over to prep Sarge and scrub-in herself. *What the hell are you doing? You don't even know his name?* Thinking back on Leon's words, she tried to remember the last time she did anything spontaneous. Or dangerous. Or out of the ordinary. *Well, Leon, you won't believe this when you come in on Monday!*

THE SWEAT BEADED on Annie's forehead as she struggled with the surgery while keeping an eye on the anesthesia. *This is never done. Never. Jesus, what did I get myself into?* She had placed the IV catheter in Sarge's front leg and with assistance managed to administer the Propofol to make him sleepy. After intubating and hooking him up to the anesthetic machine, she gave rudimentary instructions, but she was essentially doing both the job of the vet and the tech at the same time.

Earlier, when the man had walked into the brightly

lit surgical room, washed clean and wearing fresh scrubs, she couldn't help but notice how handsome he was. Tall, muscular, a strong jaw covered in a beard, but somehow it looked sexy. His eyes were so dark though. They didn't seem to fit his face, but she found herself not wanting to be on the end of an angry glare from him.

Looking back up at the x-rays after making the midline incision she felt confident that she could get to the object, but her focus was divided. Glancing over at the man, seeing the concern for his dog on his face, she realized she did not know anything about him.

Without looking up, she asked, "So, what's your name? I mean, if we are in this together, I should know who's helping Sarge."

"Stoney," came the solitary response.

Confusion wrinkled her brow. "Stoney? What's stoney?"

"No. My name is Stoney."

Annie was too good of a veterinarian to look away from where her scalpel was, but the look on her face showed her surprise. "Stoney? Your name is Stoney? Or is that a nickname?"

"It's what I'm called," he answered truthfully.

Sparing a glance at the anesthesia machine, she noticed that his eyes had not left the machine he was monitoring and admiration for his diligence filled her. "I'm Annie. Annie Donavan."

Her attention was back on Sarge's surgery, so she

missed the slight smile curving his lips.

He watched her in between watching the machine carefully. Copper hair pulled up and tucked in a surgical cap. Perfect complexion – pale with a hint of pink on her cheeks. Her green eyes, sharp and clear, never wavered from her task. In the past couple of years, the only women he had been around had the glassy eyes of users. But Annie Donavan...*Smart. Beautiful. Caring. Trusting. Damn!* It was the trusting part that bothered him. She was trusting him now and he'd have to betray that trust.

"So, I haven't seen you around the neighborhood Stoney. Do you live around here?"

"I come through sometimes."

"Do you work around here?"

"I meet some friends near here sometimes."

"You don't give very informative answers, do you?" she asked glancing up at him.

Stoney took his eyes off of the anesthesia machine just long enough to look at her, surprised to see her smiling at him.

"It's okay. I mean, you don't have to tell me anything. I'm just curious."

Nodding, he went back to watching Sarge.

"I'm used to my techs being in here with me, so I'm used to some noise. Leon tends to prattle on and on, so sometimes I just tune him out, but my other tech is quiet so I usually have to do the talking when she is helping me. We can turn the music on if you would like."

Stoney moved his eyes back over to her. Her voice was soft and clear, not harsh with too many years of smoking or slurred with alcohol. *I could listen to her all day. God, I forgot what that was like.* He watched as her brow furrowed with concentration as she was bent over his dog. Her green eyes clear and shining not, dulled with drugs.

"Got it!" came the excited shout from Annie as she was removing a small object that looked like a sausage from the intestines. "This is crazy. I removed something like this a couple of weeks ago from a dog. What is that?" she wondered out loud.

Stoney watched her remove the object and then kept his eyes on her to see what she did next. Glancing quickly between the anesthetic machine and the object, he watched her actions carefully.

She laid the object in the tray next to the surgical table then turned back to concentrate on suturing the incision.

"What'd you do with what you found last week?" he asked softly.

Annie, not looking up from her work, answered, "I threw it away."

"Is he gonna' be okay?" Stoney asked, looking back down and running his hands over Sarge's coat.

Smiling up at him, she answered, "Yeah. He seems to be doing great." Sparing Stoney a glance she couldn't help notice that his attention was on her, dark eyes piercing her. Licking her lips nervously, she looked back down at her patient.

She walked over to the anesthesia and turned it off. Stoney did not move but oddly she did not feel crowded with him standing right next to her. After a moment, she pulled out the endotracheal tube.

"He's doing great," she said, sighing in relief. Feeling Stoney's heat at her back, she glanced over her shoulder then looked up as she realized how tall he actually was. His eyes met hers and the most amazing thing occurred – he smiled.

Annie stared at his mouth. Full lips, perfect white teeth. His scary persona melted away as the smile of a relieved pet owner took over. *God, he's gorgeous.* She couldn't help but smile back.

Stoney looked down at her as he stood as close as he could without touching her. He could smell her. Even through the surgical soap and medicinal smell of the clinic, he could smell the hint of floral shampoo. He wanted to bury his head in her hair. It had been so long since he had been around beauty. *Another time, another place and I'd be planning on...*

Suddenly Sarge made a slight movement, breaking the spell between them.

Jerking back, she focused her attention on Sarge once again. "We need to get him to the kennel area for recovery," she explained.

Stoney gently lifted Sarge in his arms and followed her to the next room. There were large kennels on the floor, with rows of smaller kennels higher. She quickly went to a cabinet and pulled down clean blankets for one of the large kennels.

"You can place him here," she said kneeling on the floor.

He laid a still sleeping Sarge on to the floor in the kennel.

"I'll keep the IV in for just a bit to make sure everything is all right." Her eyes moved over to Stoney as he leaned over Sarge, speaking softly to the dog. She couldn't help but smile again. Devotion to pets told her a lot about people. He looked up at her, holding her gaze. The room seemed to slowly shrink until there were just the two of them there. His eyes did not waver; neither did hers.

Suddenly self-conscious, she stood up. "I...need... um... to scrub off." Turning, she quickly walked over to the counter and sink.

Chapter 3

HANDS SHAKING, SHE washed them off in the sink just as he walked over and stood at her back. Reaching around her their hands collided under the stream of hot water. Jerking her hands back, she found them gripped in his much larger ones and placed back under the water.

He began to wash her hands, sliding the liquid soap all around, gently massaging them under the water.

The feel of his hands smoothing over hers felt sensual. The strange sensation of becoming aroused surprised her and she couldn't help but glance over her shoulder and up into his face. Less frightened now, she could see his strong jaw despite the shaggy beard. His lips were full and she found herself licking her lips just staring at his. His face was chiseled with small lines coming from his eyes. And those dark eyes. Mesmerizing. Staring at her as though looking directly into her soul. Seeing her fears. Pulling her in.

Stoney slid her hands out of the water as he turned her around. He couldn't take his eyes off of her as he continued to pull her toward him until their bodies were almost flush.

She looked up at him with a mixture of indecision and passion. As though a magnetic force pulled the two of them together, they moved forward. She on her toes and he leaning down until their lips met.

The kiss started softly. The gentle movement of lips on lips. He pulled back slightly, smiling when he saw her brow crinkle at the loss of contact. Knowing he should stop. Knowing he did not want to stop. *Her call. It's got to be her call.*

Annie's eyes sought his again, then lowered to his mouth. The mouth that had just been kissing her. *More. I shouldn't, but I want more. More kisses. More something.* Rising back up on her tiptoes she pressed her lips to his once again.

That was all the encouragement he needed. It had been too long since he had been with a woman...a good woman. Angling his head, he took the kiss deeper. Licking the seam of her lips, he plunged in as she opened. Exploring every crevice of her mouth, he drank her in. He couldn't even remember the last time he had kissed a woman. Not like this. Not where he wanted it more than his next breath. Tongues clashing, chasing each other, trying to dominate. He needed this kiss to chase away the darkness. *Just for tonight. Then I'll walk away and leave her alone.*

He slid his arms around her back and down to cup her ass. Hoisting her up he felt her wrap her legs around his waist, her center pressing onto the bulge in his jeans as he backed her up against the wall.

Annie moved on instinct, the rational voices in her head reminding her that she did not do one-night stands, she did not have sex with strangers were drowned out by the sounds of her own moans. Feeling the pressure of his jean clad dick pushing against her aching core, she began to rub on him as though her will was gone.

She was dimly aware of her scrub top being lifted and her bra cups pulled down, freeing her breasts. Her nipples were hard, but whether it was from the cool air of the surgery room or the heat from their bodies, she didn't know. She didn't care.

Stoney kissed his way down from her mouth, across her neck as she arched her back, and down to the swell of her breasts. Pulling one nipple in deeply, he sucked hard, first nipping with his teeth and then soothing it with his tongue. Lifting his eyes he saw her head thrown back against the wall, eyes closed tightly, her perfect mouth curving in a smile. Moving to the other breast he gave it equal attention, not remembering the last time he suckled a woman for the pure pleasure it gave her. Or him, for that matter.

Annie, lost in the euphoria of the feelings washing over her, gave in completely. Her hands grasped his hair as she pulled him in closer. With his mouth finding hers again, she was barely aware of being lowered to the ground until she felt her scrub bottoms being jerked down along with her panties, before being lifted back up. This time the friction of his jeans directly on her pussy was unbearable. Her undulations began again and she could feel herself close to the goal. Dimly aware, she realized *oh my god, I am going to come just dry humping this sex god,* as she heard the sound of his zipper.

Stoney pushed her back away from him just enough to unzip his jeans, releasing his swollen dick. With one hand on her ass and his body pressing hers against the door, he reached down and pulled a condom out of his back pocket. *Not gonna think about the last time I was with a woman.* With her legs wrapped around his waist he was able to free his hands to roll the condom on quickly.

Lifting her in his strong arms he seated her right at the tip of his cock. Pulling away from her kiss swollen lips, he pierced her with his look. "Last chance, Annie."

The roar of passion in her ears, drowning out all rational thinking, had Annie pulling his head back down to hers. *Whatever comes, I need this now!*

No more hesitation, he plunged his dick to the hilt in her wet pussy, the tightness of it almost making his knees buckle. *Jesus, she is so tight. I don't want to hurt her. But I just gotta...*

He watched in surprise as she threw her head back crying out as her orgasm grabbed his dick in its vice. Her inner muscles clenched around him and he began pounding in and out, his control slipping. With only a few more thrusts his neck strained, the veins standing out, and he leaned his head against the wall next to her as his orgasm ripped through him. *Fuck, she's killin' me.*

Never. It's never felt like that before. Even before he had gone down into the rough world of drug dealers and pimps. Even when he could remember what it was like to hold a decent woman. *Never before has it felt this good. This right.*

Bodies dripping in mingled sweat, breathing ragged, the two of them clung to each other in the aftermath until slowly the cool air around them began to seep into their consciousness.

Annie kept her eyes shut tight, afraid to open for fear of what she would see in his eyes. *What have I done? I don't even date, but I just let a stranger fuck me against the wall of my own clinic.* As she felt his breath even out she loosened her grip on him, hoping he would take the hint and let her go.

He felt the change in her as soon as her guilt settled in. Lifting his head from her shoulder, he peered into her face before she quickly averted her eyes. *Did I hurt her? Fuck, I took her too hard. She's not like the skanks I have had to be with for the last couple of years. Jesus, what have I done?*

He brought his hand up to cup her face, turning it back toward his. "You all right, Annie? Did I hurt you?"

She felt the fiery blush from her breasts to her hairline as embarrassment heated her skin. "I...um...I need to...um...the dog. I have to...um...check on Sarge."

"Annie. Did I hurt you?" his gravelly voice asked again softly.

"No. Um...no. I'm fine. I...um...just need

to...um. Please, put me down," she said pleadingly. *Please just go. Just go. Let me die here alone in my embarrassment.* Having no idea how to deal with a one-night fuck up against a wall, she just wanted him to leave.

Stoney slowly pulled out and with his large hands around her waist, he set her down. When he was sure her legs were steady under her he stepped back, his eyes never leaving her face. He could see the embarrassment and guilt racing across her features. *Fuck. She was too good for this. She was too good for me. Or too good for who I've become.* He stepped away tossing the used condom into the trash. With his back to her, he could hear the sounds of clothing rustling. Giving her a moment of privacy he fixed his pants before turning around. She had put her scrubs back on but had the look of a well-fucked woman about her. Long copper hair mussed and falling about her shoulders. Lips were red and kiss-swollen. And her green eyes...*fuck.* Green eyes shining with unshed tears.

Annie glanced up at him unable to discern any emotion in his eyes. Feeling the sting of tears threatening to fall she quickly skirted around him and went over to Sarge's cage. Sitting on the floor, she leaned in to ascertain his post-op condition. The anesthesia was wearing off, but the pain meds kept him quiet.

"He looks good. We were successful with the surgery and he should be ready to go home once he wakes up. If you want to call tomorrow, I'll have our tech get him ready for you." *I can do this. I can make this profes-*

sional and just pretend the last few minutes of my life didn't happen. Keeping her face away from Stoney, she did not want him to read her emotions. *But it did happen. And it was good. Hell, it was great. I felt alive for the first time in a long time.* Giving her head a quick shake, she continued her thoughts. *Stop. It was a fuck. That was all it was to him, so don't make this worse.*

Stoney walked over and squatted next to her, reaching out to touch his dog. "I'd like to stay if you don't mind. I don't want him to wake up and not know anything familiar."

Annie turned to look at the man next to her. Strong, handsome face, even with the shaggy beard. His long hair, messy but clean. His massive thighs next to her tiny ones. His large hands, gently stroking Sarge. Hands that were just as gentle when they were stroking her a few minutes earlier. Quickly sucking in her breath at the turn of her thoughts, she looked up into his eyes. Unreadable. His eyes were the only thing about his looks that just didn't fit. Dark. Almost black.

He continued, "Look, I know you don't have any reason to trust me. I show up here in the dark alley with a sick dog. I guilt you into doing surgery and then I take advantage of the moment."

At that, the blush that had gone away flamed across her face once again and she dropped her eyes from his.

His voice soft, "Annie girl. I'm all kinds of sorry that you regret what we did. I shoulda never let it go so far. But honest to God, woman. You're the brightest thing in my world right now. I don't want any trouble. I just wanna make sure my dog is okay and I need to make sure you're okay as well."

"I'm... fine, Stoney. Honestly. I haven't...well, I've never...um...done that..."

Before she could finish, he interrupted. "I know you haven't. Annie, I've been buried in the belly of the beast for a while, but don't think I don't know pure goodness when I see it."

Her eyes jerked up to his as he continued. "I don't regret it. Not one second. The only thing I regret is you thinkin' it didn't mean anything to me. I felt somethin'. Don't understand it. But I felt somethin'."

She looked back down nodding, sucking in her lips as his words poured over her. Taking a deep breath, she stood up. "I live upstairs. If you want to stay here to keep an eye on Sarge, I'll let you. I don't understand it either, but I trust you. I'll be back down in the morning."

With that, she turned and left the room, not looking back. Walking up the flight of stairs in the back to her little apartment, she could feel the exhaustion taking over. Locking her front door behind her, she walked into the kitchen, grabbed a wine bottle and headed into the bathroom. Taking a long hot shower, she scrubbed her body thinking it would take away the shame, but as her hands lathered her breasts she could still feel his hands on her. *Stop. You're not in some romance novel. You just had a one-time...whatever.*

She then crawled into bed with the bottle of wine and tried to drink the memories away. *Just my luck. The bottle was almost empty to begin with so I can't even get drunk enough to forget. To forget the way his mouth kissed as though he was sucking my breath to live himself. To forget the way his arms felt as they wrapped around me. Protecting me, or giving himself something to hold on to. To forget how is dick felt buried deep inside. And to forget that orgasm. Nope, not happening.* So she lay in bed, finally falling asleep dreaming about the mysterious man in the room directly under her.

A FEW HOURS later, Sarge was on his feet although still wobbly. Stoney rubbed his dog's ears, speaking soft words to him as his hands were being licked. "What did I do, Sarge? The first ray of sunshine that enters my world in two years and I bang her up against the wall like some two-bit hooker."

The darkness of the past couple of years swept over him. The drugs, the fights, the lawlessness he had to participate in to get up in the organization. Every one of those actions took a little bit of his soul until he wondered if he had a soul left. *Would I have gone down this path if I had known how it would have ended or how long it would take?* Rubbing his hand over his face, he pulled himself out of the darkness that was threatening to overtake him.

Sarge's large doggie eyes looked into Stoney's face as

though he understood the words.

Shaking his head he said, "What's more, she's the kind of forever girl I always wanted to find. And I have to find her in the middle of this fucked up mess. She'll never know the real me and I can't even stay around to explain it or make her feel better." The realization that he should never see her again sliced through him. "I gotta get this done. Then I gotta get out. Then maybe...ah hell."

Bending down, he wrapped the blanket around his dog, then stood to his full height. Looking around one last time, he quietly left through the back door, slipping out into the night.

Chapter 4

T HE NEXT MORNING, Annie jumped out of bed at the sound of the alarm without hitting the snooze button. Anxious to get downstairs to check on Sarge, she hurried through her morning routine. Looking in the mirror, she spent an extra minute on her simple makeup and smoothing her hair. *What do I say to Stoney? What do you say to a man that you had sex with on the first night? First night? Hell, it was an only night.* Hanging her head in embarrassment for just a moment, she shook off the feelings and looked back into the mirror. *Girl, for once you did something spontaneous. Get back down there and face him.*

Going with her pep talk, she hurried down the stairs and entered the clinic through the back door. "Stoney?" she called. "How's our patient this morning?"

The silent clinic was her only greeting. Walking into the recovery area her eyes darted around as she realized it was empty. No Sarge. No Stoney. The room looked just as she left it last night. Everything in its place. It looked as though there had never been any activity. Stunned, she walked over and peered into the laundry bin. There were the blood covered scrubs. *It wasn't a dream. He was here.* The realization dawned on her. *He couldn't wait to get out. He didn't want to see me this morning.*

A strange feeling of disappointment filled her. She walked slowly over to the wall where just hours earlier she had been with him. Placing her hand up against the cold surface, she wanted to feel some of the heat that she had felt then. But all that was left from last night was the cold on her fingertips and the memories. *You are such a fool.*

Her eyes caught an envelope taped to the door that led to the alley. Walking over and with shaky hands, she opened it. Five one-hundred dollar bills were inside along with a note. Pulling the note out, she read: **Thanks for the help. Sarge seems fine. I hope this covers the cost of the surgery. I needed to leave before the morning. Stay safe. Stoney**

Eyes closed, she clutched the money and note in her hand. Sucking in a huge breath, she suddenly turned and walked to the reception area. Putting the money in the bank bag, she headed out the front door. *There is no way I can explain this to Suzanne. First stop, bank. Fine. I can do this. I had my one spontaneous one-night stand. No more. From now on, I play it safe and if I'm destined to be a cat lady, then so be it!*

After her trip to the bank, Annie ran to the butcher shop and then to the market down the street. Greeting the storeowners as she went, she tried to lighten her mood. Mr. Tochi at the market was always trying to set her up with his nephew.

"But he's an accountant and wears a suit to work," he pleaded. "You're a doctor. You would make a good match and make pretty babies."

Smiling indulgently, she answered, "Mr. Tochi, you know I don't have time to date. I'm up to my elbows in dogs and cats."

Shaking his head, he looked at her with sad eyes and said, "You listen to this wise old man. Don't let life pass you by, doctor."

Annie felt the smile slip from her face. *Yeah, well, sometimes we let life in and it bites us in the butt!*

Waving goodbye, she headed home. Her apartment on the second floor could be entered by going through the clinic where a staircase went from the back work area to the living room, or by the old metal stairs attached to the side of the building in the back alley and enter through her kitchen. Deciding to walk through the alley since it was daylight, she headed around the building. Balancing the bags with her purse, she managed to get up the stairs and through the door into her kitchen.

She never saw the eyes watching her. Eyes that couldn't believe that a single woman would walk through an alley to go upstairs to her apartment. Alone. Without checking her surroundings. Completely oblivious to possible danger.

Stoney stayed in the background, his teeth on edge as he watched her. Wanting to go to her. Wanting to help her. Wanting to take care of her. Wanting to…damn! *I fucked things up! But I gotta make sure there is no blow-back on her.* He found himself wondering what could have happened if he had met her earlier. Before. Before the darkness. Before the secrets. Angry at his thoughts and his situation, he slipped back down the alley careful not to be seen.

ANNIE SPENT THE rest of her afternoon in the clinic after cleaning her own apartment. Wandering among the rooms, she made sure that the surgery room was once again sterile. *Certainly didn't worry about that last night* she thought, as her eyes moved over to the wall where Stoney had pushed her up against it.

To get those thoughts out of her mind, she flipped on the radio in the clinic letting the country music blast through the speakers. Scrubbing the surgical area she made sure to put everything back in its place, not wanting Leon or Suzanne to suspect that anything had happened.

When she was sure that everything was ready for Monday morning clients again she walked up the stairs to her apartment.

"Come on babies," she called to her cats as she put food in their dishes. Rubbing their heads, she looked up as her cell phone rang. Glancing at the display she saw **Mom**.

"Hey mom, what's up?" she answered.

"I just wanted to see how you're doing."

She loved her mother dearly, but knew that she was hoping Annie was going to have news of a great date for the evening. Her parents were proud of her being a vet but kept dropping the 'when are you going to meet someone and give us grandbabies' hints. *Hints? More like demands.*

"I'm fine, mom. How are you and dad?"

"We're good. Just haven't heard from you lately so I thought I would call and see if you had any plans for tonight."

Sighing, Annie plopped down on her sofa allowing Boo to climb into her lap. "No, mom. No hot date tonight."

"Well dear, why don't you drive out to our place? Your dad is playing golf with a very nice young man from my office. We could have him stay for dinner and you could meet him. Who knows? You might hit it off."

"Mom, stop trying to set me up. And honestly, I have no interest in meeting someone who works in your office."

"What's wrong with meeting a financial consultant?" her mom huffed.

Images of a muscular, tattooed man kissing her until her toes curled ran through her mind. Dangerous. Wild. Untamed.

"I don't know, mom. It just isn't the right time. Anyway, I'll probably meet some friends later."

"All right, dear. But the invitation stands open for any weekend."

She could hear the disappointment in her mother's voice as she hung up the phone. Looking down at the large cat in her lap, "Looks like another night of just us." She wanted to forget Stoney. Be angry with him. But she couldn't. *Just for once, I wanted something wild and unpredictable.* Grabbing her Kindle, she lay on the couch reading as the evening sun began to lower in the sky.

That night as she slept, black eyes haunted her dreams.

ANNIE ROUNDED THE corner, jogging back toward her apartment. Determined to get outdoors today, she decided to get back into running. *Jesus, how out of shape am I?* She pounded the pavement, breathing heavily. She had forgotten her iPod and without music her mind was racing with thoughts of Stoney and Friday night. *You've never had a one-night stand. What were you thinking? What if he wasn't trustworthy?* She remembered him asking her if she was sure. *He was trustworthy. I don't know how I know that, but he was. But it was done and over. He left. He just left.* She shook her head in anger, whether more at him or herself she wasn't sure. Making it to her building she ran into the alley, slowing down as she approached the stairs. At the bottom of the stairs, she came to a stop and began her stretching.

Moving toward the staircase she was startled when Stoney stepped in front of her.

Shrieking in fright, she dropped her keys as she stumbled backward. His arms reached out to grab her, but held on longer than just to steady her. Jerking back, eyes snapping in anger, she pulled from his grasp and bent to pick up her keys.

"What are you doing here?" she asked, confusion warring with anger and a dose of embarrassment.

"I need your help again."

His eyes darted to the side, under the stairs where Sarge lay wrapped in a blanket.

Forgetting her irritation she darted around Stoney and knelt at the dog. Her sure hand ran over Sarge and she lifted the blanket to look at the incision site. "He seems a little feverish, but the incision site looks good. Let's move him inside so that I can get a better look at him."

Stoney leaned closely to her as he gathered the dog up in his arms and followed her inside the back door to the clinic.

She flipped on the lights in the clinic and had him lay Sarge down on the examining table in the back lab area. Quickly, but thoroughly, examining him, she looked up at Stoney's face, noting the concern etched on his features. Her ire lessened. *He really does love this dog.*

Placing her hand on his arm, she pulled his eyes toward hers. "Stoney, he's going to be fine. His surgical site looks good, but I think he's in some pain from the surgery. I'll give him some fluids and pain meds and he really just needs to rest."

Stoney's dark eyes captured hers. "I'm sorry I left the other night. I thought it was best to not be here the next morning."

Determined to keep things professional, she spoke quickly. "It's fine. It was nothing. No worries."

He noted her blush, as well as her fast-paced breathing. *She's not as unaffected as she pretends.* Smiling at this knowledge, he looked back down at his dog. "So, what should I do about him?"

"You need to leave him here overnight. Let him get some rest where I can keep an eye on him. You can come back tomorrow and check on him."

"Can I stay with him?"

Seeing Annie's look of doubt, he quickly added, "I promise I won't leave and I won't move him. I'll stay right here and keep an eye on him."

"It doesn't matter to me if you leave," she said defiantly, looking back down at the now sleeping dog as she reached out to gently rub Sarge's fur. "It's up to you. But I'm telling you this dog needs to rest." Raising her gaze back to his dark one, she nodded. "Well...I'll be upstairs if you need something."

Standing at the same time, he moved into her space. Refusing to step away or show fear, Annie leaned her head back as he came nearer, holding his eyes. His hand came up and cupped her face as his thumb moved across her flushed cheeks.

"Thanks," was all he said, but his face had gentled. The harsh lines seemed to smooth out as he continued to stroke her cheek. Leaning down slowly, giving her a chance to back away, he touched his lips to hers. She stayed. He took this as a sign and deepened the kiss, angling his head for better access. Licking her lips, he plunged in as she opened her mouth to him. Wanting to control the situation, but knowing he still had a job to do, Stoney reluctantly pulled back, noting her slight whimper as his lips left hers.

Confusion in her eyes quickly morphed into distress. Turning sharply, she walked on shaky legs to the door leading up to her apartment. Refusing to turn around she closed the door behind her and walked up the stairs, not stopping until she collapsed on her couch.

Jesus. What is wrong with me? I don't know anything about him, but I would have let him take me again! Remembering his lips, his strong arms, the hands that stroked Sarge with just as much care as they stroked her face, she felt a tingle of desire pulse through her. *What am I doing?* Hearing no answer, she lay on the couch staring at the ceiling fan. Moving her hands over her stomach and up toward her breasts, she remembered the feel of his hands on her body. *I want that. Again.*

HEARING THE APARTMENT door above close, Stoney moved to the back door leading to the alley. Slipping out, he walked over to the dumpster behind her building. Quietly lifting the top, he pulled himself up and peered down into the dark, stinking pit. Shining his light down on the garbage bags below, he saw a few smaller bags under some of the larger ones. Knowing that she had already thrown out the clinic's garbage before he showed up on Friday night, anything that she would have thrown out after that would be in a smaller bag.

Sliding down into the dumpster, he took out his knife and slit a few of them open. The filled sausage casing was visible, and he pulled it out. Still intact. *Fuckin' hell. She was telling the truth. She threw it away just like she must have thrown away the other one. She has no fuckin' clue.* Stoney slipped the sausage into a plastic bag and zipped it up. Pulling himself back out of the dumpster, he quietly lowered the lid and walked back into the clinic, making sure to lock the door behind him.

Pulling his cell out of his pocket, he placed a call as he knelt by Sarge to rub his dog's ears.

"Got it. Yeah. Bringin' it in. Tomorrow. Yeah, I know." *Fuck*

Sliding the phone back into his pocket, he shook his head. "Sarge, this shit just got worse. Looks like we'll be stickin' around for a bit, and that sure as hell won't be hard. But when she finds out...fuck. Just gotta make sure that goes the way it needs to."

His hand touched his pocket where the plastic bag contained the red sausage. Filled with a quarter of a million dollars of cocaine. *And she fuckin' threw it away.*

Hearing footsteps on the stairs, he shoved the bag

deeper in his jean's pocket. Settling quickly on the floor by Sarge, he assumed the relaxed position as though he had been there all along. The door opened and he looked over as she walked back into the room carrying a small tray.

Long hair, wet from her shower, pulled back away from her face. The light smell of flowers drifted in the air as she moved over toward him. Her face devoid of makeup was more beautiful than the painted women he had been hanging with. No longer in scrubs, her yoga pants cupped her ass making him remember what it felt like in his hands. Her t-shirt hung on her breasts, not overtly sexy, but showcasing her rack to perfection. He looked at her questioningly as his eyes traveled down to the tray in her hands containing a sandwich, an apple, some chips, and a beer.

"I thought you might be hungry," she said with a simple shrug.

He started to stand, but she was already on her way squatting down on the floor next to him. "This is for me?"

"Well, I didn't bring the beer for Sarge," she said, laughing as she set the tray on the floor.

Laughter. True, gentle laughter. Not the sound of a hard-pressed woman trying to get a man's attention. Not the sound of a drunk, stoned woman giggling because they're high out of their mind. Just pure amusement. Shaking his head, he realized it had been a long time since he had heard that sound.

Clean. Pure. Light.

Needing her more than he could believe at that moment, he reached over and quickly pulled her into his lap. Her eyes opened wide but as his lips latched onto hers, he saw her eyes warm with desire.

Tongues dueling, he explored every crevice of her mouth tasting the fresh mint of her toothpaste. The taste shot straight to his dick, feeling it swell uncomfortably in his jeans. His hands placed on either side of her head as he angled his mouth for deeper access began to slide down. One around her back to hold her to him and the other down over her breast to the bottom of her t-shirt, where it slipped under and began its path back up. Pulling the t-shirt over her head, their lips separated for the second it took the material to pass between them.

She was slender but had an amazing body. Her breasts, full and round, spilling over the tops of her bra cups, which he quickly pulled down. Now released, her nipples hardened to points, beckoning, to which his lips quickly obliged.

As his lips attached themselves to her nipple, Annie felt the electric jolt down to her pussy. Desperate for the friction that would ease the ache between her legs she quickly straddled him, rubbing her core on his jean-clad dick. Sliding one hand down she released the button on his jeans and began to unzip them as he leaned back pulling her with him. With his cock free she fisted him, stroking him gently and then with more firmness.

"Fuck, girl. You're gonna' have me come before I'm ready."

His words, meant to dissuade, only seemed to inflame her more. Sliding down, she took him in her mouth. Never having given head before, she only hoped that her romance novels had taught her something. Swirling her tongue around the tip, she heard the sharp intake of his breath. Encouraged, she continued to take him in her mouth. He was large. Much larger than her few sexual experiences in college. She moved her mouth over him, gently fondling his balls with one hand while the other pumped him at the base.

Suddenly, he lifted her off of him and laid her on her back. His hands grabbed the top of her yoga pants and panties and jerked them down and off in seconds. Pulling a condom from his back pocket he sheathed himself as her legs fell naturally open.

Stoney fingered her quickly, feeling the slick moisture that had pooled between her folds. "Fuck. You're already wet for me, baby." Looking down at her face, wanting to ascertain that she wanted this as much as he did, he found her eyes staring into his. Not with question. Not with concern. The look on her face was one of trust. *Fuck! She goddamn trusts me.* Not willing to stop, he plunged into her waiting body, feeling her tightness surround him. Cushion him. Hold him.

Stoney never lost control. With his job. With a woman. Everything he did was about control. But Annie undid him. Thrusting into her, he felt her tight walls pulling at his dick as he leaned over and clasped his lips over a swollen nipple. Sucking deeply, he felt her body buck under his. Nipping with his teeth, he quickly licked the pain away then moved up toward her mouth. His tongue slipped in and began thrusting in time to his dick.

He couldn't remember the last time he kissed a woman, certainly not like this. Before Annie, his last fuck had been pounding into some junkie, a woman who worked for a supplier. She wasn't too hard to look at, but she'd been a job. Part of the job. Part of dealing the drugs that kept coming.

But Annie. She was no fuck. Looking down at her face as she leaned her head back and screamed his name as the orgasm ripped through her, he knew that no matter what else happened, she was no fuck. Thrusting a few more times was all it took and he pushed through his release, his neck straining. Collapsing on top of her but quickly rolling to the side, he gathered her in his arms, cradling her gently. Listening to their breathing as it slowly regulated, he saw her looking at him. Those gorgeous green eyes, staring into his darkness. With trust. *I am so fucked. Don't know how, but I gotta protect her.* He tried to convince himself that he would protect her for his job, but he knew as that thought flitted through his mind that it was shit. *Clean. Pure. The one. I gotta protect her from everything.* Trying to figure out how was killing him.

Annie looked up into his dark eyes, wishing she

could tell what he was thinking. This time she felt no guilt. This time she felt no embarrassment. If a few stolen minutes with Stoney was all she would get, she wanted them. Reaching her hand to cup his face, she pulled him down for a soft kiss.

Looking down at the still sleeping Sarge, she asked Stoney, "Do you want to come upstairs? You could have your sandwich there." Her eyes raised to his face, knowing that she couldn't keep the hope out of them.

Stoney, realizing that he just fucked her on the floor, was almost overcome with disgust. Knowing that he should get the hell out of her clinic and her life, he also knew he was never going to do that. "Yeah, baby. I'd like that," he answered softly. Getting to his feet while adjusting his pants, he assisted her up from the floor.

Annie pulled her bra cups back into place and scooped her t-shirt, panties, and yoga pants off of the floor. She noticed Stoney picking up the tray while she quickly dressed. Smiling up at his face, she turned and walked to the door leading to her apartment. "Come on up," she said as she disappeared through the doorway.

Stoney hesitated for only a second. *Fucked up timing* was all that he could think, but he followed her anyway.

Chapter 5

A FTER THEY BOTH had eaten, Annie and Stoney settled into comfortable positions on her sofa. Tucking her feet up under her, she twisted her body so that she could see him at the other end. At the moment, he was looking down at his rough-worn hands rubbing Boo's fur and she wondered what was going through his mind.

"What are you thinking, Stoney?" she asked softly.

He lifted his face to hers. "Honestly?" he asked. When she nodded, he answered, "Glad I'm here, but kinda' pissed you'd bring a strange man up to your apartment, doc. You're too trusting and this ain't the smart play."

Annie's eyes narrowed at his words. "Are you saying I'm dumb?" her voice not hiding her irritation.

"Just sayin' you don't know anything about me, yet you bring me up here where anything dangerous could happen. You do that often?" His dark eyes held hers until she looked away.

Taking a deep breath, she slowly let it out. "I want to be angry about what you just said, but I can't. You're right." Turning her gaze back to him, she continued. "I don't bring men here. Ever. But I think...I mean...I just feel that I can trust you."

Right then, another cat strolled into the room, weaving its body around Stoney's legs.

"Damn, doc. How many strays do you pick up?"

Laughing, she scooped up the cat and rubbed its ears. "It's hard not to care for a stranded animal. They just want to be loved."

"Is that how you see me and Sarge? Are we strays to you?"

Shrugging, Annie answered honestly. "Kind of. You needed my help. I couldn't turn you away."

His eyebrows raised. "Help is one thing, baby. What we did went way beyond help."

Annie's blush returned as she buried her face in the cat's fur. Looking back at him, she replied, "You probably won't believe this, but I've never done that before. I've never slept with a man I just met. I've never been someone's one-night stand."

Stoney leaned over, closing the distance between them, saying, "Baby, you don't gotta convince me. Men can tell these things and believe me, there is nothing fake about you at all. You are pure sunshine."

Smiling, she set her cat on the floor, then leaned back into the sofa cushions. "So what do you do? I mean, I kind of thought you might be homeless when you showed up in the alley, but homeless men don't leave five hundred dollars for vet expenses."

Holding her gaze, he answered, "I solve problems."

Waiting for him to elaborate, she quickly realized that nothing else was forthcoming. Wrinkling her brow, she cocked her head as she asked, "Solve problems? What kind of problems?"

Sighing, he continued, "Simple. People have problems. I'm sent in to fix them. Any way I can. Any way that gets the job done."

Not having any idea what he was talking about, she probed. "Who do you work for, solving problems?"

"Different people. Some better than others, but they all know I can take care of things."

By this time, Annie realized that he wasn't going to give her any more information and what he had given her seemed a little scary. *What kind of man have I invited up to my apartment?*

Recognizing that she was beginning to question his motives, Stoney knew that he needed to move the conversation to her. "So, tell me about being a vet."

Immediately the smile that lit her face took his breath away once again. Green eyes, bright and alert, turned on him as she effused. "I love it. It is the only job I ever wanted. My parents were afraid that if it didn't work out, I would have no plan B. But I never needed a plan B."

"How long have you been in practice?" Stoney found himself wanting her to keep talking. He no longer cared about her talking so that they focus was off of him; he simply wanted that smile to continue to beam his way.

"I've been out of vet school for two years. The practice downstairs was owned by Dr. Cranston and he took me in then made me a partner. He died six months ago and left me the practice and this apartment. His practice was a good one, but it has been hard to keep things going."

"Business is bad?"

"No, actually there is a lot of business, but I had vet school loans to pay off and can only afford my two employees right now. And this apartment is free, but we work all the time."

Looking around at the old, minimally furnished apartment, he noted that it was clean and well kept. But still...facing an alley in an area not populated with other apartments for neighbors.

"Do you feel safe here?" he asked with bite in his tone, his irritation showing.

"It's not so bad," Annie admitted reluctantly. "I don't go out at night. If I'm in the clinic late, then I use the inside staircase and I always keep the outside door locked." Shrugging, she continued, "It works for now. Sometime, when there is more money, I can move out. But it keeps me close to the animals if we have a patient that has to stay over, like Sarge. That way my employees don't have to try to come back."

"Who works for you?" As he asked, he found himself thinking *when was the last time I gave a fuck about talking to a woman for any reason other than sex or information?*

"Suzanne is a dream. She is almost finished with her vet tech degree and we've become good friends. She could work anywhere but said she wanted to work for a female vet. She's kind of quiet and doesn't go out much, so she is willing to work for me as she finishes her classes. Leon is my vet tech and surgical assistant and they both are my receptionists for now. I'm hoping to move her to a full-time vet tech position when she graduates and then be able to hire a full-time receptionist."

"Money a problem?" Stoney asked cautiously.

Laughing, Annie replied, "Who doesn't have money problems?"

She really didn't know she was in possession of a quarter of a million dollars of cocaine. Twice. Throwing that shit out in the garbage.

"But you know what is nice?" she asked as she looked into his face. "Suzanne and Leon aren't just employees. It seems as though we are starting from the ground up, building something special. We work closely and we have fun. So even though I can't pay them what they are worth, and after the business expenses and my loan payments are paid each month, there is very little for me to live on…I love what I'm doing and who I'm doing it with. That makes it special, don't you think?"

Stoney looked into the face of the woman sitting next to him. Eyes bright with excitement, not dull with drugs. Taking in a man and his dog, not expecting him to pay instead of trying to figure out exactly what she could extract from him. Stoney tried to remember a time when he knew women like Annie. But right now, all he could see in his mind was her. Her goodness.

They stared at each other for a few minutes, the street noises fading away until the only sound they heard was their breathing. Slowly drawing toward each other as though a magnet was pulling, they met in the middle of the sofa.

"Doc, I've fucked you up against a wall and then on the floor. A woman like you deserves to be taken in a bed by a man who cares. You got a problem with that?"

Annie's eyes registered surprise. "You care?"

Stoney's lips moved toward hers, stopping only when they were a breath away. "Girl, I'm so fucked, but yeah. I care."

Seeing the slight smile curve the edges of her lips, he couldn't wait any longer. Pulling her toward him forcefully, he took her mouth in a possessive kiss. *I need this now. The rest of this shit, I'll figure out later.* His tongue plunged into her mouth and she moaned as he sucked on her tongue.

He stood, pulling her up with him, then scooped her up and walked past the kitchen counter. There were two doors, one obviously the bathroom. Turning right into her bedroom, he continued to kiss her as he slowly let her slide down his body. He could feel his dick tightly pressing into his jeans and knew she could feel it as well, as her body was pressed full frontal into his. Just as quickly as earlier he divested her of her clothes and for the first time perused her completely naked body.

Petite, she couldn't be over five feet five inches tall. But curvy. Tits, ass, and long coppery hair that waved down her back. Green eyes that stared directly into his. He felt her hand raise up underneath his shirt, sliding her fingers along his abs. Closing his eyes, he wanted to take it slow. Savor the feeling. Savor her.

Annie watched as he leaned his head back, eyes closed as her fingers caressed his chest. She pushed his shirt up but was too short to take it off over his head. He completed the task for her. She placed her hands on the waistband of his jeans, unbuttoning the top and sliding the zipper once again over his swollen cock. She pushed them down and as he kicked his pants and boxers off she ran her fingers back over his chest, up toward his shoulders. Standing on her tiptoes, she reached her fingers to the back of his head, pulling him down for a kiss.

Breath mingling, tongues tangling, the kiss took on a life force of its own. What started as a soft, gentle kiss soon became a roaring flame, consuming both of them.

He lifted her up in his arms and leaned forward planting her on her back on the bed, covering her body with his own. For the first time, with no clothing barriers between them, he reveled in the feel of her breasts pressed against his chest and his dick pressed against her mound. *Jesus, I could lose myself in this woman.* Then the realization hit him. *I have lost myself in this woman.* Holding himself up on one elbow, he moved his other hand to her breast, rolling the nipple between his finger and thumb, swallowing the moan elicited.

She felt the jolt from her nipple to her pussy as his hands did amazing things to her breasts. Her hips began to undulate in the age-old mating dance as she desperately sought to ease the pressure building. She slid her hand between them to grasp his cock, feeling the bead of pre-cum pooling at the end. Sliding her legs open she moved to place the head of his cock at her entrance, but he stilled.

"Not yet, baby. Wanna taste you first."

Before she could protest he slid down her body placing his face against her slick folds and used his tongue in ways she had only read about. His beard tickled her thighs and she squirmed as the sensations raced over her.

"Never. I've never had…" was all she could say, before the building pressure exploded and she found herself flying over the edge. Crying out his name again, she felt the orgasm rip through her as he kept his head between her legs licking her juices.

"Sweetest pussy I've ever had," he said as he moved up her body, kissing her from navel to breasts again. Capturing her mouth he kissed her, desperate for more of her sweetness.

Tasting herself on his kiss, she found she was turned on even more than she thought possible, while wanting to protest his reference to other pussy he had had. She heard moaning again before realizing it was coming from her. Eyes closed, she let his kiss take her away. Away from her tiny apartment with no view. Away from her loneliness. Away from her money concerns. Away to a place where her body vibrated with need. Pressing her hips up toward his once again, she just knew that she wanted him. Inside of her. Now.

Stoney chuckled as he reached for the condom packet. Her need seemed to match his. Her wants were exactly what he was wanting also. Quickly sheathing himself he plunged in, burying to the hilt. He watched her face as he moved in and out, the feeling of her inner muscles clenching him tightly almost taking him over the edge way too quickly. Her trusting eyes stared into his as he felt her arms tighten around his neck.

Annie felt the friction of his large cock sliding in and out of her tightness. She felt as though she were running a race toward the finish line knowing that the elation of crossing was going to be mind-blowing. She felt his pace increase and she raised her legs to his back to open herself as wide as possible.

Stoney reached between them fingering her clit and pushed her over the edge.

Annie's orgasm exploded, taking her whole body in its wake. She was still floating when she felt him tense and she opened her eyes just in time to see him rear his head back, neck muscles straining as he powered through his release.

He continued to pump slowly several more times before collapsing on the bed, rolling to the side taking her with him. He stayed inside of her with his arms wrapped tightly, pressing them full frontal together.

Bodies slick with sweat, legs tangled, breathing ragged, they slowly pulled their lips away from each other. He smoothed his hand along her back, from her neck to her ass and back again. She cupped his face in her hand, running her fingers along the stubble on his jaw.

"Do you want to stay the night?" she asked on a whisper. There was no reply, just his dark eyes staring into hers. Licking her lips nervously, she quickly amended, "You don't have to. I just thought...well, maybe...um"

"No, I want to," he said. Leaning forward to touch his lips to hers, he repeated, "I. Want. To."

Smiling up at him, she simply nodded as she snuggled closer. She closed her eyes and felt his body settle around her. Arms around her, one leg slung over hers, as though he was afraid that she would slip away. *Just a one-night stand. I got that. But I can pretend, can't I? Just for now.* Drifting off to sleep, well sated for the first time ever, she found herself feeling drawn in. Wishing it could be more. Wanting more.

Stoney snagged the covers to pull over their bodies. Tucking her in closely, he wrapped his arms around her with her head pressed to his chest. He couldn't remember the last time he spent the night with a woman. Certainly not within the last two years. But even before that, he didn't spend the night. Sex was physical, for pleasure. He had dated before, but never found the right person. He liked control and it was hard to find a good woman who liked to give that control over. But the last two years? He shuttered thinking about some of the things he had done and some of the women he had been with.

Smoothing his hand over her silky hair, he found a part of himself relaxing. Allowing Annie's beauty and peace to sneak inside of him. Into the dark corners. Into the secret places. Trying to figure out how to make this work, he lay awake, listening to her steady breathing. *She's got to understand. She's just got to. I'm not gonna let her walk away. Not without a fight.*

Chapter 6

"**D**OC ANNIE? DOC Annie?" Leon's voice yelled up the stairway to her apartment. "Where are you? And whose dog is this down here?"

Annie's eyes flew open and she looked at the clock. *Shit!* "Oh my god, it's after eight o'clock. I'm late," she said scrambling over Stoney's body, jolting him from his sleep.

He couldn't believe it. He hadn't slept that sound or that late in several years. Looking over to the side of the room, Annie worked in a blur, throwing her scrubs on and pulling her hair up in a ponytail.

"Leon, sorry!" she screamed down the hall. "I overslept and will be down in a minute. Can you start the preps for me?"

"Sure, doc. You need me to come up and help with anything?"

"NO! I'm fine," she yelled back down, eyes darting over to the bed where the gorgeous man smiling at her was lounging against the headboard.

"You can't come down," she whispered. "At least not to the clinic. Or maybe in a little while. Or maybe I can let you know when the coast is clear. Or maybe…"

Stoney threw his legs over the side of the bed and stood, comfortable with his nudity. Walking over to her, taking in her wide eyes and stammering, he just laughed. "Doc darlin'. It's obvious you have no experience in slipping men in and out of your apartment."

She was pulled in for a hug, feeling his chuckle deep in his chest against her cheek. "Of course I'm not used to it. I've never done it before!"

Stoney tightened his hold, feeling her words sink into his soul, knowing she let him in and that was something she didn't do lightly. Let him into her apartment. Let him into her emotions. Let him into her body. He looked down as he felt her turn her face up toward him.

"I've got to go, but you can stay here and have some breakfast. I'll check on Sarge for you. Then I'll figure out how to get you out."

"Annie relax. You've got a back door. I'll go that way and leave by the alley. No one will see."

Blushing, she dropped her forehead down to his chest. "I'm such an idiot. I forgot about that door." Quickly looking back up, she said, "Stoney, I know what last night was and I don't want you to feel any pressure. You can come in to pick up Sarge anytime."

His eyes darkened even more, if that was possible. "And just what in the hell do you think last night was, doc?" he growled.

"I thought...that we...I... it was..." Her blush had deepened and her eyes grew wide at the tone of his voice.

"What?" he growled louder.

"I just thought that you... thought of me...as... convenient," she stammered.

Lifting his hands to cup both sides of her face he pulled her in close as he lowered her head. "Let me spell it out for you, darlin'. You're no fuck. You got that? I don't spend the night with a fuck. You let me in. You talked to me and you let me in. That means something to me. Things between us may be fucked up for a while until I can get some shit settled in my life, but last night was no fuck. You with me?"

Slowly nodding, she stood on her tiptoes again to press a kiss against his lips. "I gotta go, Stoney. I gotta get down to the clinic."

He let his hands drift down to her sides as he released her.

"But if you want to come back later... or tonight... that would be fine," she whispered. Annie then witnessed a sight that stole her breath. Stoney smiled. His face which was handsome, but always so stern, broke into a smile and it moved right through her.

"You get to work, but I gotta let you know, you spendin' the night in my arms was the best thing that has happened to me in a long time, baby. You lettin' me come back again, makes my fuckin' day."

She jumped as Leon yelled back up the stairs. "I've got to go. See you later?"

Touching his lips to hers once again, he replied, "Absolutely darlin'. I'll be back."

AFTER CHECKING ON Sarge and giving Suzanne and Leon an abbreviated explanation of how the dog ended up in their clinic, she started to walk to the front rooms.

"Are you going to tell us what you've really been doin' this weekend?" Leon asked with his hands on his hips, staring her down.

Annie turned, looking at him. "Wh…what? What do you mean?"

"Doc, you've got a look about you that you haven't had since I met you."

Suzanne's lips twitched upwards as she stood next to Leon.

"And just what look is that?" Annie asked.

"Honey, you've got well-kissed lips and sex hair."

Annie's hand immediately went to her hair, unconsciously smoothing it back down into her ponytail. "I don't know what you are talking about," she protested.

Leon laughed as he walked to her, leaned down to kiss her forehead, and said, "Don't worry Doc. You haven't had a man since I've worked here and it is high time you got some!" With that, he headed out to the front desk.

Annie's eyes latched onto Suzanne's face. "Does it really show?" she whispered.

Suzanne walked over, following Leon's direction. "Annie," she said, remembering to not call her Dr. Donavan, "It only shows to those of us who know you.

You look great. You just look...happy." She squeezed Annie's hand and walked to the front rooms.

With that revelation flowing through her head, Annie began seeing the scheduled patients. Monday wasn't surgery day, so she just needed to get through the rooms of appointments.

By lunch time, she was tired and hungry. "Leon, are you going to the deli?"

"You want me to pick you up something?" he asked. "Suzanne, you want something too?"

Just then the front door opened and Leon swung his gaze around. Seeing the tall, well-built man entering without an animal, he quickly said, "We're closed for lunch. But can I make an appointment for you?"

"I'm just here to check on my dog, see if I can take him home."

Leon's eyes widened, as did his smile. "So you're the mystery man?"

Stoney looked at him, lifting an eyebrow, not saying a word.

Leon nodded, his smile getting even wider. "You're Sarge's owner. The one Dr. Donavan helped over the weekend. Makes sense now." Looking down at the bag Stoney was carrying, he saw the familiar logo from the deli. "And you brought her lunch. I'm liking you so far, Mr...?

Stoney, lifting the deli bag in his hands, said, "I brought sandwiches for everyone. And the name is Stoney."

Suzanne walked from the back and came to a stop next to Leon, staring up into Stoney's dark eyes. She wasn't smiling. Instead, she seemed to be evaluating him, measuring him, trying to figure him out.

"I'll get the doc," Leon said. "Suzanne and I can eat here where we can keep an eye on the front and you can have lunch with doc and Sarge." Leon headed toward the back rooms, calling, "Hey, Doc. Guess who's here for lunch?" in a sing-song voice.

Stoney swung his gaze back down to Suzanne. She definitely wasn't giving off a happy vibe. Tall, beautiful, with long black hair and piercing blue eyes, she seemed to still be deciding on him.

"You must be Suzanne. Annie told me about you. Said you were friends as well as co-workers."

"Yes," Suzanne said softly. "Don't hurt her."

Surprised at the words that just left her mouth, he cocked his head to the side. "You think I want to hurt her?"

Her eyes looked back into his face as though she were struggling with something. "Maybe not intentionally. But she has a lot going on and you seem like…pardon me, but you seem like trouble."

Softening his voice, he assured, "I appreciate your concern for her. I don't want any trouble. And if any comes her way, I'll take care of it."

Suzanne nodded. "Yes, you seem like a man who could do that. But my experience is that men bring trouble, don't stay around long enough to fix it, and then they're gone." She looked past his shoulder as her mind drifted off somewhere, another time, another place.

"I plan on sticking around. And I plan on taking care of anything that comes her way. Keep that in mind. No matter what it may seem like. Keep that in mind."

Suzanne swung her gaze back to him, her brow wrinkled at his cryptic words, but before she could question him further, Annie walked in from the back rooms.

Smiling at Stoney, she walked over to him as he leaned down to press a simple kiss on her lips, cognizant of their audience.

"Come on back. Sarge is up and around, eating and drinking. He's doing great."

Stoney followed Annie to the back area where the kennel cages for post-surgery animals were housed. He couldn't help but notice her ass swaying in front of him as she walked. *How can an ass covered in scrubs be that scrumptious?* Looking down at her croc covered feet all the way up to her copper ponytail with tendrils falling out, he was struck once again by her beauty. *And she has no clue.* His attention was quickly diverted when he heard a familiar bark.

"Hey buddy. Good to see you," he said as he knelt to the floor, grabbing his dog's head in his hands. Ruffling his fur, he gladly accepted the dog licks to his face, knowing that he was alive and well.

Annie knelt down next to him smiling, as she also

reached out her hand to Sarge. "He's doing great. Fever is gone. Incision is fine. He's anxious to go home with you." This last statement was made softly, as though Annie felt that the only connection between them was the dog at her clinic.

Stoney leaned over and touched his lips to hers, keeping it light knowing that Suzanne or Leon could come back at any time. "Let's eat," he said to her lips.

Sitting at her desk in her tiny office, Stoney unwrapped the deli sandwiches and they shared lunch. Annie looked over at him whenever he would focus on Sarge sitting at his feet. *'Stoney' doesn't quite fit him. He's quiet, but only when he doesn't need to say anything.* She stared at his mouth as he spoke to Sarge. *God, he can kiss.* She found herself touching her lips, remembering the tingle from a night of kissing. *I wonder...*

Just then, Stoney lifted his dark eyes to her, noticing the look on her face. "Baby, you keep lookin' at me that way, and I'll find a way for us to get creative right here on this desk and won't give a fuck if Suzanne or Leon are outside listenin'. You got me?"

Startled out of her daydreams, Annie jumped. "Stoney! Hush, they may hear you!" Then she couldn't help but smile at the thoughts she had been having. "Are you taking Sarge home?"

"Yeah. But I'll be back tonight. It'll be late. I'll use the alley stairs, but baby?" He waited until he had her attention. "You don't open the door until you know for sure it is me. Got it?"

Annie nodded at the change in his demeanor.

"Annie. I wanna hear it. You got it?"

"I'm not dumb, Stoney. I don't ever open that door to anyone."

"Didn't say you were stupid, doc. I just don't want anything bad to happen, so I gotta hear that you get me."

Sucking her lips in as she attempted a glare his way, she agreed. "Yes, Stoney. I will only open the door when I'm sure it is you."

Chuckling, he leaned over and captured her lips in the kiss. One that started out slow, then he shifted so that he could pull her body over into his lap and the kiss deepened. When he slanted his head for deeper access, the kiss went wild. Tongues tangling, fighting for dominance, until Annie couldn't remember why she was irritated.

Pulling back, he said softly, "Got to go, baby. Got shit to take care of today, but I'll be back tonight."

As Annie walked he and Sarge out, Leon looked up from the front desk. "Damn, man. You don't waste any time. You've been back there with lunch and I can see our doc has been kissed thoroughly again!" Leon was smart enough to see the warning glare in Stoney's expression. "Don't worry, man. It's high time this beautiful lady met a man who could give her something to think about other than this place!"

Smiling in understanding, Stoney gave a head jerk to Leon, said goodbye to Suzanne, and planted a big kiss on Annie right in front of them all. "See you tonight, baby," he whispered against her lips. Then he and Sarge were out the door.

"ARE YOU FUCKIN' kiddin' me?" Stoney asked the man standing near him. "I bring you the shit, lay it out for you, and you want to dick with her?"

"You know how it is. Can't take any chances. It's gotta be done." The man talking looked at Stoney's face for a moment, before leaning in close. "Are you fuckin' her? Oh, Jesus. How fuckin' crazy are you? You can't leave her tail alone?"

A growl was all the man heard before he was pressed up against the wall with Stoney's hand around this throat. "Don't call her tail. Don't speak of her."

"Calm the fuck down, man," another voice came from the side. Stoney let him go.

"Hope to God you know what you are doing, 'cause we're on the brink of the biggest deal we've ever scored and you can't fuck this up 'cause you can't keep your dick in your pants."

"It's covered," Stoney answered to both men.

"She know who you are? She know what you do?" the first man asked. "You sayin' she is more than tail, then you gotta know when this shit blows and she's is in the dark, you're gonna lose big."

"Told you. It's covered," Stoney replied again. "Now, let's get to work. Tonight, it happens." *In more ways than one.*

THAT NIGHT, JUST as he said he would, Stoney showed up at the back door about eight o'clock. Annie's back door had glass in the top half that she had covered with curtains. Pulling them back so that she could see who it was, she smiled when she saw him. She opened the door but never got out a greeting before he pushed her inside, kicked the door closed, and pulled her close latching on to her lips.

"Been wantin' to do that since I left here this mornin'." He snaked one arm around her back and the other hand held the back of her head firmly. Moving his lips over hers, he wasted no time in plunging his tongue deep inside, eliciting moans that went straight to his dick.

Pulling away, Annie looked into his eyes, wondering once again how it was so hard to read his expressions. Before having a chance to ponder that thought further, he scooped her up and headed to her bedroom.

She pulled his tight black t-shirt up and he jerked it off as quickly as he pulled her camisole off of her. She moved her hands to the waist of his jeans, but he moved them out of the way as his hands went to her shorts and he pulled them down. Once again, she found herself completely nude, but strangely felt no shame.

Stoney cupped her jaw, rubbing his rough thumb over her lips, watching the emotions cross her face even as passion lit her eyes. "Baby, feelin' the need to be adventurous. Can you take it?" Seeing her questioning look, he leaned in. "Wanna eat you first...been dyin' to taste you. Then want you on your back and then on your knees. Want you to come so hard you'll feel me long after we're done. Wanna make it so that you remember this night and who I am. You with me?"

Annie felt the jolt between her legs at his words. Licking her lips, knowing the most adventurous thing she had ever done in the bedroom was...well, she couldn't think of anything but plain missionary sex and that was only with a couple of partners.

"Yeah," she whispered. "I'm with you."

That was all the encouragement he needed. He backed her up to the bed until she felt the mattress, and then he gently pushed her down. Pulling her to the edge of the bed, he lifted her legs to his shoulders and brought his mouth to her. Diving in, he licked her wet folds, reveling in the taste of her, using his talented tongue while the fingers of one hand rolled her nipple and the other hand pressed her stomach flat on the bed to keep her in place.

Wanting to move, Annie protested. And then begged. "More," she panted, feeling the orgasm building. She could feel his chuckle vibrate through her pussy and it was the most amazing feeling. Higher and higher she climbed as she tried to move her hips closer to his face, but his hand kept her still. Finally with one last deep suck on her clit she arched her back as the tremors shook her from deep inside radiating out. Lying on the bed, sated, she barely registered that he had removed his jeans and towered over her. She opened her eyes just long enough to see him lick his fingers.

Before she could move, he leaned in, grabbing her knees to spread her legs as wide as they would go before slamming into her. Leaning up as he pounded into her, he watched her breasts move up and down with his thrusts, enflaming him even more. "I own this, baby. Just me. Remember that." With those words, he leaned down, capturing a nipple in his mouth and sucking deeply.

Annie had never had a man tell her he owned her, but she was too far gone to protest. *If this is what it means to be owned, then hell yeah!* She didn't think she would be able to have a second orgasm so closely to the first, but she could tell it was coming.

"You close, baby?" he asked, his voice rough with need.

"Yes, yes," she panted back.

Suddenly he pulled out, leaving her bereft. Her eyes flew open to question, but before she could think, she was flipped over onto her stomach.

"Up on your knees, Annie. Stick that sweet ass in the air."

She obeyed quickly, because the thought of what she was about to experience overrode any thought of protesting against the alpha-man-in-charge. She felt him plunge from the back, hitting a place deep inside that had never been touched before. This angle was her new favorite position, but before she could express this, she felt a hard slap on her ass, then it was quickly smoothed by his hand.

"That okay for you, baby. Won't do if is you don't like it, but gotta' say, I like to play."

She nodded because as surprised as she was at the spanking, she felt herself tingle all through her core and wanted him to do it again.

"Don't just nod, baby. You want it, I need to hear you say it, so there's no mistake."

"Yeah, honey. I want it."

The words had no sooner left her mouth than she felt another sharp stinging slap. Several more rapid spanks followed, then the sting was smoothed by his rough hand.

"Goddamn, you're tight. I can feel your pussy grab my cock every time I spank you. Are you close again?"

"Yes," she panted out once more, desperately hoping he was not going to pull out again. She was not disappointed. His thrusts increased and as he leaned over her back to roll her nipple once again, she screamed out his name as she came harder than she had ever come. A few more thrusts and he joined her, his head thrown back, neck muscles straining as he released into her body.

They both collapsed, he almost crushing her until he could roll to the side, pulling her with him. Hearts pounding, they lay silent for a few minutes until the fog of bliss slowly lifted.

Turning to face him, she raised her hand to his

strong, stubbled jaw, and then she placed the softest kiss he had ever experienced on his lips.

Staring into her green eyes, he said, "Annie, I need you to remember this. No matter what else happens, this, right here, between us, is real."

Her brow crinkled, but before she could ask any questions, he reiterated, "Got shit in my life. Shit I have to deal with. And I'm trying to keep that from you. But you gotta know that this is real. What we're doin'. What we're feelin'. It's real. You with me?"

Not sure what he was talking about, she knew that she felt the same way so she simply agreed. "Yeah, Stoney. I'm with you."

He closed his eyes tightly as he pulled her head into his chest, tucked under his chin. Wrapping his other arm around her, he pressed her into him as he held on as though his life depended on her.

"Baby? I've gotta go take care of some business. I don't know when I'll be back, but as soon as I can, I'm comin' back to you."

She jerked her head back. "You're leaving? Where are you going? For how long?" She could hear her voice rising with each question. *I've just found you and you're leaving me?*

"Shhh, baby. It shouldn't be long. I've got some work I need to take care of and hopefully it will be done soon. Then I'll be back. I promise. And we will continue this, only it will be better."

Her eyes searched his, but the darkness staring back

at her gave no expression. Knowing he had work to do just as she had her practice to run, she could hardly blame him.

"Are these some of the problems that you fix?" she asked.

"Yeah, baby. These are definitely problems that I have to go fix, but it will end soon, and then I can devote my time to lettin' you know you are the one."

Still not knowing what he was talking about, she allowed him to pull her head back into his chest. Relaxed, sated, warm next to his body and tired from a long day, sleep overtook her.

Stoney lay there, listening to her easy breathing, knowing that this may be the last time he held her. *I come out of this alive, I'm comin' back, baby. We come out of this unscathed, we'll be together and stronger.* Kissing the top of her head, he slid out of bed. Grabbing his clothes, he slipped out of her apartment, making sure to have the door lock behind him.

Then once again, he moved through the shadows, his survival depending on him staying out of sight. Rubbing his hand over his face, he realized how tired he was of the game he was playing. Finding a woman he cared about…really cared about, made him know the game needed to end. Glancing back down the alley at her apartment, he couldn't help but wonder. *Will we get out of this unscathed? And if so, will she forgive me?*

THAT NIGHT, A combined task force of Richland police, DEA, and FBI raided several warehouses arresting a large number of people involved in an organized illegal drug operation. With search warrants in hand, they effectively shut down a huge portion of the gang's drug activities, including drug sales through prostitution and strip clubs and transporting drugs across state lines.

Processing the gang members lined up, handcuffed, and being loaded into transports, the officers smiled knowing the hard work and diligence of each of them culminated in a huge investigation finally coming to an end. As they carefully noted the ones arrested, a tall, tattoed, bearded man with dark eyes and his hands cuffed behind him glared back at them just before he was loaded onto the RDP bus.

Chapter 7

A WEEK PASSED without a word heard from Stoney. Annie kept running their last time together over and over in her mind, searching for clues as to what his words meant. "*Got shit in my life. Shit I have to deal with. And I'm trying to keep that from you. But you gotta know that this is real. What we're doin'. What we're feelin'. It's real.*"

If it was so real, why did he leave in the middle of the night? Wanting to hope that he came back and being angry at being left warred inside of her until she was exhausted from sleepless nights.

"Doc, don't be offended, but you look like shit," Leon said as he came back toward the lab, carrying a large fat cat in his arms. Putting the cat on the table, he and Suzanne expertly drew blood from the yowling cat, while Annie looked over from staring at x-rays.

"Gee thanks, Leon." She glared at him while knowing he was right. She had seen the evidence this morning when she looked in the bathroom mirror at the dark circles under her eyes.

"Leon! You know never to tell a lady that she looks bad. Shirley would slap you silly if you ever told her that!" Suzanne admonished.

He cut his eyes over to Suzanne. "I'm not that big of a fool! You think I'd ever tell my Shirley that? Hell no. I need my balls to stay right where they are!"

Suzanne and Annie couldn't help but laugh, knowing that he was exactly right about Shirley. As Leon headed back to the front with the fat cat, Suzanne walked over to Annie and put her hand on her shoulder.

"Seriously though, Dr. Donavan. You don't look like you have slept in a week."

Barking out a rude noise, Annie confessed, "I haven't."

Suzanne speaking softly, "Is it him? Sarge's owner? I noticed I haven't seen him around and well...I just wondered."

A pithy reply on her lips, Annie looked at Suzanne's face. True concern shown and Annie knew that only honesty was worthy of their friendship.

"Honestly? I don't know. He said he had some business to take care of and when he got back, things would be even better. But it's been a week and I've heard nothing. So..." she replied.

"I'm sorry. If you want to talk, just call," Suzanne said.

The lab phone rang and Annie picked it up, surprised to see that *Reception* came on the screen.

"Dr. Donavan? You're needed up front."

Suzanne and Annie looked at each other in confusion. Usually Leon just yelled to the back since the clinic wasn't very large.

"Wow, he's being very efficient. Must be important," Annie said as she got off her stool and walked to the front.

Annie rounded the corner and saw two men, dressed in suits standing at the counter. One was middle aged, with graying hair and a kind face that was lined with what Annie thought looked like fatigue. The other was tall, huge in fact. He looked as though he felt out of place in his suit, although it fit his muscular frame very well. He was younger, with dark hair, slightly mussed as though his hand had been running through it. He had a vicious scar that ran from the middle of his forehead down toward his eye.

Leon had placed himself between the men and the hallway as though to protect her. Moving to his side, she looked at them curiously.

"I'm Dr. Annie Donavan. May I help you?"

"Dr. Donavan," the shorter of the two men greeted. "I'm Detective Lawrence Carter and this is Detective Matt Dixon." Both men held out their badges for her to see.

Annie, not knowing what to say to their introductions just nodded to the two men. Licking her lips, she began to feel the nausea rising as she wondered if these detectives coming into her clinic had anything to do with Stoney. *Oh, Jesus. Please don't let him be in trouble.*

"What can I do for you?" she asked, trying to steady her voice. She felt a presence at her back and realized that Leon and Suzanne has moved forward to flank her, providing her with whatever comfort they could.

"We have some questions for you and would like you to come down to the station with us."

"Questions?" Her voice was definitely shaky now, "Questions about what?"

Before they could answer, Suzanne piped up from behind. "Do you have a warrant? Is she under arrest? Should she have a lawyer?"

Turning to shush her tech, Annie couldn't help but wonder about the answer to those questions herself. Turning back to the detectives, she squared her shoulders and looked them in the eye.

"Detectives, as you can see, I have a business to run, and as I am the only veterinarian here, my business depends on my being in this clinic. Is this something that can wait? What is this in regards to?"

"No Dr. Donavan. You are not under arrest, but you are a person of interest in a case. We do need to speak to you and we need you to come with us as soon as possible."

A person of interest? What the hell are they talking about? Pulling herself together, she turned to Leon and Suzanne. "I want to get this over with as soon as possible. Please call the afternoon appointments and tell them that we have to reschedule. I'll be back when I can, please just lock up when you're finished."

Leon put his hands on her shoulders, pulling her in. "Doc, you don't have to go now. We can find out what is going on and we can call the lawyer that drew up the contract for the business. Don't know if he is that kind of lawyer, but he can suggest someone."

"I'll be fine," she whispered. Giving Suzanne a quick hug, she retrieved her purse and turned to the detectives. "Gentlemen? Shall we go?" she said with her most authoritative voice, but even as she spoke she knew the tremors in her voice gave her fear away.

WITHIN THE HOUR, Annie found herself seated at a gray metal table in a gray metal chair in a grey painted room – as uncomfortable to sit in as it was to look at. Detective Carter was seated in front of her with a file folder on the table and Detective Dixon was standing next to the door, arms crossed over his chest. He had ditched the jacket as soon as they had arrived at the police station and she noticed that his biceps were straining the material of his short sleeve dress shirt. *I wonder if he busts out of his clothes like the Incredible Hulk.* As quickly as that bizarre thought came, she shook her head to clear her thought tangled mind. *Focus. Answer their questions and get the hell out of here.*

"Dr. Donavan, have you seen anything like this before?" He pulled a photograph out of his file and pushed it forward to her.

Looking down at the picture, she was surprised. Certain that she was going to be seeing a picture of Stoney, she was looking instead at a sausage link.

Crinkling her brow, she raised her eyes back to Detective Carter. "It's sausage. A sausage link. It looks like sausage?" She realized that she was babbling, but her surprise over the picture had stolen her ability to think straight. "You brought me here to ask about this?"

Hearing a growl near the door, she turned her confused look over to Detective Dixon as he peered at her, unsmiling. Licking her lips nervously, she looked back down at the picture.

"Anything else it reminds you of?" Detective Carter prodded. "Anything recently?"

"I removed some links like this in two dogs recently. But you have to understand, dogs will eat anything. I've removed rocks, baby toys, paper, string, even half a steak with the bone in it... everything you can imagine. A dog swallowing a whole sausage link isn't that unusual."

"What made you decide to remove it?" Detective Carter continued.

Entering an area that Annie felt confident in, her voice was stronger as she explained. "When an animal eats a foreign object, the best we hope for is that it will pass. If it doesn't, the animal needs surgery to remove the object. I had a dog dropped off at the clinic about a month ago. It was near death. Some kids in the neighborhood found it and brought it in. They just left it and I couldn't just let it die, so I did the surgery. After it recuperated, I had it taken to a local pet adoption service."

"Where is the...sausage?" Detective Carter asked.

Crinkling her brow once again, she asked, "The sausage? That I removed? You want to know where the sausage is?"

"Yes," was the only answer she received.

"I threw it away. Why would I keep a dog ingested sausage?" she asked incredulously.

"You had another recent case like this?"

Stoney. She knew this had something to do with Stoney. *But what the hell could a dog swallowing a sausage link have to do with the police and Stoney?*

"Yes. It was a week ago. A man came to the clinic late in the evening with his sick dog. I examined the dog, took radiographs, and saw a foreign object. He wanted me to do emergency surgery so I agreed."

"Wasn't it unusual to do surgery late at night, without your assistants?"

"Yes, but the dog was in a great deal of pain and the owner insisted that we help Sarge."

"Sarge?" came a growl from near the door. "And who was the owner?"

Annie looked over sharply at Detective Dixon, who was stalking toward her, stopping only to place his fists on the table as he leaned it. "I didn't know him. He said his name was Stoney. He didn't tell me his last name." *I never knew his last name. I slept with a man wanted by the police and I never knew his name.*

"So what did you do with that *sausage*?" Detective Dixon asked, interrupting her thoughts.

"I threw it away also." Feeling closed in, she felt her

fear slide away, replaced by anger. "Look, I don't know why you are so interested in them, but I don't keep objects that I pull out of dog intestines! I threw them away. If I could go get them to show you, I would, but I can't. They went into the garbage and tossed in my dumpster. They are probably buried under a ton of garbage at the dump. I don't know what this is about. You haven't told me anything, but your attitude makes me think that maybe I do need a lawyer."

At that, Detective Carter opened his file again, pulling out more photographs. Pushing them across the table to her, he lined them up.

Annie looked at them, first in confusion, then in horror. Radiographs of dogs with numerous packets inside of their stomachs and intestines. The sausage-like packets split open with white powder spilling out. Pictures of knives. Guns. Dogs lying in an open grave, their bodies hacked and stomachs slit. The bile rose in her throat as she looked at the devastation. Bringing her fingers to her lips, she tried to swallow down the nausea. "Oh, Jesus. Oh, Jesus," she said, as the sting of tears filled her eyes.

Lifting her gaze up to the Detectives watching her closely, she shook her head. "What is this?" she whispered, visibly shaken. "What happened here?"

Watching her reaction, Detective Carter spoke. "Dr. Donavan, this is one of the ways that drugs are trafficked from one area to another. These aren't sausages. At least not in the traditional sense. They are packets of cocaine, wrapped so that a dog can swallow them. The dogs are then shipped from one area to another and then the drugs are retrieved."

"Retrieved?" she asked, her head shaking back and forth as her voice cracked.

"They are taken, their guts slit open, the drugs removed, and the dog carcasses dumped," came the growl from Detective Dixon.

Detective Carter looked at him sharply, then swung his eyes back to Annie.

"H...How? How c...can someone do this?" she stammered, with her fingers still pressed to her lips. Lifting her eyes from the horrible pictures to their faces, her eyes went wide. "You think I did this? You think I knew about this?" her voice rising.

"No, Doctor. We don't think you had anything to do with this. We have been watching you since we got a tip about that surgery a month ago. You have been on our radar and we've been including you in our investigation. We don't think that you had any prior knowledge of what you were operating on and we have no evidence that you had any plans to sell the cocaine."

"There was really cocaine in those dogs?" *Stoney. Did Stoney know what was happening? Is this what he said he had to take care of? Oh my God – did the detective just say I've been watched?*

Leaning back in the uncomfortable chair, she tried to stop her swirling thoughts. "Am I free to go now?"

"Yes, doctor, you are. You may be called as a witness when this goes to trial, and we would like you to stay in town in case we have more questions. But yes, you may go."

Standing on shaky legs, she rose from the table. Nodding to both of them, she walked passed scary Detective Dixon on her way out into the hall.

"Doctor?"

She turned to look at Detective Carter as he approached her.

"I'll drive you back to your clinic."

Nodding numbly, she began to walk down the hall toward the front door of the station. Hearing noises coming from the doors ahead, she looked up to see a familiar figure walking through the doors, entering the station. Though his hair and beard were now close-cropped, she recognized his build. His tight black t-shirt that barely contained his muscles. The faded jeans that were worn in just the right places. The way he held his body. The way he walked as though he commanded all around him.

Before she could call his name, he turned toward her and she stopped. And stared. His eyes. It was Stoney, but it wasn't. It wasn't his eyes. The dark eyes were gone. In their place were eyes as blue as a summer sky. Piercing blue eyes that penetrated hers. For the first time, she could see emotion in them. But hers were too full of tears to read what emotions were in his. Staring at his face that looked so familiar and yet now so different, she glanced down to see a badge hanging on his belt. Police. He's police. He wasn't interested in her. He was investigating her.

And that makes her...used.

Chapter 8

"**A**NNIE," THE PLEA came.

She heard his voice call her name at the same time she felt a hand on her arm. Turning, she saw Detective Carter still standing next to her, kindness in his eyes. And sympathy. *Oh Jesus, he knows.* Her eyes quickly scanned the room, finding most pairs of curious eyes on the unfolding drama in front of them. *Who else knows? Do they all know?*

Her eyes landed back on Stoney as he started walking toward her. She backed up. For every step he took forward she took a step back, until she hit the wall. The air felt thick, as though she couldn't pull it into her lungs quickly enough.

"Annie, let me explain." The voice came again as his blue eyes never wavered from hers. Detective Dixon stepped in, placing his hand on Stoney's chest holding him in place. "Shane," he said. "Don't do this now. She doesn't need this now."

Shane? He called him Shane? I didn't even know his real name.

Turning quickly, she scooted around Detective Carter toward the entrance. "I have to go. I have to get out of here. I have to go," she kept repeating.

Detective Carter jogged after her. "Dr. Donavan, let me take you back. Please, it's raining outside. I'll drive you to your clinic."

Shaking her head, not speaking, she picked up her pace trying to run past Stoney/Shane being held by Detective Dixon.

"Annie, come back," Shane yelled, then looked at the man holding him and warned, "Matt, get your fuckin' hands off of me."

Suddenly, Annie stopped just as she was almost to the door. Turning slowly, she walked closer to the men, her arms wrapped tightly around her waist as though to protect herself from whatever was coming.

Looking up into the blue eyes that seemed so different and yet so much more natural than the dark contacts he had obviously been wearing, she thought she saw regret. But regret over what, she didn't know and didn't want to know.

"Shane." The word sounded strange to her, but she noticed his eyes latched onto hers as she spoke. "You don't have to explain. There's...nothing...nothing," her voice cracked.

"Baby," he said softly, his blue eyes full of longing.

Shaking her head quickly to unclutter her mind, she drew in a deep breath before letting it out slowly. Pulling herself up to her full height, which she knew wasn't very much, but it gave her a sense of control, she looked straight into his eyes.

"No. Shane. You don't get to call me baby. I think I know exactly what happened and can't believe how gullible I was. You obviously had a job to do, and I get that. I'm just sorry that I was the collateral damage to you doing your job."

He started to move forward again, growling as Detective Carter stepped up to stop him if necessary. "Annie, it wasn't like that. Please, let me explain," he begged.

"Do not come near me. If I have to file a restraining order, I will." Her bravado was fading, and she knew she needed to get out of there.

Turning quickly, she ran the last few steps to the door and disappeared through it.

"Fuck!" Shane bit out.

Matt released his hold on Shane but cautioned him. "You gotta pull your shit together, man. We just scored the biggest hit against these mother-fuckers, got some of their asses in jail, and you cannot fuck up this case 'cause you couldn't keep from fuckin' over some witness while undercover."

Shane rounded on his friend, shoving him up against the wall. "You don't have a fuckin' clue what you're talkin' about. I never meant to fuck her over. She was never that." Shane let go of Matt and stared at the closed door. "She was never that," he said softly, to no one in particular.

Matt and Larry looked at each other, understanding passing between them. Matt clapped Shane on the back and said, "Come on. We gotta get the reports finished. Until this is over, you can't do anything about the doc anyway or you'll really fuck up the case."

Shane stood, his head hanging for a moment, fighting the urge to run after her. Make her listen. Make her understand. *She stopped being a mark the moment she talked and laughed while saving his dog's life. The moment she opened herself to him, she became more than just a witness.* But he knew. He had always known. He'd been buried so deep undercover, letting all that shit touch him for two years. Having to live the life of a drug runner, just to get enough evidence to get them. Right now, he still had to focus on the job. Right now, he had to let her go.

Looking back at the closed door she had left through, he sighed, then turned back to his friends. "I stink with this shit right now. I've been living it and stink with it."

Matt got right in his face and said, "Get that outta your mind, man. You did what you had to do."

"Maybe," Shane replied. "But it cost. And it cost me fuckin' huge. And when this is over, I'm going back to get her. And hope to God, she gives me a chance."

ANNIE RAN OUT of the station, heedless of the pouring rain, right out into the street. A car honked, and she heard cursing.

"Lady, what the fuck? You gotta death wish?"

Pushing on through to the other side of the road, she continued to run several more blocks until soaked and breathless, she stopped under a shop awning. Tears mingled with raindrops. Shivering from cold or anger or heartache, she wasn't sure, but she knew she needed to pull herself together.

Looking up, she saw a taxi drive up letting its passenger out. Racing toward it she hopped in, giving the address of her clinic.

The driver looked in his rear-view mirror at the wet, bedraggled passenger in the back. "You okay, miss? You need me to take you to the hospital or the police?"

Barking out a rude noise, Annie leaned back in the seat, aware that she was dripping water all over the inside of his cab. "Thank you, but no. I think I've had enough of the police to last me a lifetime!" With that, she closed her tear swollen eyes and tried to still her racing thoughts, unaware that she was being followed.

"WELL, I THINK it completely sucks!" announced Suzanne. "Jesus, they haul you out of here like some criminal when they knew all along you didn't keep the drugs. What the hell was that all about anyway?"

Annie and Leon looked at each other, shock plainly written on their faces. They were all sitting in the lab area on stools trying to process what Annie had divulged.

"Girl, that is the most emotion I have ever heard

come outta your mouth since you been workin' here," Leon announced as Annie tried not to grin.

Patting Suzanne's arm, she said, "Don't worry. I haven't felt like grinning since this nightmare started, so that felt good."

Suzanne rolled her eyes, then wrapped her fingers around Annie's as well. "I'm just upset. I can't believe you had to go through that." A grimace crossed her face. "And Stoney. Or Shane. Or whoever the hell he is. I just knew he looked like trouble."

Leon stood and walked over to Suzanne and kissed the top of her head before heading over and doing the same to Annie. "Doc, what do you need us to do? I know this mess is hurting right now, and I can't fix that. Well, I could go try to find Shane's bad-ass and kick some sense into him. But then since he is a big badass, I don't know that I could."

Annie looked up at Leon and smiled a slow, soft smile. "Shirley's lucky, you know?"

Smiling his dazzling white smile, he laughed. "Yeah, well. I think I'm the lucky one."

Annie and Suzanne shared a look before turning their attention back to him. "And that is exactly why she is so lucky," Annie said as she rose from her stool and wrapped her arms around him. Suzanne joined them in a group hug, and Annie felt the familiar sting of tears returning.

Sucking in a deep breath, she pulled away. "Guys, go home. I'm fine. It's Friday, and we have two days off.

Don't worry about me. I'm just going to eat junk food, pull myself together, and come Monday morning it will be business as usual."

"You sure? 'Cause I can call Shirley, and we'll hit up some bars and get totally smashed, if it would help!" Leon offered.

"Nah. You guys head on out. I'll lock up after you and then head up to bed. Truthfully, I am exhausted. Bed is exactly what I need." She thought for a second and then amended, "Well, copious amounts of wine and then bed."

She walked them to the front door, watched as Leon made sure that Suzanne was in her car safely, and then locked the door. Making her way toward the back, she caught a glimpse of herself in the glass window of the lab. Her coppery hair had dried from its earlier drenching and now was frizzing out of control from her ponytail. Green eyes, still red-rimmed, stared back at her.

I am such a loser. I gave myself to man I didn't even know and actually starting falling for him. In a week. What the hell is wrong with me? I never do that. Determined to go back to her well-ordered life she drew herself up, wiping the last of her tears. At least the last of them for now. She had no doubt that more would follow once she hit the wine.

Walking toward the back stairs to her apartment, she clicked off the lights in the clinic, one by one.

Suddenly a figure loomed in front of her. Screaming, she jumped back in fright, but found herself held in place by a large arm with a hand held over her mouth. Without thinking of anything other than escape, she bit down on the hand. She was flung away only to be backhanded across the face. Her head snapped to the side and she tasted blood as she was once again pinned in someone's arms.

Heart pounding, she blinked as the lights came back on in the room. Two men stood in front of her, with the third man at her back holding her tightly. One of the men was tall, distinguished looking in a dark suit, with an air of danger swirling around him. Perhaps it was the scar that ran down the length of his face from brow to chin. His eyes bore into hers. They were cold. Dead. The second man was dressed much more casually. Black pants, black t-shirt. And a smile. A smile that was not friendly. A smile directed at her.

"Who… are you? Wh…what do you want?" her voice weakly asked. Trying to pull herself together, licking her split lips, she continued. "There's no cash in the drawer. It has already gone to the bank."

The smaller of the two men chuckled. Fear trickled down her back and if it wasn't for the arm around her waist, she was sure she would have collapsed to the floor.

The man in the suit spoke. Quietly. Softly. "Dr. Donavan. You have cost us a considerable amount of money. I assure you that whatever was in your cash drawer would not even cover my expenses for an hour."

"I...I don't know wh...what you are talking about?" she replied, terrified to move. "I don't know you." She tried to swallow but found that her throat was closing with fear. Her chest heaved as her breathing became more rapid.

"My needs are simple, doctor. You found something that belonged to me, and I want to know where it is."

"I don...don't have anything." Her eyes darted around as though looking for something that she might have that belonged to someone else. Clarity struck her as she looked back into his sinister gaze. "The drugs. Oh Jesus, you want the drugs."

"With the police now involved, I am sure you don't have my possessions here, but surely you knew what you had. Surely you are hiding it to see how much I will pay to get it back."

"I didn't keep it. I thr...threw it away," she stated, hoping this would give them a reason to leave.

The smaller man's mouth curved into a slow smile, as his eyes seemed to glimmer. His hand had slipped into his pocket drawing out out an object that she did not recognize until he flipped it and realized that he was wielding a knife. Oh my God. She began to shake with fear, but the man holding her only tightened his arms.

"My dear doctor. Are you trying to tell me that you did not know you were holding a quarter of a million dollars in your hands? I highly doubt that. But..." he held her gaze. "If it is true, that would be very unfortunate for you."

"I don't have it. Honestly, I threw it out."

The man with the knife approached her slowly, the smile never leaving his face. He drew the flat surface of the blade down her cheek. Annie felt a tear slid down her cheek, mingling with the path of the metal.

The man in charge watched her carefully. "You know, Jose, I think I believe her. I don't think she knew what she had at all."

Her eyes sought his, looking for a reprieve from her terror. But it wasn't going to come.

"My dear, you may have tossed out a fortune in cocaine, but you will still have to be an example. I can't have everyone acting with such cavalier ignorance."

A loud noise came from the front of the clinic. "Annie! Are you still here? I forgot my cell phone," yelled Leon.

Jerking up, Annie began screaming. "Leon, call 911, I'm being robbed. 911. 911."

The man holding her tried to put his hand over her mouth again, but she was too quick. Ducking her head, she continued screaming. Kicking out, her shoes hit his shins, causing him to loosen his grip just enough for her to wiggle away. The taller man was already at the alley door, making his escape. The shorter man's glare was no longer smiling as she now saw a gun in his hand aimed at the hall.

"Nooooo!" she screamed, terrified that Leon would come into the room, then found herself being thrown to the floor as the man who had been holding her pushed her down so he could escape. "Stay back, Leon! They have a gun!" she yelled.

She looked up just in time to see the gun pointing at her as the man called Jose was at the alley door. His eyes, soulless, pulled the trigger just as she tried to roll away. The sound of gun blast in the small area deafened her as a pain sliced through her side.

She lay on the floor, seeing Leon's anxious face above hers.

"Oh God, doc. What the hell happened? Stay with me. I've got you, honey."

The sound of sirens filled the night air. Leon's face seemed fuzzy. Far away. Then another face appeared above her. *Shane.* Then blackness.

Chapter 9

FLOATING. ON THE ocean. On a blow-up pool lounger. Warm sun on her face. Working on her tan.

It's not warm. It's dark.

Strange noises seeped into Annie's consciousness. Noises that did not sound like waves.

Opening her eyes, the harsh lights had her closing them quickly, but not before her brain registered that she was in the hospital. A flood of memories rushed back as she remembered the events in her clinic. Panic rose in her chest as her eyes opened wide and she tried to sit up. The pain in her side sliced through her and she fell back to the bed, a gasp escaping her lips.

"Baby?" a familiar voice sounded right next to her. She opened her eyes again, seeing Shane bending over her, worry lines scoring his face.

Confusion melded with fear and as much as she hated to cry in front of him, tears slid down her face.

Shane cupped her face with his hands, wiping her tears with the rough pads of his thumbs. "You're okay, baby. You're gonna be fine."

"I was shot," her voice croaked.

"I know. I'm so sorry, Annie."

"How bad?"

"The bullet just barely grazed your side. Honestly, baby, it did not hit anything major. It is more like a bad burn."

"Hurts."

"I know, baby. I know," he answered as he leaned over and kissed her forehead.

She looked into his blue eyes, so expressive, so different from the dark contacts he had been wearing. She saw concern...and care. *No, I do not see care. He does not care about me.*

She did not want to ask, but found the words coming out anyway. "Why are you here?"

Shane's gaze did not waver. "Annie, there's nowhere else I would wanna be than right by your side." He saw the doubt in her eyes. "Baby, you ran out yesterday and didn't give me a chance to explain."

Just then there was a commotion at the door as Leon and Suzanne hustled in.

"Explain what? That you are a complete asshole who used Annie to get what you wanted? Forcing her into your world of drugs and men with guns and...and ...your shit!" Suzanne yelled as she got right in Shane's face.

Before he could react, Suzanne was pulled back into Leon's front as he wrapped his arms around her. "Down wild-girl," he said calmly. "Annie doesn't need this right now."

Suzanne burst into tears as she looked down at Annie. "I couldn't believe it when Leon called, I just couldn't believe it."

Leon's voice, soft and gentle, said, "Annie, I called your mom." At this, Annie's eyes grew wide, but he continued before she could say anything. "It's okay, doc. Your mom was freaked, but I got your dad on the phone. I told him what the doctor said and that you can go home tomorrow. They wanted to come immediately, but I told them to wait. I figured you might need them later."

He then turned his gaze to Shane and his gentle look was replaced with a hard one. "You want to step outside with me?"

Shane shifted his stance, arms crossing his massive chest, legs apart. "No one knows what went down between Annie and me, but Annie and me. I get that you care and I get that you're a friend. I respect that. But I'm not leaving her side now. I let her walk away earlier and I'm not making that mistake again."

Leon stared at him for a moment, as though measuring Shane's honesty. Finally giving a head jerk, he turned his gaze back to Annie, offering her his dazzling smile. Tucking a still sniffling Suzanne into his side, he said, "Doc, don't worry about the clinic. We'll call the appointments for the week and reschedule..."

"No!" Annie protested. All eyes turned to her in surprise. "I'll be there on Monday morning. We have to keep the clinic open," she explained.

"Baby, you gotta have time to heal," Shane said.

She looked at him sharply. "Do not call me *baby*. And do not tell me what I have to do. You made your play. I get it, Sto...Shane. You had a job and you did it. I was just collateral damage."

Shane's look went from concern to scary as he leaned down in her face. "You were not a play," he growled. "You know exactly what happened between us was real. No play. No game. It was in the middle of a fuckin' mess, but it was real."

Staring into his face that still made her long to kiss his jaw, she whispered, "I didn't even know your name."

He closed his eyes and dropped his head for a second before bringing it back and leveling his blue eyes onto hers. "Annie, it wasn't a lie. I was a quiet kid growin' up, known as Stoney in the neighborhood. I needed a name when I went under, but I wanted to hold on to something that was real. I went with Stoney. So baby, when you got Stoney, you were still getting me.

"I know you're in pain and I didn't want to do this here, but you wouldn't give me a chance yesterday, so I'm takin' my chance now. Can't give you too many details, but you're gonna let me tell you how it is.

"I've been workin' vice for several years, gettin' more and more frustrated, 'cause no matter how many dealers we would get, we couldn't get the top. Two and a half years ago, a good friend's woman was kidnapped and hurt by these fuckers. We got her out, but I saw what that did. Fuckin' almost lost his woman and thought for sure we were gonna fuckin' lose him too."

Annie lay quiet, listening to his story, unable to look away. Unable to turn it off. Unable to shut it down. *Oh my God. He's witnessed this and been hurt by it.* Softly she asked, "Was the woman all right?"

He looked down at her face that had gentled, seeing her brow wrinkle in concern. Placing his hand on her cheek, he smoothed his fingers over her brow, willing her to relax. "Yeah, baby. She was fine. Drugged and hurt, but she came out all right, with a good man by her side to make sure she would stay all right.

"I decided then that a big play needed to be made. I thought that goin' undercover would work for me. So I volunteered."

"Your eyes," she whispered.

"Yeah. I been wearing dark contacts 'cause my eyes give me away."

"I didn't like the dark eyes. They didn't tell me anything when I looked at you."

Shane smiled, relieved that Annie was talking, giving him a chance.

"So I went in. Two years, baby. No contact with family." At this, her eyes widened, but he continued. "My family knew. They get it, 'cause this job is who I am. But it sucked all the same. I thought maybe six months, but it fuckin' kept draggin' out. And livin' in that world for two years was fuckin' killin' me."

The room was quiet for a moment until Leon spoke. "So what about doc? Where did she fit into your world?"

Annie's eyes shifted to Leon and Suzanne in the corner, having forgotten they were still there. Suzanne was no longer sniffling, but eyes wide, attentively listening.

Shane glanced to the corner also, taking in the two friends. Rubbing his hand over his face, he continued. "Been watchin' them torture dogs to get the shit in and around the country. Finally got a tip that a vet in the area was helpin' them. Didn't know how. Findin' easier ways for the dogs to ingest the drug packets. Started watchin' some of the vets. I ended up with you," he said as he leaned back over the bed, placing his fists on either side of her.

"Annie baby, you were the first ray of sunshine I had in almost two years. It wasn't hard followin' you, watchin' you. I'd been buried deep in the belly of the beast. Forgot what clean livin' looked like. Smelled like. Felt like. But you, you lived that clean every fuckin' day. I had the urge to make contact just so I could have a little of that clean back. It didn't take long to figure out you weren't the vet we were lookin' for. But baby, couldn't give you up."

"What do you mean?" she asked, peering into his sky blue eyes, looking for understanding.

"I kept followin' you. Just to see you. Just to have that sunshine, even from a distance. Not too close. Not enough to get burned. But just enough to feel the warmth."

The room was silent. No one spoke. No one moved. The only sounds came from the heart monitor that Annie could swear was beating faster.

"We were gettin' close to havin' the evidence we needed, when one of the fuckers decided to test some of us by havin' us use our own personal dogs. I'd rescued one not long after takin' this assignment. It fuckin' killed me to have them get Sarge to swallow that shit, but I knew that would give us the evidence."

Shaking his head at the memory, he continued, "So I let them do that, but only 'cause I knew I could get him out and get him to you. I wasn't testin' you. I wasn't settin' you up. I already knew you were clean. Annie baby, I came to you 'cause I knew you would save his life. Without thinkin'. Without askin' for the moon. Without throwin' a shitfit 'cause it was late and I might not have money. I came to you 'cause I knew you were the only one I wanted to trust with my dog."

Shane finished by bending his elbows and leaning the rest of the way down, placing his lips gently on hers. It wasn't a kiss of passion. But one of promise.

"I hate to interrupt this touchin' scene, but I gotta witness I need to interview," came a voice from the doorway.

Growling, Shane stood up, recognizing Matt's voice. "You got shit timing friend."

"Yeah well, add it to my list of other transgressions." Matt's eyes cut over to Leon and Suzanne. "You Leon?" Receiving a nod, he added, "I gotta interview you too, since you were at the crime scene."

"Crime scene?" Suzanne asked in confusion.

"The clinic," came the terse answer.

She slid back into Leon's embrace unnerved to hear the clinic being called a crime scene.

Annie looked up at Detective Dixon, suddenly fearful of reliving the events of last night, while hearing the heart monitor speed up again. Shane caught that look and slid his hand down to hers, holding it tightly.

"It's gonna be all right, baby. I'm right here," he said.

Her eyes cut over to his expressive blue ones and she gave a quick nod. Linking her fingers with his, she turned her attention back to the detective.

"Okay, Detective Dixon. I'm ready," she said, trying to not show that she was shaking.

Matt's face gentled as he said, "Considerin' you're holdin' my friend's hand, how about you call me Matt?" Seeing a small smile cross her face, he continued his questions.

She answered everything, giving as detailed a description as she could. Occasionally she saw a glance between Matt and Shane, but didn't know how to interpret it. Several times she heard her voice waver, met each time with a squeeze to her hand. Shane was willing his strength to her and she gladly accepted it.

"Det...I mean Matt. What happens now? I mean they know me. They know where I work. Where I live."

Before Matt could answer, Shane swung back

around planting himself firmly in her line of vision as he leaned over the bed again. "Baby, that shit does not touch you again."

"But…"

"No fuckin' buts. That shit does not touch you."

Pulling her lips in, she wanted to know more, but Shane didn't seem to be in a mood to share.

Matt spoke and she looked around Shane's body so that she could see his face. Realizing that Shane was holding on by a thread he moved to the other side of her bed so that she could see him easier.

"Doc, with your statement and Leon's, we are already picking those three up. The main man with you last night was higher up than we have gotten and we've been after him. I know it doesn't feel good right now and it wasn't planned, but you have just helped us close the loop tighter around the top of the chain."

"But she's still in danger," Suzanne bit out from the corner. "You all don't seem to get that she is now in the middle of this mess!"

Shane swung around, piercing her with his glare. "Suzanne, I get that you're her friend and you care, but what you don't get is that I'm sayin' this shit doesn't touch her again." Seeing that Suzanne was about to argue, he cut her off. "I'm out now, back on the force as vice. We got police protection for the clinic and she will have it 'round the clock. When she's not with me, then she's got someone on her."

At that, Suzanne mouth dropped open, but not before Annie looked up sharply. "What do you mean I've got someone on me?"

Shane's eyes penetrated hers as she heard Matt chuckle in the background. "Baby, you're with me," he explained. "I got outta this shit life by takin' them down. Now I'm livin' for me, not goin' back under, and I'm doin' it with the sunshine that I found. This shit wasn't supposed to blow back on you. It did and they're gonna pay for that and pay big. And until that happens, I'm callin' in all my markers and you got protection when I'm not around and all of me when I am."

Suddenly exhausted, Annie slid back into the pillows, all the fight gone out of her. Shane's blue eyes warmed and he pushed her hair back away from her face. "You need to rest, baby, and I'm gonna be right here. You can rest easy, 'cause I'm not leavin'."

The nurse walked in, checking her vitals and giving her another dose of pain meds. Eyeing the group, she announced that she thought the patient needed more rest and less visitors, before marching out of the door.

Leon and Suzanne walked over to the side of the bed where Matt had been standing. Suzanne kissed her cheek and whispered, "Be safe, doc."

Leon followed suit as he kissed her too, but whispered, "You've hooked a wild one, doc. But I think he's all right. If you can hold on to his wild ride and tame him at the same time, you're gonna find what you been looking for."

At this, Annie closed her eyes, letting the pain meds place her back on her float on the water in the warm sun.

Chapter 10

THE NEXT MORNING Annie woke groggy, but as she turned the stitches in her side were a stark reminder of what had happened. She lay on her uninjured side, but felt something at her back. It was too hard to be pillows. As she twisted her head around to look, she saw a large arm come around carefully and pull her back into his embrace. *Shane?*

"Mornin', Annie baby," came his sleepy voice. "Do you need some more pain medicine now before they discharge you?"

"Why are you in bed with me?" she asked, a blush firing across her face.

"You kept moving in your sleep and when you did, you would whimper in pain. If I lay here beside you, it would keep you from moving to your injured side."

Annie warmed, not because of the blush, but because she liked his explanation. A lot. She still had not had time to process everything that he told her yesterday, but she understood his motives.

Dealing with the uncomfortable feeling of a full bladder, she tried to move herself to a sitting position, but found herself pinned down.

"Baby, you need to keep resting."

"Um, I um…need…," the blush came back as she tried to figure out how to get to the bathroom without telling him she needed to go to the bathroom.

Before she could decide how to get him to leave, she felt him leave the bed and walk around to her side of the bed. Leaning down he scooped her gently and set her feet on the floor, steadying her until he was sure she could stand, and then started walking with her toward the bathroom.

Looking up sharply, she asked, "How did you know what I needed?"

Smiling, Shane answered, "Baby, you've been hooked up to an IV since yesterday, and they took the catheter out last night, so it only figures you gotta go." By the time he finished, they were at the door. "You need help?"

"No. But thanks," she said softly as she let go of his arm, and hobbled into the bathroom.

A couple of minutes later, Shane knocked on the door. "Annie? The nurse is bringing in your discharge papers so I've got your clothes here for you. I'm gonna just set them inside," he said as he barely opened the door and laid her clothes on the sink. Shutting the door quickly, he hovered in case she needed something.

After a moment, she cracked open the door and peered out. "Shane?"

"Right here, baby."

"I…need…"

"Annie baby, let me in," he said gently as he carefully pushed her back and slid into the bathroom. She was holding onto the sink for balance and had managed to get the hospital gown off, but was clutching it in front of her, blushing furiously once again. Bruises covered her arms.

Shane stepped up to her, wrapped his arms around her and pulled her in close. One hand cupped the back of her head as he pressed her into his chest. The other wrapped around her body, holding her protectively. They stood this way for a moment, Shane offering comfort. Annie taking it.

She finally pulled back slightly and looked up to say, "I can't get my clothes on."

He peered into her tear filled eyes. "I'll take care of you, baby. In all ways. Promise."

Sucking air in through her nose to still the threatening tears, she nodded. She stepped back, still clutching the hospital gown to her front. "I can't twist my body to even get my bra on and I can't bend to get my pants on."

Nodding, Shane reached over and snagged her bra off the counter, then turned her so that her back was to him. He held the bra out in front of her as she dropped the gown to slide her arms in so that he could pull the back pieces and hook them in place. It was not lost on her that he did all of this while preserving her modesty at the same time.

Grateful, she glanced over her shoulder, seeing his

blue eyes full of concern. "I'm okay. Really."

Growling, he replied, "No, you're fuckin' not okay. You're strong. You'll survive. You'll get through this. But baby, what you aren't, is fuckin' okay."

Pulling her lips in as she saw anger in his intense look, she just nodded and said nothing.

Shane took her scrub bottoms and helped her slide them on as well. Holding up her scrub top, he just shook his head. The material was shredded and bloodied. Tossing it in the trash, he left the bathroom and shortly returned with a white t-shirt. Seeing her questioning gaze, he explained, "Had Matt bring over a change of shirts for me early this morning. It'll be big, but you'll be covered."

Nodding her gratitude, she allowed him to slip it over her head and work her arms through it, being careful of the stitches in her side.

"Thank you Shane. I don't know what I would have done..." her voice trailed off as her eyes slid to the side and her mind wandered.

Shane, not wanting to lose the connection, placed his large hand on her face, pulling it gently back to his. "Don't be thanking me baby. I brought this shit to your door and I'm fuckin' pissed at myself about that." Shaking his head as he looked down toward his feet, "I was fuckin' stupid to bring Sarge to you. I just..."

Annie reached up and mimicked his actions by cupping his strong jaw in her hand, pulling his face back up to hers. "I would have never wanted anything to have happened to Sarge. Or you." At that, she saw Shane's face gentle as he looked deeply into her eyes.

Leaning down, he placed a soft kiss on her lips. "Let's get you home, baby."

AFTER HELPING HER up the stairs to her apartment, he looked around carefully to see what work had been done.

"Shane, what is this?" Annie was looking at a box next to her front door.

"Security system, baby."

"Since when do I have a security system?"

"Since this shit-storm hit you and your clinic. Now, I'm workin' to keep that from blowin' back on you again."

Her eyes cut over to a similar box on the wall next to the kitchen...*door?* "What happened to my kitchen door?"

"Baby. The one you had was old, coulda been kicked in easily, and was half glass. Seriously? A shit door, baby."

"But, it had a window. I could look out."

"Baby, what the fuck? Yeah, you could look out, but then anyone could look in." Shane saw the irritated look on her face and rubbed his hand through his hair. Not used to explaining himself to anyone, he realized that he needed to get her on board with the new security changes.

Walking over to where she stood, he held her in his arms, feeling the tension radiating from her. Sighing, he began again. "Annie baby. The door you had was an old wooden door with a full window at the top. Yes, it let in some light, but it also offered no privacy or protection. This is a steel door, with a peep-hole at the exact height that you are so that you can easily see who is on the other side. It even has one-eighty degree viewing so that you can see if there is someone on the steps."

Turning his body to face the front door, with her still tucked in his embrace, he continued. "You got a security system on both doors. You arm them when you leave, even if you are goin' down to the clinic, and then you arm them again when you come back in."

Annie shifted in his embrace, wincing slightly, a movement that did not go unnoticed by him. Looking up, she said, "I appreciate all that you have done. Really. But, I can't afford this. The clinic is doing well, but once all the clinic expenses are paid and my student loan payment is sent off, there isn't a lot left over right now."

Looking down, he felt lost in her green eyes. Cooper hair fell in waves framing her face. Shiny. Clean. Sunshine. "What I said in the hospital is true, Annie. What happened with us was real. We're gonna ride that as far as we can and see where it takes us. Things go the way I think they will, you and I will be movin' out and you'll get that clinic in the country, and we'll leave this shit behind. Something happens and we decide we're not an *us*, then you still got a security system that'll give me peace of mind. One way or the other, I want you safe."

Confusion wrinkled her brow as she murmured in his chest. "You think we're an *us*?"

She felt his chuckle rumble against her cheek.

"Hell yeah, baby. I know we're an *us*. Told you, I never played you. We were an *us* from the moment you let me in to take care of Sarge. We continued to be an *us* when we first kissed. And we were solidly an *us* when my dick was inside of you."

Gasping, she looked back up into his face ready to give a pissed off retort then she looked into his eyes. Blue eyes that no longer hid his thoughts. Blue eyes that she could now read. Blue eyes that were twinkling. *I didn't know they could twinkle.* Deciding that she liked that look, she gave in.

"Okay, the security system stays."

"Thank fuck," he replied, "cause I sure as hell wasn't callin' my friends back in to remove it." He moved her over to the sofa where he sat and gently settled her down on his lap, carefully avoiding her injured side.

"Friends?" she asked.

"Yeah, baby. I got friends. I'm enjoyin' spending some time with them since I've been under and off the radar for two years. Got some friends workin' in security systems and they jumped at the chance to help me make you safe."

"Why would they do that?" she wondered out loud. "They don't know me."

"No, but they know me. Know I haven't had a woman I cared about in years. Know I've been drownin' in shit for two years and am just now comin' up for air. Know I've got a woman that needs protection and one call was all it took. They were over here yesterday makin' sure my woman was safe."

"You keep saying *your woman*. I've never said I was your woman. In fact, I don't recall you asking."

"I told you, baby. You became my woman, the first time my dick was in you."

She looked up and pierced him with a glare. "So you're saying that any woman you have slept with has been 'your woman'?"

His expressive eyes changed from amused to something else she couldn't read, but was very visible nonetheless.

"Baby, part of us seein' where this goes is hammering out things from the past. But that is not a conversation we want to be havin' right now." Seeing her eyes narrow he continued,

"At some point, we'll share about our pasts. Gonna let you know right now, mine is not pretty, but you already know a lot of that. I'm no saint when it comes to past women, but again, that is not a conversation we want to have now. But you were different from the moment I laid eyes on you. Never felt that before. Never cared about watching a woman come before. So yeah, since our first time, you've been my woman." He paused, spearing her with his sharp gaze. "Now can you honestly say you don't want that?"

Sighing loudly, she agreed. "You're right. I'm too tired to have a conversation that will undoubtedly piss me off. She lowered her head, studying her shoes for a moment.

"What's goin' on in that pretty head of yours, baby?" he asked gently.

She lifted her eyes back to his, feeling as though she could really see him now that she had expressive blue eyes to peer into. "Shane, I've never done any of this. I barely date much less have the craziness that we have had. Leon told me that I should be more spontaneous and have some fun. Look where that got me? Questioned by the police, men breaking into my clinic trying to kill me, me needing a security system…" Shaking her head again, she sighed. "It just seems so backwards. We should have met. Been honest. Got to know each other. Then and only then, if we were sure there was a connection, have sex."

"In a perfect world, baby, that's exactly what I would have wanted to do with you." He leaned closer until they were almost touching, keeping his eyes on her the whole time.

"Shane, how do I know that I'm not just the first girl that gave in to you that wasn't in that other world? I mean, this could all seem bigger to you because you're not undercover anymore."

He could see self-doubt cloud her expression as he lifted his hands to cup her face. "Annie, I haven't been undercover my whole life. Hell yeah, the last two years sucked. But before that, I dated, and never met anyone that made me want to know them the way that I want to know you. I can't give you promises right now, but I can honestly say I want to explore what we have."

Peering up into his eyes, she nodded and whispered, "I'd like to see where this goes too. But I want to back up, Shane. I need us to do this slower."

Smiling, he pulled her in for a kiss. One that started out slow. Gentle. Then with a touch of her tongue, went wild. Untamed. Wet. Unrestrained. Just like him.

Chapter 11

THAT EVENING, SHANE ordered Chinese and he and Annie sat at her little table eating. He noticed that she was quiet. Almost uncomfortable.

"What's up baby?"

A guilty look crossed her face as she raised her eyes to his. "I'm sorry," she said.

"Don't want you to be sorry, Annie. I just wanna know what is goin' through that beautiful head of yours."

"Shane, I don't know anything about you. I was just thinking that I'm sitting here with someone that I know intimately, but don't know at all." Shrugging, she added, "It just seems weird that's all."

Finishing his food, he stood and took their plates to the sink and rinsed them out. Returning to the table, he took her hand and assisted her to her feet before leading her over to the old sofa. Sitting down he pulled her down into his lap. "So let's talk, baby. What do you want to know?"

Smiling, she said, "Now I can't think of anything with you staring at me like that."

"Okay, how about I just start out telling you what I

think you might want to know."

Giving him a curious look, she agreed.

Shane settled one hand on her hips while the other rubbed lazy circles on her back, willing her to relax.

"Okay, baby, here it is. My full name is Shane Patrick Douglas. I grew up outside of Richland in a suburb and my mom still lives there. I've got a younger brother, Rick, in college. He's thinkin' about going to the police academy but mom's hoping he decides to go into something safer. I've got one sister. Megan. She's the middle one. Married to a good guy and they've got a couple of kids. They live near mom so I know they're close if she needs anything."

He paused, watching her carefully. Her brow crinkled as she pondered what he had just said.

"You didn't mention your dad," she said.

Shane inhaled deeply and let his breath out slowly. "Yeah. My dad. He was a policeman and was killed about seven years ago while on duty." He heard the gasp from Annie's lips as he continued. "Drug bust gone bad."

The silence loomed between them, each lost to their own thoughts.

"Is that why you do it? Why you go after them so hard?" she asked softly.

He looked beyond her for a moment, then pulled his gaze back to hers. "Baby, I can't tell you exactly why I went into police work. It just seemed like the right thing to do. Dad saw me graduate from the academy and hoped I would come work with him on the force."

Annie looked at him sharply. "You don't blame yourself, do you? For what happened to your dad?"

"Maybe if I had been there with him instead of here, things would have been different."

"Shane, you can't possibly believe that. Who knows what would have happened, but you can't blame yourself," she said adamantly.

He gave her hips a squeeze while shaking his head. "Don't know, baby. But I know I can't go back and change anything, so I just decided to do whatever it took to bring those fuckers down."

"What does your family think?"

His hand continued to move up and down her back as he continued. "Rick? He gets it. Understands it. Hell, he may even be after it himself. Megan and mom? They wish I'd do something else. Mom knows I gotta do what I gotta do, but I know she's afraid of the phone call in the night, just like with dad. But she gets it."

They sat quietly for a few moments, each to their own thoughts. His hands drifted upward until they cupped her face, holding her gently. His pale blue eyes captured her green ones before he pulled her forward. His lips met hers in a kiss that held promise, then quickly became wild and untamed again. Just like before, sparks ignited. He pulled back, waiting to see what her reaction was going to be. He didn't have to wait long.

Annie grabbed his face in her hands, pulled him

forward and latched her lips onto his. Tired of waiting. Tired of analyzing. Tired of sitting on the sidelines. Tired of overthinking everything. In that moment, she decided that the sparks she felt every time she was with him were worth jumping into the unknown. He seemed unsafe, but when she was with him, she never felt safer. Slanting her head to give him better access to her mouth, she kissed him with all that she had.

Feeling her moan in his mouth he immediately stood, lifting her in his arms with his hands on her ass. Striding to the bedroom, his mouth never left hers. He slowly lowered her, holding her steady until she was standing. Feeling her breasts pressed into his chest, he slid his hands up under her shirt moving it upward until he peeled it off of her. His hand quickly divested her of her bra and it landed in the floor next to the shirt.

While she was being undressed, her hands were pulling his t-shirt off of him as well. She began to unbutton his jeans when his hands came to hers and covered them.

"Hold on, Sunshine. We keep goin' this fast and it'll be over before I'm ready." Looking deeply into her eyes, he continued, "You asked me earlier about bein' my woman. We do what we're gettin' ready to do and this time will be different. This time, make no mistake, I will be makin' you my woman. Just want to check, Annie girl, you with me on this?"

She peered into his pale blue eyes…eyes that no longer seemed hidden, unexpressive. Her breath caught in her throat as she saw into the depths. He was looking at her with compassion. She could actually see the care in his eyes. Warm. Glowing. Just for her.

Nodding slowly, she replied, "Yeah, I'm with you."

Closing his eyes he lowered his head, touching his forehead to hers. "My sunshine," he whispered. "Only light in my darkness."

Before she had a chance to speak he took her mouth again, this time possessively. His lips latched onto hers, kissing her with a force that threatened to overtake both of them. Plunging his tongue deeply, he explored every crevice. Sucking on her tongue, nipping her lips. She wasn't aware he laid her back on the bed until he stopped kissing long enough to slide her pants and panties off of her legs, tossing them into the ever growing pile of clothes on the floor.

While standing, he quickly divested himself of his jeans and boxers after pulling a condom out of his pocket. Sliding it over his impressive cock, he joined her back on the bed, covering her body with his own.

He looked down at the woman beneath him, knowing she was different. Knowing she was the one he wanted. Knowing she was the one who saved him. And yet frightened. This one tiny beauty held so much power over him. *What if she's repulsed once she knows what I have had to do for the past two years? What if she decides that I'm too much of a wild card? What if…*

He felt hands gripping his face as his eyes moved back to hers.

"Hey, where'd you go?" she asked. "You were laying with me but your mind was somewhere else."

Smiling down into her perfect face, "Sorry Sunshine. I was chasing shadows, I guess. But I promise, right now with your body underneath mine, there is nowhere I'd rather be."

He watched her face a few minutes later as his long lazy strokes drove her wild and she came apart in his arms, screaming his name. Dipping his head back down, he sucked her nipple in his mouth, prolonging her orgasm as he quickly followed in his release.

This time it was making love. She felt it. He knew it.

LYING IN BED tangled up in each other, they listened to their hearts beating in unison.

"Sunshine, as much as I hate to do this now, we got some things to talk about."

Annie turned so that she was facing him, a questioning look on her face. "What is it?" she asked with fear in her voice.

He quickly looked down at her and assured her, "It's nothin' bad, baby. I just need to let you know where things stand right now with me 'cause it's gonna affect the next week." He slid up in the bed, leaned against the headboard, and pulled her up with him. Tucking her in his embrace, he began.

"I'm gonna be leaving tomorrow morning and be

gone for most of the week."

She twisted around to look into his face, deciding that when they talked she wanted to see his eyes. Eyes that could now let her know how he was doing.

Smiling he continued, "I've got two days of debriefing since coming back from undercover. Got meetings about the big takedown we did last week and need to check on the progress of the three goons we picked up from your assault. Right after that, I want to head to Jefferstown to see my family. I'd love for you to go with me, but I know you can't close the clinic right now."

"Honey, you need this time with your family. You need to see them and focus on just you and them right now."

Giving her a squeeze, he nodded. "Yeah, I want to spend more time with you before throwing my mom into the mix."

Annie's eyes widened. "You don't think she'll like me?"

Shane threw his head back and laughed. "Like you? Sunshine, she'll be picking out china patterns the minute she lays eyes on you!"

Rolling her eyes, she lay her head back on his chest. "Is there more?"

"Yeah, there is. For one thing, my stuff is in storage 'cause I had to give up my apartment when I went under. When I get back, I gotta find another place to live."

"You can stay here until you find a place," she offered quietly, keeping her face pressed to his chest.

Shane lifted her chin with his fingers and looked into her eyes. "Sunshine, there's nowhere I'd rather be than spendin' my nights in your bed, but I was thinkin' more along the lines of getting a nicer place and hopin' you'd move in with me."

"What's wrong with this place?" she asked, giggling while pretending to be insulted.

"Baby, it'd take more time than we've got to go over what all is wrong with this place."

"Well, I'm not moving in with you now. Remember, we said we would take it a bit slower?"

Shane pulled her so that she was straddling his lap. Feasting his eyes on her nude form, he asked, "Don't you think its a little late to go slow?"

"You know what I mean. The past two weeks have been a whirlwind and we just need more time to get to know each other." She leaned in and licked his lips before pulling back. "But that doesn't mean we don't get to enjoy this."

Growling, he took over the kiss, once again plundering her mouth until they could no longer tell where one ended and the other began. Pulling back, he rasped, "Sunshine, we got more shit to talk about. We keep this up, we'll never get it done."

Pouting, Annie settled once again on his chest. "Okay, what's next?"

"We need to talk about where this case is and how it affects you."

This had her immediately sitting back up, peering into his eyes with fear. "I thought it was over. I thought they were all in jail."

Wrapping his arms around her, he pulled her back into his embrace. "Slow down, Sunshine. Here's the deal. I told you that when I went under I thought the mission would only last six months, a year at most. But the shit kept draggin' on and on. The bastards were slick and trusted real slow. It took almost a year for me to even get close to them. I was gettin' the dirt on them, but my superiors wanted an air-tight case so they kept me in, wanting me to get as much as I could. DEA was also in on it. They had their own undercover agents in as well."

Annie pulled herself back to where she could peer into his eyes, swearing she could see shadows passing through them. "Was it bad?" she whispered.

"Most of it I can't tell you, but yeah baby. It was bad. And that was before I even knew about the dogs. Then that shit took me over the edge. I knew I had to get out, and when they involved my own dog for me to prove my loyalty after almost two years of doing their shit. I knew I had to get it shut down before I completely lost myself."

He pulled her face back to his, smoothing his hands over her cheeks. "I never lied when I said that your sunshine was the first ray of light I had seen in two years. I wanted you then and I want you now. So I also wasn't lying when I said I want to see where this goes."

This time her wild, untamed man kissed her with the softest kiss filled with gentle promises. Promises of more to come. Promises of protection. Promises of ...*love?* Before she could ponder that last thought, he pulled back again.

"So Sunshine, I'm gonna be gone this week, but my security buddies and the police will have you under surveillance. We have a huge number of the gang in jail, but there are still a slippery few that got away. They've dug in deep and gone way down under. I want you protected, but they won't risk anything now. Still, you gotta be smart."

Her eyes went back to his face. "Smart?"

"Yeah. No runnin' in the neighborhood alone. No opening the back door to anyone. Use the security system in the clinic and in this apartment. You gotta do all of that, promise?"

Seeing the concern in his eyes, she agreed. "Yeah honey, I can do that."

Hearing the word "honey" on her lips, he allowed the warmth to slide though him, reaching the dark corners that for two years had not seen the light of day.

"And when I come back...we continue this," he said. "You and me. Gettin' to know more about each other. Nothin' between us. We will lay all our shit out and deal, so nothin' will come back on us." Seeing her questioning look, he said, "Annie, there's shit I had to do for the past couple of years. No way am I gonna tell you all of it, but I don't want anything to come up later and bite us in the ass. So when I come back, I will give you as much as I can give you. But you'll hear it from me, not someone else. You with me?"

"You're kind of freaking me out right now, Shane, but I get where you're coming from. So yeah honey, I'm with you."

With that, he was through talking and he showed her just how much when he took her mouth. Then he took her body and showed her just how wonderful untamed can be.

Chapter 12

TRUE TO HIS word, Shane left that next morning with promises to be back at the end of the week. Annie, anxious to get back into her routine, took over-the-counter pain meds so that she could perform all the duties necessary to keep the clinic running.

Leon and Suzanne were just as determined to assist in every way possible. The end result was that they often ran into each other as they were all trying to do the same task.

Finally, in frustration after Annie crashed into Leon as they were both attempting to pick up a dog from the lab table, she snapped. "Stop! Just stop you two!"

Suzanne and Leon looked at her in surprise.

"Look guys. I know you are trying to help, but I am fine. Honestly. My side hurts just a little, but other than that, I'm back to normal. We will work more efficiently if we resume our normal duties." Smiling at both of them, she added, "But thank you. Both of you."

"Group hug," Leon shouted as he rushed forward with Suzanne in tow, lightening the mood. The girls couldn't help but giggle, then broke apart quickly as they heard the sound of a client in the front jingling the bell numerous time.

"Oh dear. It's Mrs. Scarsdale and Precious," Suzanne moaned. "Her incredibly fat pug."

The three laughed as Suzanne and Annie headed back to the examining rooms. After fifteen minutes of trying to get the client to stop feeding Precious treats, she finally resorted to threats.

"Mrs. Scarsdale, giving Precious treats all the time would be like you going to Mrs. Greenwold's Bakery and eating a pastry every day."

The silence in the room was deafening. Looking up from Precious on the examining table, she met the icy glare coming from the irate client.

"And just what is so bad about having a pastry from the bakery every day?" Mrs. Scarsdale asked.

Annie looked at the plump client and tried to find a way to soften the blow. "Well…I'm sure you are… in very good health, but an…overweight dog can have many health issues such as diabetes, joint, problems, liver issues, even an increased risk of cancer. I know you don't want Precious to have any of those problems."

Mollified, Mrs. Scarsdale finally agreed to place Precious on a diet then picked up her pug and headed back to the reception area to check out. As the pug and its owner left the building, she could hear Leon and Suzanne in the back laughing.

"Oh my God, it's true!" Leon said between chuckles. "Owners really do look like their pets."

"When you tried to compare his treats to Mrs.

Scarsdale going to the bakery every day and it was obvious she did…I almost lost it," Suzanne joined in.

Annie, always trying to maintain professionalism, couldn't help but join in the laughter. "I'm afraid it's a lost cause. Precious is destined to become one of the fattest pugs in history."

By five o'clock, the last of the clients had left and the three were involved in the clinic clean-up.

"So…doc," Leon started as he was gathering trash. "What's going on with your hot detective?"

Suzanne, overhearing his question, moved closer so that she did not miss out on the conversation.

Annie looked at her two friends and smiled. "We're just taking it slow. In fact, he had to go out of town and will be gone for this week."

"With the drug case?" Leon asked.

Shrugging, she replied, "I don't really know. After he got me settled in from the hospital yesterday, he just said that he would be gone for most of this week. I was sort of overwhelmed, so I didn't ask much."

Suzanne spoke up sharply, "I thought he was supposed to protect you, not run out of town."

"Believe me, my apartment and this clinic are totally secure with the new system he had put in. Plus, haven't you seen the number of cop cars driving by!"

Just then there was a knock on the front door of the clinic. The three friends looked at each other in dread.

"Oh lordy, don't let that be another Labrador that ate little Johnny's toy or a cat that got in a fight!" Leon moaned.

Peeking around the corner, Suzanne called for Annie. "Hey doc. It's a delivery and I just bet it is for you."

Annie walked to the door seeing a huge bouquet of flowers being delivered. Taking them from the delivery boy, she placed the riot of color on the reception counter. Pulling the note out, she read **Miss you already, Sunshine. Thinking of you. We'll go on a real date this weekend. Shane**

Smiling, she looked over to Leon and Suzanne as they stood admiring the bouquet.

"Yep, looks like I might need to step up my game. Shirley gets wind that your new beau gave you flowers, she's gonna put me in the doghouse until I do the same," Leon complained.

Suzanne laughed, then looked wistfully at the beautiful arrangement. Sighing she admitted, "It's been a long time since I've gotten flowers."

Leon and Annie exchanged glances. Suzanne rarely talked about her past other than her family, and she never mentioned any men in her life at all.

Throwing his arm around Suzanne's shoulders he commiserated. "Darlin' girl, with your smarts and your looks, men will come sniffing around if you'd just get out there."

Suzanne raised her eyebrows at him and just retorted, "No thanks, Leon. Not putting myself out there for anyone. Been there, done that, and believe me the heartache is not worth it!"

The three quickly finished the evening clean up and Annie said goodbye before locking up the clinic and setting the alarms. Taking her flowers up to her apartment, she settled in for the night. Keeping her cell phone close at hand, she was hopeful that Shane would be able to call or text. The evening hours seemed to go slowly with no contact from him. Boo, Rags, and Tiddles began circling her legs letting her know it was time to go to bed. Used to sleeping with her they expected their final treat before getting comfortable for the night.

"Okay fine, guys. It looks like he isn't going to be able to call tonight," she sighed as she got off the sofa. "Let's go to bed," she said as she herded the cats to the back of the apartment.

Lying in bed, she realized how quickly she missed him. The bed seemed cold and lonely without his presence. Just a few more days, she told herself. Once he gets to his mom's house later this week, he can call. With that thought, she scooted over for the cats and fell asleep.

"ARE YOU SHITTIN' me?"

Shane's growl had the others around the table glancing his way. Those who knew him best knew that he was barely containing his anger. His debriefing was now going to take all week and was not going in the direction he wanted.

"I gave up two years of my life for this assignment, getting very little help from you all, and you are questioning how it ended? I handed you everything I had. You have enough to convict most of the traffickers in this area and significantly tightened the noose around the top man, Gerard Washington, and his right-hand man, Xavier Thomas. And you are dickin' me around 'cause I saved my dog's life by goin' to a vet that we already knew wasn't involved. And then I was able to confirm that she wasn't involved."

"Detective Douglas, we are simply questioning your decision to start a relationship with a possible witness. She has already been injured and now we have to spend taxpayer money insuring her safety until the case is over."

Shane looked across the table at the Internal Affairs investigator. Tailored suit. Immaculate haircut. *Hell, even his fingernails look buffed.*

Shane stood putting his fists on the table and leaned forward. "You spend two years of your life on an assignment that was originally going to take only six months. You spend two years of your life with the lowest scum of the earth. You spend two years of your life away from family and friends and spend them with unclean, unwashed junkies, addicts, and the pimps that pass around women like joints at one of their parties. You spend two years doing unspeakable things just to get on the inside and high up enough for them to trust you. And you do NOT want me telling you what those things were. You spend two years of your life finally getting high up enough to see how they move the drugs in and out and in doin' so, watch dogs being hacked up. You spend two years of your life that you cannot ever get back and then come sit at this table with me. Until you do that, I've got nothin' more to say to you that isn't in my reports."

With that, he turned and stalked out of the room, slamming the door behind him. The silence in the room was broken when Matt and the chief also stood as they moved to leave the room. Before reaching the door, Matt turned and spoke to the small assembly.

"He ended it because it needed to be ended. In the process, he found somethin' worth more than that hell he'd been livin' in. If you can't understand that, then you've been off the street too long." Then he and the chief followed Shane out of the room.

They walked outside to find Shane standing with his back next to the building, his head hanging down. He looked up as they approached.

Matt walked straight up to him, getting in his space, and said, "Do not let those fuckers get in your head. You did what you did. You made the calls no one else wanted to make. That asshole IA dick has his hands in the pocket of the District Attorney and he just wants his job to be easier."

Shane looked into the eyes of his one-time partner seeing anger as well as honesty. "Thanks man. Jesus, how cocked up can something get?" Swinging his gaze over to his chief, he asked, "How long do you think this shit is going to go on? I was headin' out of town to see my family in a couple of days and then told Annie I'd be back to take her out on an actual date this weekend."

The chief shook his head saying, "Don't hold your breath waiting on them. They're up there right now seeing which play they want to make. But you should be done soon. Just hold on, Shane. Just a little bit longer."

"Goddamn, this is so fucked," he growled. Sucking in a huge breath, he pulled himself away from the wall and said, "Let's go back in and get this over with."

By the end of the day, Shane's debriefing was coming to an end while his fury had increased. He and Matt sat talking as he tried to process what had happened.

Matt said, "You know you had no choice. It's only for another couple of weeks."

Shane's eyes cut sharply to Matt's. "Tell that to the woman I am having to leave behind for several more weeks. Weeks, I might add, I can't have any fuckin' contact with her. And weeks I am supposed to be with another woman."

Shane's superiors and the DEA wanted a few more weeks to tie up their case and while he wasn't going back undercover, they wanted to make sure he did not fully integrate back into his old life immediately, possibly tipping off the top of the drug chain they were still hoping to catch. They impressed upon him the necessity of separating himself from Dr. Donavan for a few weeks for her own protection. And that was the only reason he agreed. Her protection. Her safety.

Their DEA cover had been a woman, one that he had been involved with while they were both under and lonely. Rochelle. *Fuck.* She was gorgeous and it hadn't been hard to get physical with her, but that was all it was for him. The last time he saw her it had gone badly and the idea of having to spend more time with her instead of Annie was eating at him.

Looking at the smug expression on the IA's face as all the details were being hammered out, he gave them his own ultimatum. "I've given this force eight years of my life and two of those were in hell. You've got two weeks. Two more weeks to tie up this shit. For two weeks, I'll stay away. For two weeks, I'll continue to play your game. But that's it. Non-negotiable. Two weeks. Then my life is my own."

Now that it was just the two of them, Matt offered, "I'll try to get some word to her."

Dread began to circle Shane's heart; the fear of something he could not put his finger on threatened to choke him. Sucking in a deep breath, he acknowledged Matt's offer. "Appreciate it, man. Could you just let mom know I'll be around in a few weeks?"

"You got it." The two men sat quietly for a few minutes. "What're you gonna do?"

"I'm spending the next two weeks on the edge of hell. Can't go back in, but if they see me in a different part of town, acting like I've moved on, it'll take their eyes off of Annie."

"You've gotta be careful, man. The last thing you need is for Gerard or Xavier to see you with the doc or think you're vice."

"Yeah, but now they'll be willing to make a deal. They may start rollin' on each other. I honestly don't give a fuck. As long as the rest of the force gets what they need – and I was serious about givin' them only two weeks – then I don't give a fuck if I make any deals at all. I'm doin' this to keep her safe. I just hope she understands and gives me a chance to make it up to her when it is all over."

"If she feels about you the way you feel about her, it'll be fine, man."

Glaring into his partner's eyes, Shane just bit out, "How much more can she take? She's felt used since I met her and now I gotta jerk her around again? Jesus fuck, Matt." He rubbed his hand over his face, the fatigue no longer hidden. *Please sunshine, when this is over, come back to me.*

Chapter 13

AFTER FIVE DAYS of not hearing from Shane, Annie was getting worried. Trying not to show it was wearing on her and it wasn't fooling either Leon or Suzanne. As they finished their last appointments on Friday, Leon was not giving up on trying to spread some cheer.

"I'm telling you two, you need to go out with Shirley and me tonight. We're meetin' up and having a drink to celebrate the weekend. Come on…good food, good music…good company. What's not to love?"

Suzanne looked torn. She never went out and Annie knew the idea did not appeal to her. And she didn't really want to go…what if Shane called or came by.

Leon's eyes cut back and forth between the two of them. "You two are not backing out! I'm not suggesting you go clubbing. Let's just do something together that doesn't involve blood, piss, or anal glands!"

Annie couldn't help but laugh as Suzanne joined in.

Leon walked over to Annie, pulling her in for a hug. "Look doc, I know you're upset that Shane hasn't called. You'll have your phone with you and you can leave him a message telling him where you are."

"His phone is no longer taking messages. It says that it is not a working number."

"Oh," was the reply that Leon and Suzanne said in unison. They shared a glance then quickly looked back at Annie.

"I had a voicemail this week from some man, but the message kept cutting in and out so I don't know what that was about, but it wasn't Shane's voice so I didn't worry about it."

"All the more reason to go out with us for just a little while. I promise I will see you home safely."

Annie debated for just a moment before agreeing. "You're right. I need a diversion and going out for drink together will be nice. And hanging with Shirley is always fun," she said smiling.

Leon had brought a change of clothes since he had planned on meeting Shirley after work and since Suzanne was about the same size as Annie, they headed upstairs to quickly get ready. Soon the three of them headed out.

"Where are we going?" Suzanne asked.

"There are some good bars in the Brookmont area that aren't pricey."

"Brookmont?" Annie said incredulously. "That's kind of a seedy side of town, isn't it?"

"Yeah, well that's why we are taking a taxi and not my car," Leon joked. "But seriously, they have some great music. We'll just stick together and we'll be fine."

Suzanne leaned over and whispered to Annie, "I

hope this isn't a mistake!" Annie did not reply, but couldn't help the feeling of uneasiness that crawled over her.

The inside of the bar was crowded, but Shirley had gotten there before them and snagged a table. She greeted Leon with a kiss and then turned to Suzanne and Annie.

"Girls, I haven't seen ya'll in a month of Sundays. It's 'bout time Leon got you two out of that clinic to have some fun." Grabbing Annie in a hug, Shirley whispered in her ear, "It'll be fine, doc. Just relax a little tonight and try to enjoy yourself."

Annie felt the sting of tears threaten, knowing that Leon had shared her situation with her and that she had support from all of them. Settling in their seats, they ordered drinks and sat back to enjoy the music.

Leon kept an eye on the women, wanting to make sure that Suzanne was comfortable and Annie wasn't bothered. By the time the second round of drinks were finished, Annie excused herself. "Guys, I'm heading to the ladies' room. I'll stop at the bar on the way back and grab more drinks. The next round is on me."

Getting nods from everyone, she headed down the hall. Standing at the crowded sink in the restroom, she couldn't help but notice the woman beside her. Blond, statuesque, with plenty of tits, ass, heavy makeup, and big hair that made Annie feel dwarfish and frumpy. Skin tight pants, low-cut shirt, and cowboy boots. She was conversing with another woman waiting in line.

"Rocky, I saw you with your man out there. Damn he's fine. And big. Jesus, he's big."

"You're right about him. Stoney is one helluva man. Been with him a while now and there's nothin' small about that man at all. Not his arms, not his chest, not his legs, not his ego, and sure as hell not his dick."

"Your names even fit – Rocky and Stoney."

"Honey, that's not the only thing that fits. His dick hits the spot every time!"

The women laughed outrageously before the one named Rocky left.

Stoney. There must be a lot of Stoneys. Big Stoneys. Nausea started in the pitt of her stomach rising slowly until Annie thought she would choke. *It can't be him. I couldn't have gotten played twice.*

Moving on wooden legs, Annie maneuvered her way out of the crowded restroom and back into the bar. Pushing her way through the crowd it was hard to see since she was short, but she managed to make it to the edge of the sunken dance floor. There was the statuesque blonde. A man was standing behind her with his hands on her hips as she was grinding into his crotch. The man leaned over putting his mouth on her neck and the blonde began to laugh as she turned in his arms, pressing her impressive chest tightly against…Stoney. *My Stoney.*

Annie couldn't move. Couldn't tear her eyes away from the scene in front of her. Couldn't stop her heart from hurting. *I am such a fool. I was never more than part of a case to him. It's over and now we're over.* The sting of tears that she felt earlier came rushing back. Blinking rapidly to try to stop them, the bar seemed blurry for a moment. Quickly wiping them away, she looked back to the dance floor. There he stood. Immobile. Staring. Right. At. Her. With dark, black eyes.

Whirling around quickly, she ran to the table and grabbed her purse. "I've got to go," she said in a rush. "I've got to get out of here."

Her three companions jumped up without question and hustled out of the bar with her.

"You don't have to come," she said, her tears now falling freely once outside the bar. Leon flagged down a taxi, and the four of them piled in. Suzanne's arms were wrapped tightly around her.

"Don't be silly, doc. We're not about to stay when you are upset," Shirley said.

"What happened back there?" Leon demanded. "We didn't even stay long enough for me to see if I needed to kick someone's ass!"

Annie wanted to keep her secret. Admitting what she witnessed would be humiliating but she knew her friends deserved the truth.

"I saw Shane."

"What?" came the exclamations from the other three.

"He was there with another woman."

The silence in the taxi was broken only by the traffic that passed them by. Even the driver just looked in his rear-view mirror, knowing to keep his mouth shut.

The silent tears slid down Annie's cheeks as Suzanne held her close. "I'm such a fool," she whispered on a sob.

The three friends immediately jumped to her defense, each clambering that she was duped. Finally, Suzanne couldn't hold it in any longer. "That rat bastard! How dare he do this to you!"

The taxi finally pulled up to the clinic and Leon told him to wait. "Doc are you gonna be okay?" he asked with concern.

"I'm staying with her," Suzanne announced.

Annie quickly hugged her friend but said, "No, really. I'd rather be alone."

Shirley chimed in, "Nothing like bein' alone when you just need a good cry."

Annie nodded, glad that Shirley understood. She turned to Suzanne, "But thank you. Thank all of you. I just need to have a good cry, pitch a fit, and forget all about him."

Leon saw her safely in, making sure she set her alarm. "You be strong, doc. You'll be fine," he said softly hugging her goodbye. Nodding, she felt the tears wet his shirt before pulling away.

SHANE STARED AT the woman he had fallen in love with watching him let another woman grind up on him. *Jesus, fuck, NO!* Before he had a chance to react, she was gone. The desire to run after her warred with the desire to distance himself to keep her safe. *I just have to see if she is all right.* Pushing Rochelle away from him, he tried to make his way through the crowd, but was hampered by the crush of people. Finally arriving at the doors, he saw Annie and her co-workers in a taxi pulling away from the curb.

Standing outside the club, he hung his head for a moment then turned around quickly and pulled out his cell.

"Matt. Did you call her?"

"Yeah, man. I called her cell from the road after I left you. Why? What's up?"

"She just showed up with some friends where I'm tryin' to be visible tonight and just got an eyeful of me with Rocky."

"Fuck Shane. How is she?"

"How the hell do you think she is? Took one look, then bolted out of the door with her friends. Jesus, Matt. How much more of this shit am I expected to take?"

"Look, I'll go over tomorrow and talk to her. See if I can make things right. Make her understand."

"One more week, Matt. That's all I'm giving."

"I hear they've got evidence against one more man up the chain."

"Well, they better go for it, 'cause I'm done with this in a week." With that, he put his phone back in his pocket and leaned up against the wall. Hearing a noise to his side, he watched as Rochelle walked out to of the bar and over to him.

"You okay," she asked pressing close.

He moved away as he turned toward her. "Rocky, this is a job, nothin' else."

"It used to be more than a job, for both of us," she said with sadness. "We used to be good."

"Rocky, we met in shit circumstances. We did what we needed to do to keep our cover and make it work. But you know it was fucked from the start."

Her eyes flashed pain as she glanced down. "I thought it could've been more. I was willing for it to be more."

"Rocky, you were married. You may not have been happy, but you went under even though you were married. And, I might add, a fact you never shared with me when we were actually fuckin'."

"Shane, my marriage was over before I volunteered for this job. Maybe not officially, but I wanted out. Meeting you just made that decision more real."

Shane looked at the beautiful, desperate woman standing in front of him. Gorgeous. Built. Smart. Tough. *But no sunshine.*

"The bottom line is this. We both used each other for sex. It worked for our cover, but you always knew it was nothin' but physical for me. Wasn't ever gonna be anything else. Lookin' back that was a mistake on my part. I should have kept with the illusion that we were together without us actually hookin' up. But at the time, the physical won out. But you gotta know...if I had known you were married, I'd a never gone there. That's on you. You made that call and you gotta live with the fact that your husband left you because of it. And you gotta live with the fact that my heart is somewhere else. Somewhere clean. Somewhere light."

"The doctor?" she asked softly. "You're in love with her."

"Yeah. But she saw us here tonight. Fuckin' mess. She never goes out clubbin' and the one night her friends drag her out, she comes here and sees us."

Rochelle stepped back over to Shane and placed her hand on his arm. "I'm sorry. I'm sorry for a lot of things." She looked away for a moment, seeming to gather her thoughts. "When this is over, I can go talk to her. Try to explain."

Shane peered into her eyes, seeing honesty. "Rocky, you think a woman wants another woman to show up on her doorstep and tell her not to worry, it was all just physical? You really think that would make this fucked up shit any better?"

Rochelle shook her head. "No, you're right. No woman wants that in her face." Stepping back, she looked up and asked, "So what are we gonna do?"

Sighing deeply, he replied, "For one more week, we're gonna keep the attention on us and not on her. By the end of the week, the force and DEA will get whatever they can out of this case and wrap the rest of the shit up. I'll walk away knowing I did the best I could to bring down the top men, but the bottom line is that at the end of the week, I. Walk. Away."

She nodded. "Yeah, me too. I want to keep climbing higher in the DEA, so I am hoping this punches my ticket. I'm just sorry for the collateral damage to a friend."

With this, the two of them parted ways as Shane slipped off into the night. He had something to take care of and nothing was going to stand in his way.

Chapter 14

ANNIE MADE IT up the stairs to her apartment before letting the tears take over. Making her way over to her sofa she collapsed, sobbing into the cushions. *How could I have been so gullible? How can I be so book-smart and so man-dumb? How could I have given myself to him over and over and not even known who he really was?* The silence of the night gave no answers to her questions. As her sobs began to slow, she stayed face-planted on the sofa.

After a few minutes, a wet nose pressed into her ear. Turning her head, she saw the familiar face of Boo nuzzling her face. Moving her hand down off of the sofa, she felt the other two pressing against her.

Sitting up, she leaned back. Her eyes landed on the security box next to the back door. She slid her glance over looking at the one next to the front door. *Why would he set up an expensive security system if he was just playing me?*

Snorting as she stood up, she looked down at Boo saying, "I guess even a player can feel guilty."

"Meow," was the only response she received as three cats swirled around her legs.

"Oh babies, I'm sorry," she sniffled. "I forgot to feed you before I left." She walked into the little kitchen, getting their food out of the cabinet. Scooping it into their individual dishes, she watched as they lined up side by side to eat, each keeping an eye on the others to make sure they didn't snatch food from their bowl. Once finished, they swirled around her legs for a moment before they plopped down in the living room to bathe.

"Oh, to be a cat. One owned by me," she said wistfully. *Needs always met. Life always stable. Food. Water. A warm bed. A sunspot occasionally. If only my life could be so easy.*

Grabbing a bottle of wine from the fridge, she headed to her to her bathroom. Stripping, she quickly showered wishing the hot water could wash off the night's memories. *He looked so amazing. Tall and handsome. Moving to the music. His hands on the woman's hips. She was grinding on him. Stop! Stop thinking about it!*

Turning off the water, she stepped out of the shower and quickly pulled on short pajama bottoms with a matching camisole. Brushing her teeth, her mind wandered back. *He wasn't smiling. He didn't look like he was enjoying himself.* Her reflection stared back at her in the mirror. "What are you doing?" she asked herself. "Are you trying to find excuses for his behavior?"

Leaning in closer to the mirror, she said, "Face it, girl. You got played. Huge. So pull up your big-girl panties and get over him." Slamming her toothbrush back into the holder, she flipped off the light and headed to bed.

Crawling under the covers, she wondered if sleep would come. Unable to stop its path, another tear slid down her face onto the pillow just as sleep claimed her.

SOMETIME DURING NIGHT, Annie dreamed of being visited. She was vaguely aware of having a warm, hard body pressed up to her back. A heavy leg thrown over hers with an arm across her waist pulling her in tightly. Warm. Cocooned. Safe. *What a strange dream* she thought, as her exhausted mind slid back into sleep.

Awaking the next morning, her swollen eyes tried to open to the little bit of light that was coming in through her bedroom window. Lying in bed for a few minutes, she slowly allowed her mind to wander. Suddenly remembering the feeling of having someone in bed with her last night, her eyes flew open as she jerked her body around.

The bed was empty. *I must be losing my mind.* Pressing her fingers to her eyes, she noticed Boo lying on the end of the bed. She leaned over to make the bed when she noticed that the other pillow was indented as though someone's head had lain there.

"Boo, did you sleep with me last night?" she asked. Unable to stop herself, she picked up the pillow noticing that it had no cat hair on it. But it had a scent. *Shane.*

Tossing the pillow down she sprinted into the living room to see if he was there. Empty. The room looked just like she left it last night. Wrapping her arms around her middle, she stood and stared. At the room. At nothing. *Was it a dream?*

COMING IN FROM a run to clear her mind as much as to keep in shape, she rounded the corner of her block. Mr. Tochi was waving at her so she slowed down to greet him.

"You ready to meet my nephew? He is coming to town this afternoon to visit me. You should come by market and I will make introductions."

"Oh, Mr. Tochi. I don't think I am ready to meet any man now. I'm kind of a disaster when it comes to men."

"Well, just stop by the market. You don't have to do anything but say hello."

Smiling at the kindness in his eyes, she agreed. "Okay. If I get a chance, I'll come by, but just to say hello."

Jogging the rest of the way to the door of the clinic, she was surprised to see Detective Dixon leaning against his car parked in the front. Slowing her pace, she made her way over to him.

Eying him suspiciously, she greeted, "Detective Dixon."

The man in front of her was ruggedly handsome and

she wondered what his story was as her eyes glanced up to the scar running across his forehead. Slightly taller than Shane, his dark hair was neatly trimmed and his brown eyes seemed to take all of her in quickly.

"I see we have gone from Matt to Detective Dixon," he said.

Pressing her lips together, she weighed her answer. "I think the time for friendliness has passed, don't you? I'm assuming this is an official visit since that's the only visit that would be necessary between us."

Sighing, Matt stared at the woman in front of him. Hurt, more than anger, seemed to be coming from her.

"Doctor, I tried to call the other day. It seems you may not have gotten my message."

Her brow crinkled as she pondered his words. "A message? Here at the clinic?"

"No. Your cell phone."

"There was a message the other day, but the signal kept coming in and out so the message was mostly garbled." Looking up into his face, she asked, "Was that from you?"

"Yeah. I was driving and didn't know the signal was weak. Fuck."

"What was the message you were trying to leave? I'm assuming it was about Shane, but I can assure you that if you were going to tell me he was alive and well, I already know that. Believe me, I saw with my own eyes that he is alive and very well it seems. So if there is nothing else, you will excuse me." She turned to open the clinic door.

"Why are you going to your apartment through the clinic? You have an outside entrance."

Turning back around, she looked at him questioningly. "Because...I don't know. It's just safer." Thinking momentarily, she continued, "You should know as well as anyone that I was threatened and attacked. I try to avoid the alley and just use the clinic entrance now."

"Are you safe there? In the clinic? That is where you were attacked."

Facing him fully, anger showing on her face, she asked, "What are you getting at? Why are you asking me these questions?"

"Humor me. Just answer," was his reply, as his gaze never wavered from hers.

Licking her lips, she looked to the side. "Yes, I feel safe in the clinic. Before he left, Shane had a security system put in. The clinic is wired and my apartment is wired. He said it was top-line security, patched into the police station as well as his friend's security business." Walking straight up to him, she poked her finger into his chest. "Yes, I feel safe inside. Not the alley. That I avoid. Does that answer your question, Detective Dixon?"

Looking down at the beautiful woman poking her finger at him, he smiled. "Shane did that for you?"

Putting her hands on her hips, she glared up. "What are you getting at? Yes, Shane did that before he left to go back to what is obviously his real life. Or pretend life. Or whatever the hell other life he has that doesn't involve me!"

Matt let the silence stretch out between them for a moment. Then he answered, "My message the other day was to let you know that not everything is what it seems. Trust in him and trust in what you actually know. Not what you think is happening."

Annie stepped back keeping her eyes on his. Confusion showed on her face as she tried to decipher his words. "I don't...I don't know what you mean."

Leaning down close to her face he simply said, "Think about it." With that piece of cryptic advice, he turned and climbed back into his car. With a nod of his head, he pulled out and headed down the street leaving her standing on the sidewalk bewildered.

Walking through the door and up to her apartment, she stared at the security system panel on the wall again. *Why would he do that if he did not care?* She walked to the kitchen to make a sandwich and noticed the empty bottle of wine from last night in the trash can. *That was left on my nightstand when I went to bed.* Whirling around, her eyes scanned the room looking for more evidence that he had been there while she slept.

Not everything is what it seems. Trust in him and trust in what you know, not what you think is happening.

The sting of tears threatened once again as she thought back to the scene in the bar from last night. *Shane, I don't know what you want me to think. I don't know what is real anymore.* Dashing her hands against her eyes to keep any more tears from falling, she show-

ered and then headed back out. To the market. To meet
Mr. Tochi's nephew.

SEVERAL HOURS LATER, sitting at a neighborhood
Italian restaurant with Ricardo, Annie found herself
wishing that the man across from her was someone else.
Ricardo was delightful, but there was no spark. He was
well-mannered but seemed shy. He was handsome, but
there was nothing that made her want to take him home
and rip his clothes off. Ricardo was predictable, not wild
and untamed. *Jesus, stop comparing him to Shane.* But
the more she sat with Ricardo, the harder it was to not
think of Shane when things were good.

"You seem preoccupied. Am I boring you?" Ricardo
asked politely.

Blushing, she hastened to assure him. "No, I'm so
sorry. There's just a lot on my mind today. I have
enjoyed lunch, but I really should be getting back. I
have some work that needs to be done today."

He placed his hand on hers and said smiling, "I have
had a delightful time, Annie. Perhaps we can have lunch
again sometime soon."

Smiling back, she could not think of a reason to not
acquiesce, even though her heart was not there. "Sure,
that would be fine."

Walking back down the street to the clinic, she kept
glancing behind her. The uncomfortable feeling that
someone was watching her made her uneasy.

Ricardo, noticing her behavior, asked if she were all right, as he placed his arm around her shoulder.

"I'm sorry, I am just a little nervous." They had reached the clinic, but she hesitated at the door. Looking up into his handsome face, she asked, "Ricardo, would you mind stepping in with me for a moment. I'd feel better if someone was with me to make sure no one is in the clinic. I know it is silly, but there have been some robberies," she lied. The uneasy feeling of being followed had continued and she felt desperate to make sure the clinic was empty.

"Of course," he said with concern. He walked through each room with her, making sure the door to the alley was locked and secure.

"Thank you so much for a lovely afternoon," she said truthfully while knowing she would not be seeing him again.

Ricardo leaned down and placed a chaste kiss on her lips. "The pleasure was all mine. I'll call you the next time I'm in town."

Watching him walk back down the sidewalk, she shut the clinic door leaning her head against it for moment. "God you are such a fool," she said to the empty clinic.

"Have a good time?" a deep growl came from behind her.

Screaming as she whirled around, she stood stunned looking at a very pissed off Shane standing in the middle of her reception area. Heart pounding, she took him all in. The close-cropped hair, strong jaw that was tight with emotion, the muscles straining his t-shirt, right down to his old, faded jeans tight across his thighs. And anger. Pouring off of him. Directed at her. *What the fuck?*

"Shane, Jesus you scared the crap out of me!" she exclaimed. "What the hell are you doing here?" She threw up her hand as she attempted to walk by him saying, "Wait. I don't want to know. I don't care. But you can just leave the way you came, however that was!"

He grabbed her arm as she attempted to pass him and swung her around so that she was plastered to his front. Both arms encircled her essentially trapping her into place.

"Oh no you don't, you jerk. You let go of me right now or I swear, I'll scream the house down!"

"Not until you listen to what I've gotta say," he growled again.

"I don't want to listen to you, Shane. I'm done playing stupid and being played. You think this is a game, well here's a tip buster. I don't like this game. It hurts!"

Grabbing her by the arms, he pushed her away from his body just enough to lean down into her face. "A game? You think I'm playin' a fuckin' game? You think I've spent two years of my life in hell, all for a game?" His voice started low but rose to a roar, giving her a little shake, "A fuckin' game?"

Eyes wide, she stared up into his face. A face that had kissed her sweetly and gentled when he came inside of her. Now she had poked the bear and had no idea what to say. Bringing her hands up, she placed them on his chest. "You're scaring me," she whispered, tears starting to spill down her cheeks.

A look of anguish crossed his face before he pulled her back into his chest, pressing her head gently against his heart. "Jesus. What a fuckin' mess," he said quietly. Rubbing her back, nothing was said for a moment as her tears quieted. "I'm sorry, baby. Let's just go upstairs and talk. Please give me that. Please."

The sound of his anguished voice pleading broke through to her. Nodding her head against his chest, he bent and picked her up and she wrapped her legs around his waist as he carried her upstairs.

Chapter 15

MANEUVERING INTO HER apartment, Shane relished the feel of her in his arms, but once inside she wiggled to be let down. "Not happenin' baby."

Her head snapped back, eyes narrowing on his face. "Shane, you need to put me down."

His ice blue eyes held her green ones in a stare-down that she was not going to win.

"Told you, baby. Not happenin'."

He held her firmly as he walked over to the sofa, sitting down with her straddling his lap. "We're gonna talk. There's too much shit happenin' and I'm not wastin' anymore of my life."

Not everything is what it seems. Trust in him and trust in what you know, not what you think is happening.

Annie was angry, but she had to admit she was curious about Matt's words. Pulling her lips in, she lifted her eyes back to his. "Why?" was the only whisper from her mouth.

With that one word, Shane felt her wrap around his heart again. No screaming, no yelling. No throwing things, sobbing uncontrollably. No shouting insults, no tossing accusations. Just one simple word and his anger left him. The beast inside that had been raging felt tamed.

One large hand came to the back of her head, pulling her forward as his lips found her forehead. Holding her tightly, he whispered back, "Please give me a chance."

He heard a sigh leave her body as her breath hitched with unshed tears. He waited for a moment before feeling her nod her head against his chest. *Sunshine. Pure, fuckin' sunshine.*

"Annie baby. I've got a lot to tell you and not a lot of time right now."

She pulled her head off of his chest, her eyes full of questions.

He continued, "I know you've got questions, but baby, let me tell you what I can and then we'll deal. Can you do that?"

Breathing deeply again she just nodded, curiosity winning over anger.

"Everything I ever told you was true. About my job. About goin' under. About my family. Everything." He held her eyes. "Includin' everything I ever said about you and about us.

"I went in last Monday for the debriefing. What I wasn't expectin' was to be raked over the coals about you."

"Me?" she asked, startled.

"Baby, when I came to you with Sarge, I knew it

was a risk. A huge fuckin' risk. I was tellin' the truth when I said you were the first ray of sunshine I'd had in two years. But I never wanted to involve you in this. Never wanted to put you at risk. But one look and I had to take a shot. I had to pull you in. But then the shit hit the fan. The one fuckin' thing that made my life worth livin' was about to blow everything to hell."

Shaking her head, she said, "I still don't understand."

"My superiors weren't thrilled that I had almost blown cover by gettin' involved with you. Then you get hurt, which tellin' you right now baby, someone is still gonna pay for that. You're on the radar and I put you there. So when we pulled off the takedown, we got most of the ones we were after, but there are still some slick-shits at the top we didn't get. The PD and DEA want them and held me by the balls to go back under for two more weeks. I'm not in tight with the gang, but I knew that if I showed back up as Stoney and stayed away from you it could pull some of the attention off of you. So I got pissed, but I told them I'd give 'em two weeks and that was it. Two weeks to finish their case and then the DEA can takedown whoever they can. I don't give a fuck."

He slid his hand to her cheek, his thumb tracing the dried trail of a tear. "Baby, it was no fuckin' game. I've never played you. I'm wild and untamed, but I'm yours."

"I saw you. With her. She was in the restroom talking about you," Annie said, the pain in her voice evident, her eyes looking down at his chest.

Using his fingers to lift her chin, "When we talk, I wanna see your eyes, baby. That tells me how you're doin' and right now they tell me you are hurtin' and goddammit, that fuckin' kills me."

He took a breath, then said, "I told you a while back that there were things about my past I was gonna share. Things that I knew would hurt, but I didn't want there to be shadows between us. No doubts. I just figured that we could talk about it, lay it to rest, and then never have to deal with it again." He shook his head cursing, "Fuck! You should never have to have seen that shit last night. You should never have to deal with that part of my past."

"Shane, last night wasn't part of your past. Last night was last night. You were with her after I let you…have me last week and the week before that!"

"It wasn't what you thought it was, baby. It's all just an act."

Silence greeted him. Her eyes held his. "Shane. Can you honestly tell me that you have never been intimate with her?"

Another sigh. "I don't want to have this conversation now, baby. We don't have enough time to talk it out, deal with it, and move on."

"Well, guess what? I don't care! Let me tell you where I am coming from. You drop into my boring life, giving me a glimpse of what life could be outside this apartment and this clinic. I let you in and you've got to know I never do that. I let you in my bed and I let you in my life. We have a couple of weeks of a whirlwind that includes me finding out that you weren't who you said you were. Then bam, you're gone with promises that you don't keep. Then I see you, practically having sex on the dance floor with another woman, one you've obviously been involved with before. So here is me telling you, I don't give a shit whether or not you want to have this conversation!"

Slowly nodding, he sighed heavily as he admitted, "You're right. Rocky and I worked together on this case. She is DEA and went under about a year after I did. She was workin' the drugged out prostitutes while I was working the transporters and the dogs. You want it baby, here it is. Sometimes when you're under, you gotta' act like the animals you're associating with to get information or just to prove loyalty. There were some skanks I fucked just to keep up my cover or get infor-mation. It was physical, and I made sure I was protected 'cause I had no idea what diseases they probably had."

Annie winced as though in pain, but he held her fast to him with his hands to her hips and kept going.

"It was dark and fucked up, but I was determined to do what I had to do to get the information I needed. I met Rocky and found out she was undercover too. We worked the relationship that was advantageous to both of us. We made it look like we hooked up and that kept others from sniffin' around too much. And yeah, it got physical. But that was still all it was to me. Just physical. I liked her, but I didn't love her. I respected the work she did, but baby, she did not share my bed all night."

"Stop. I don't want to hear anymore." Annie shook her head from side to side, not able to hide the pain that sliced across her features. "Just stop. I thought I could do wild and unpredictable. I thought that's what I needed in my life, but Shane, newsflash – I can't. You've got me so twisted and turned, I don't know what is real anymore. All I know is I fell for you and this," pointing between them, "hurts."

"No baby. This isn't finished and I'm not about to leave this shit in the middle. Found out later that she was married."

Annie looked up sharply at that revelation.

"Yeah. She went undercover as a married woman, which is all kinds of fucked up. Turns out she was wantin' to leave her marriage anyway, but she was still married when fuckin' me. I was pissed when I found out. Found out later that her husband got wind of what was happening and filed for divorce."

"She wanted you," Annie said simply, understanding instinctively why a woman would want Shane.

"Yeah, but it wasn't gonna happen." He peered deeply into her eyes, as he continued. "I didn't love her. And I was never gonna love her. She wasn't it for me. And I sure as hell couldn't be with a woman who was a cheater. And most of all...ah hell baby...*she* wasn't sunshine."

Annie's brow crinkled in thought as she tried to take in all he was saying, feeling overwhelmed by their conversation.

"Told you baby. I lived in darkness for two years. I did shit I'm not proud of to fit into that world, and yes that included other women. But none of them gave me sunshine. Not one. Not ever. Not until you."

Placing his hands on either side of her face, he leaned forward until his breath was mingling with hers. "Felt that sunshine on my face and baby, I can't live without it." With that, he kissed her gently, slowly moving his lips over hers. Feeling moisture on his face, he leaned back seeing silent tears slide down her cheeks.

Her breathing hitched as she said, "I don't know what to do with all of this. I can barely take it all in, much less process it."

Leaning forward again so that his forehead touched hers, they sat in silence for a few minutes.

"Just to let you know about last night. We were just out to be seen by anyone who might still have eyes out for me or her. I wasn't given a choice in my debriefing. I had to pull away from you and keep attention off of you for two more weeks to keep you safe while the DEA is getting ready to move in again. That's all it was for me. A job. Rocky knows the deal. She knows she was never it for me and never will be. She may have cheated on her husband, but she truly felt bad about last night. Before I went under, I never even came close to fallin' in love. Never took a woman home to meet my family. Couple of years ago I got to meet the woman my friend Tom fell in love with and knew then that one day I wanted that. Just didn't find it until you."

They continued to sit in silence for a few more minutes. *Come on, baby. Please give me a chance to prove I'm the man for you,* he thought while watching emotions flit across her eyes.

"Shane, I honest to God have no idea what to do with all of this." Biting her bottom lip, she fought back tears. "My life was so tame before you. It may have been boring, but I knew each day what was happening. You've entered my world and turned it upside down. I've been happier with you around than I've been in forever." Giving a rude snort, she continued, "I've also been more hurt since meeting you too. It's like a damn roller coaster."

Smiling, he held her face close to his. "Yeah, but baby it's livin'. Being on that roller coaster with someone you love makes the ride worth it."

Silence ensued again as Annie pondered all she had heard. Lifting her eyes back to his, she gazed deeply. She was so used to four-legged animals. When they are in pain, you can see it in their eyes. When they are happy and healthy, that shows as well. But humans? That was always harder for her to read. But staring into his blue eyes, she saw nothing but sincerity staring back.

"What now?" she asked in a small voice, afraid of the answer.

"Baby, I've got one more week to get through then I

am done." He watched shadows pass through her eyes. "Nope, not going back there. I'm done with Rocky. She's DEA and is on her own now with her own orders from them. I am just working the dog issue now. Just still trying to get a lock on where they get them and where they house them before shipping them out. Took me a year and a half to get high up enough in their organization to be trusted with just knowin' about the dogs, and I've got a pretty good idea, but one way or another baby, one week."

"Then what, Shane?"

"Do you remember what we talked about before I left? Me livin' here while I find a place. A place for both of us. And we were goin' to keep finding out where this goes," he said as he pointed between them. "That's still my plan. Nothin's changed for me. I want this life and I want you and I'm goddamn tired of all of the bullshit bein' thrown at us that is gettin' between us."

"What about the next time one of your past women comes back to haunt us? I don't want to live as though I'm constantly in fear of having your past thrown in my face."

"That's not gonna happen, baby. I'm out and no one from that hell comes into our world."

Annie raised her hand up to rub her temple, feeling as though she were on a mental overload. Sighing deeply, she said, "I swear I can handle a vet emergency with calm assurance that I know exactly what I'm doing. I can handle irate clients and don't mind getting down and dirty with my hands in an animal that I'm trying to save. But this...Shane, I don't even know what to think."

"Baby, what do you feel? Stop thinking and just feel."

"I don't know how. I'm trained to think analytically. I take a problem and break it down. Then find the best solution. I'm not equipped for this. If I break this down, my head says that this," pointing between the two of them, "Is a fucking mess and I should run for cover!"

"But what do you feel?"

"Feel? Shane, feelings are what got me in this mess to begin with. I give in to feelings and that gives you the power to stomp all over my heart. One. More. Time. I can't protect myself from hurt if I give in to feelings." Her eyes glimmered with unshed tears while hope and fear warred within her.

"Annie," he said softly, wrapping his arms around her. "Tell me what you feel."

She leaned her head down on his shoulder, pressing her face into his neck. She felt his strong arms holding her closely. She felt his breath on her neck as he leaned his head over toward hers. She felt his heartbeat against her chest. She remembered how wonderful she felt before he left and how devastated she was last night. She felt...

"I feel...safe," she replied. She felt his arms tighten. "I feel safe," she repeated as he moved his hand up to cup her head. Sighing deeply, she admitted, "I feel... like I want this. I want us. It may be a rollercoaster and I have to tell you that I'm afraid of heights and scared to death of falling off...but this feels...right."

Shane closed his eyes as he buried his face in her hair, the tightness in his chest at the thought of having almost lost her made him think of Tom. No wonder Tom was desperate to get his fiancé, Carol, back safely. *I almost lost her before we really had a chance to begin. No more. I'm done.*

The sun began to go down behind the buildings across the street, casting long shadows across the floor. The two of them sat, holding each other, saying nothing for a while. Letting the silence give them peace. The kind of peace that seeps into the deep crevices of one's soul.

After a while, Shane felt something furry rub up against his leg. Back and forth, making a figure-eight between his feet. Glancing down, he saw three pairs of eyes staring intently at him. "Baby?"

"Um hum," she answered not moving.

"I hate like hell to move from this position, but we've got company and I think they want to be fed."

On cue, Boo led the others in a chorus of "meows", letting Annie know that they had reached the end of their patience for dinner.

Leaning away from Shane, she twisted around to look at them before swinging her gaze back to him. Suddenly the thought of the rollercoaster wasn't so bad if it was Shane sitting on the ride beside her. Grabbing his face with her hands, she pulled him in for a kiss. Plunging her tongue in his mouth, she latched on as though she needed him for her very existence.

Growling, he angled her head for better access and plundered her mouth as well. For several minutes, the kiss took on a life-force of its own. Needy, possessive, untamed.

Pulling back, she once again looked into his face, a smile curving her lips.

Watching this, he smiled back. "Oh baby. Seeing you smile...pure, fuckin' sunshine."

Her smile reached her eyes as it grew wider, spearing him with its brilliance.

"Meeeooow."

Wiping the rest of her tears off of her cheeks, she moved off of Shane's lap saying, "Let me take care of them." He followed her into the kitchen as she fed them. Standing at the sink, she felt him come up behind her, pressing her into the counter. The unmistaken bulge pressing into her ass as he placed his hands on either side of her had her panties begin to get wet. He leaned down, kissing her neck as he moved his hips back and forth against her ass.

Twisting her head around to look at him, she smiled. "I know you have to go for another week, honey, but are you telling me you have time for something first?"

"Baby," he growled, "I will always make time for

you. Sometime in the future our make-up sex might be in the kitchen against the counter, but not now. Tonight is about you and me and us. And we're gonna do it in your bed." And with that he took her by the hand and led her into the bedroom. Closing the door behind him, he looked down at Boo. "Not now, buddy. Right now, she's all mine."

Chapter 16

THE NEXT WEEK went without incident and by Friday Shane headed back into the police station. Walking over to Matt's desk, he plopped himself down in the chair. Matt looked up, a rare smile on his face.

"You done?" he asked.

"Yeah," was the tired reply.

"You decide what you're gonna do?"

Shane looked into his friend and partner's face, knowing Matt was reading him like a book even though Shane had not indicated any plans other than coming back to the force.

"Been thinkin' about how long I want to keep this up. Talked to Tony. He wants me to come work with him in his security business." Tony Alvarez had been a former policeman, having graduated from the police academy with Shane and Matt. After a few years, he quit the force and opened Tony Alvarez Security, specializing in providing security systems. Shane had his suspicions that Tony's company did a helluva lot more than just install security cameras, but had never confirmed that with him. He was just glad that Tony jumped at the chance to set up Annie's system.

Matt nodded in agreement. "You'd be good in security. Money's probably a shit-load better than this pension."

Shane grunted. "Yeah. I just don't know, man. My dad was vice. All I ever wanted was vice as well. Worked hard, made detective, then spent two years under. Now I'm back out and findin' I've got a life that I want. And I don't know that chasin' drug dealers is what I want to do with someone in my future."

Matt raised is eyebrow. "So it's leaning that way?"

Shane leaned forward, looking directly at his friend. "Matt, it goes the way I want, I'm talking forever. Wife, kids, home. Everything. And I sure as hell don't want anything gettin' in the way of that."

The two sat in silence for a moment, then Shane continued, "But I don't like leavin' if I'm not sure. So I'm gonna keep workin' these cases with you, see how things go with Annie, and in a few more months, we'll see how it goes."

They stood and shook hands. "Good to have you back, partner," Matt acknowledged.

ANNIE'S WEEK HAD been anything but comfortable. The moment she let Leon and Suzanne know that Shane was back in her life, the peace from the previous evening ended.

"Are you crazy?" Suzanne yelled, placing her hands on her hips as she looked at Annie while her voice rose with each word. "He lied, he cheated, he left you, he just makes up shit to get you back with him, and I think he does it 'cause he's homeless and wants a place to crash!"

Leon walked over to stand behind Suzanne. "Gotta say, doc, Suzanne's telling it like it is. I like the guy, but he's got some serious issues."

"I know what his issues are and I believe him," Annie replied. "A few more days and then he is back on the police force as a regular detective. No more undercover. No more dangerous missions." She hesitated a moment before looking back at them. "No more Rocky or other women."

Suzanne, still on a roll, continued, "Let's face it. Other than Leon, men are just shits. They lie, use you, make promises they don't keep, and then you are left high and dry to pick up the pieces of your life all on your own!"

Leon and Annie just stared at Suzanne. "Are you sure you aren't just talking about your own experiences?" Annie asked gently.

Suzanne pursed her lips together for a moment until the fight seemed to leave her. She had never talked about her past relationships.

"So the other night was just an act?" Leon asked, turning the attention back to Annie.

"Yes. And even if you don't believe him then you should at least believe me. I know he is telling me the truth. I told you what Detective Dixon said. And when

Shane laid it all out there, I admit it was overwhelming. But guys," she said looking at her two closest friends, "I believe him. I want to give this a shot."

Suzanne and Leon were silent for a moment, taking it all in.

"I just want you to be happy and honestly, he scares me," Suzanne admitted.

Annie walked over to her friends, taking their hands. "I know. Sometimes he kind of scares me too. But then the thought of him not in my life scares me more."

The two women embraced then Leon threw his arms around both of them, shouting, "Group hug!" Just then, the front doorbell sounded accompanied with the noise of dogs barking, starting a new day for the clinic.

By Thursday, Annie could feel the nervousness of waiting reaching an all-time high. Before Shane had left her last weekend, he promised her that he would be with her on Friday evening. If it wasn't for the busy work schedule, she wasn't sure she would have made it.

Suzanne passed her in the small hallway with a small Chihuahua in her arms, heading back toward the workroom. "Mrs. Greenwald's neighbor is in exam room three. Looks like his dog was in a fight, but it's not too bad."

Annie dropped off the cat in her arms to Leon to finish in exam room one, then walked in to see the dog. An elderly gentleman was standing by the examining table talking softly to his bulldog. After greeting him, Annie looked at the bite marks that Suzanne had already cleaned.

"The good news is that they are superficial and not deep. I don't think any stitches will be required, but I want to give him an antibiotic injection to make sure they don't become infected."

She looked up to see the owner smile as he leaned down to place his face next to his dog. The old bulldog lifted his sad eyes to his owner.

"You hear that Petunia. The nice doctor says you're going be just fine," he said as he continued to rub his dog's ears.

"Petunia?" Annie couldn't help but smile as she inquired about the bulldog's name.

"Yes. My wife named him after her favorite flower. Lucy's been gone a couple of years now, but me and Petunia keep her memory going just be hanging on to each other."

"Oh, I am so sorry about your wife, but I can definitely tell you that…Petunia's bites are not too bad." She looked down at the notes that Suzanne had taken, but there wasn't much information on how Petunia was attacked. "Mr. Charleston, can you tell me what happened?"

The pleasant look immediately left his face as he became animated. "Me and Petunia were just out for a walk when a stray dog came from the dumpsters in the alley behind my street. I live about five blocks over and we have never had any problem with strays before. Next thing I knew that dog rushed over and jumped on my poor Petunia, starting to bite him. I had my cane and I whaled on that dog till it ran away. I got him home and washed him off, but I knew he needed to see a vet. I took him to that emergency vet down the way, but the doc on duty that night said he'd be fine."

Annie looked up sharply from taking notes. "Mr. Charleston, we have to make a report when an animal is attacked, so surely they took down your information to do that."

"He didn't do a goddamn thing," he said, then immediately apologized. "Doc, I'm sorry about my language. I should have never cussed in front of a lady, but I guess when it comes to my Petunia, I just lose my manners."

Why would the emergency vet not take notes and file the city report? Shaking her head to clear her musings, she just replied, "Well, I can certainly understand why you wanted Petunia seen. I'm glad that Mrs. Greenwald suggested you come here."

Finishing up with his discharge instructions, she left the exam room and noticed that Leon had closed the reception area since Petunia was the last client to be seen for the day.

"Hey Leon, do you have those city animal control forms that are needed when an animal had been attacked?"

Leon found the file and handed one to her. As Annie was filling it out, she began to tell Leon about what Mr. Charleston said concerning the emergency clinic.

Suzanne walked in from the back, hearing the story.

"I'm sorry, doc. When he told me that he had taken his dog to the other clinic, I assumed that they filed the report."

Annie looked up, a crinkle above her brow, replying, "I can't imagine why they wouldn't! I'll call them once we finish up and see what the deal is." Handing the form to Leon to fax to city hall, she turned and began their end-of-day duties.

By the time Leon and Suzanne left for the evening it was after six o'clock. *Perfect time to call the evening shift at the emergency clinic.* Sitting at the desk, she reached for the phone when her cell phone rang. Looking down, she saw Shane's number. Smiling to herself, she grabbed her cell.

"Please tell me you are not calling to put things off some more," she said hastily.

She heard a deep chuckle that made her smile even more.

"Well, hello to you to, baby," Shane said, the warmth of his voice carrying across the airwaves. "And no, I am not goin' to put things off one more fuckin' moment."

"Thank God," she said.

"Tonight is my last night and then I'm finished. I'll be back to bein' Matt's partner at the station."

"Are you going to be in danger tonight?" she asked.

"I promise that there is nothin' I'm doing tonight that will put me in harm's way. I'll see you tomorrow night when the clinic closes."

"Okay," she said softly.

"And baby?"

"Yeah?"

"Be ready to change into other clothes, 'cause I'm finally takin' you to dinner. And on Saturday, be prepared for a road trip."

"A road trip? To where?"

"I'm takin' you to meet my family." Silence met this statement. "Baby, you still there?"

"Shane, are you sure? It seems too rushed. You haven't even seen them yet."

"Baby, not waitin' anymore on this shit. Stole too much from me – not lettin' it steal more. You with me?"

The warm feeling from last weekend crept back over Annie, washing away the fears. "Yeah, I'm with you."

Clicking off her cell phone, Annie sat back in the chair with what she knew was a silly grin on her face. Sighing happily, she reached for the phone to make her call to the other vet.

Reaching the vet that was on duty, she heard, "Dr. Ketchum, may I help you?"

"Phil? This is Annie Donavan."

"Annie! How good to hear from you. How've you been?"

Annie had gone to dinner several times with Phil the year before, but the spark wasn't there and they had remained professional friends.

"I'm really calling in an official capacity, Phil. I had

a client come in to the clinic this afternoon with a dog that had been attacked by a stray dog. He claimed to have brought him to your emergency clinic last night, but that no one would treat the dog, nor did they take a report."

"I was here last night but was working in the back. We have a nighttime receptionist up front, but I can tell you that they never told me that a dog had come in. I admit that the person up front is a new hire, but I don't know why they wouldn't let me know about a dog attack. Are you sure he actually came in?"

"Well, no. I am just going off of what he said. I filed the report to animal control, but I wanted to follow up with you."

"I'm glad you did, Annie. That new hire isn't working tonight, but I will talk to our clinic supervisor, Dr. Watkins, and let him know he needs to train our new hires, especially if they are going to be working the front desk by themselves at night."

"Thanks, I appreciate that," she replied.

"So...any chance we could get together for dinner sometime soon?" he asked.

Annie smiled, thinking of the difference between the dapper Dr. Ketchum and the untamed man that would be taking her to dinner instead. "Phil, I appreciate the thought, but I'm seeing someone."

"Hey, that's great Annie. Well, if you ever need me, professionally or otherwise, you know where to find me."

Hanging up the phone, she finished her reports and then headed upstairs to her apartment. Setting the alarms carefully, she turned to be greeted by her meowing trio. "Guys, this is our last night where it is just us by ourselves. Tomorrow night we will have someone else here."

After she fed the cats, she walked to the small bedroom and looked in the tiny closet. Unlike most females she knew, she did not have a lot of clothes. Her days were spent in scrubs and a lab coat. Pushing her clothes to the side, she made room for Shane to put some things in the closet. Looking down at the floor, she realized that she also had very few shoes: Dress pumps to wear to professional conferences, crocs and tennis shoes for work, running shoes, a few pairs of sandals and flip-flops, and one pair of fuck-me shoes that she wore once when going to a vet school dance.

Looking back behind her, three pairs of eyes stared at her from the bed. "Looks like the wild man has hooked up with Miss Boring, doesn't it guys? Well, at least he will have room for his clothes." Rags and Tiddles were occupied with bathing, but Boo stared as though he understood everything she said.

Walking over to her dresser, she moved her possessions around to empty some drawers as well. Noticing the full moon shining into her bedroom from the window by the dresser, she walked over to look out. The surrounding brick buildings gave off little personality, but she could hear the music coming from some of the bars down the street, giving her little area of Richland a certain energy.

Looking back at Boo, she remarked wistfullly, "I still want a clinic in the country." Somewhere where I'll have a view and you can watch birds out of the windows."

The few light posts gave off little illumination on the alley below, but she found herself looking down toward the dumpster behind the building. Her mind went back to the first time she saw Shane. Was that really just a month ago? It seemed as though the roller coaster had been longer. Smiling once again, she went to bed wondering what the ride would bring tomorrow.

She missed the silhouette of the man in the alley, looking at the woman in the window, his eyes gleaming with malice.

Chapter 17

BARELY CONTAINING HER excitement, Annie found herself wanting to rush through her appointments, but her professionalism wouldn't allow it and the time seemed to drag. At three o'clock, Leon locked the front door, two hours before closing.

Looking at him in curiosity, she asked, "What's going on?"

Suzanne walked in from the back room and stood next to Leon as he threw his arm around her. "Well," she said, "We decided to make sure you had plenty of time to get ready for your big date tonight, so we shuffled around the appointments so we are done for the day."

Beaming a huge smile, Annie ran over to grab her friends. Pulling back, she looked at Suzanne. "I thought you didn't like Shane," she said gently.

"Oh doc, I just don't want to see you hurt. He seems so…I don't know…wild and unpredictable."

Annie laughed, "Yeah, you got that right." Looking into Suzanne's worried face, she said, "But it's okay. I feel safe with him."

Leon took her by the shoulders, turned her around,

and gave her a gentle shove toward the back stairs. "You, dearest doc, need to head up to your apartment, get ready for tonight. Suzanne and I will finish up here getting the clinic ready for Monday."

Flashing a smile over her shoulder at her two friends, she jogged up the stairs. Walking into her apartment, she was met with her trio, all demanding to be fed. "Guys, it's not dinner time yet. I'm just early today."

Boo, being the ring leader, refused to be persuaded that her walking in the door was not the signal of dinner time and continued to meow loudly.

"Fine, fine. But just remember this later when you get hungry again!"

Once her furry friends were sated, they followed her into her bedroom, piling on her comforter to watch the proceedings as they licked themselves clean.

Walking into her tiny bathroom, Annie looked over at her shower. *What I wouldn't give for a bathtub. A chance to soak until I was a wrinkled prune.* Knowing that no matter how long she stared at the minuscule shower stall it was never going to turn into a large soaker tub, she stripped and hopped in. Shower, shave, and shampoo. *God, this feels good.*

After drying off with one of her fluffiest towels, she began getting ready. As she rubbed lotion on every part of her body, she imagined Shane licking along the trail that she was smoothing. Glancing to the bed where Boo was keeping his eyes on her, she thought, *if I am lucky tonight, Boo, you won't be sleeping on my bed all night!*

Looking at the clock, she was so grateful that her friends had closed the clinic early so that she would have time to get ready. Her long, thick hair took forever to dry and she wanted to have time to tame a few of the natural curls.

Once the curls hung down her back she finished her make-up, deciding to go with simple instead of something more sultry. *The dark smoky eye just isn't me.*

Walking over to her small closet filled with scrubs, two extra lab coats, a few professional looking pants, and blouses, she went to the back corner pulling out a plastic bag. Her one little black dress. It had been her extravagance when she first got out of vet school and assumed that she might actually have a night life. Or a dating life. Or any life that didn't involve fur, guts, blood, and anal glands. *Yeah, didn't exactly call that one right*, she thought ruefully.

The dress was still in its store bag with the tags attached. Pulling it out carefully, she cut the tags and then slipped it on. Twisting and turning in front of the mirror checking out her reflection, she couldn't help but smile. The dress was asymmetrical, high on one leg and flowing down lower on the other. Little straps held the top in place as it dipped low enough to show off some cleavage without screaming 'check out my knockers'. Finally pairing it with a pair of strappy, sexy heels that had been worn once, she was ready.

"So, Boo. What do ya think?" As usual, Boo just

stared before he lifted his leg to lick himself. *Nice job, Boo. Way to make a lady feel special!*

Glancing at the clock one more time, she walked into the living area to wait. Butterflies began to flit around her stomach, catching her off guard. Realizing that she did not want to just sit around, she headed back down the stairs to the clinic.

SHANE ENTERED THE clinic through the door opened by Leon. The two men shook hands and Shane noticed that Leon held his in a tight grip for a millisecond longer than necessary. Recognizing mans-speak, he raised his eyebrow in question.

Leon smiled as he dropped Shane's hand. "You good, Shane?"

Nodding, Shane replied, "Yeah. A helluva lot better now that I can move on with my life."

Suzanne slid up beside Leon, peering intently at Shane. He held her gaze, knowing that she was struggling with accepting him.

While undercover, to stay alive he learned to keep his mouth shut, giving nothing away. No emotions. No thoughts. No explanations. Fighting the desire to tell Annie's friends to fuck off and keep their opinions to themselves, he knew this was part of being back in the real world. The world of honest, clean living – normal.

Deciding to acknowledge the elephant in the room, he simply stated, "I know you're worried. Don't know what to say other than I care about Annie."

Moving her long, black hair off of her shoulder, Suzanne fixed her blue eyes on his. "I just don't want to see her hurt again. And you Shane, have the makings of hurt written all over you."

Shane noticed Leon wrap his arm around her shoulders, pulling her in gently. *That girl's been hurt. Don't know that she's shared with anyone, but that hurt runs deep.*

"I can't make any promises about where this'll go, but know this – I'm out now. Not goin' back under. I plan on movin' in with Annie just until I can find a place for me and Sarge. Things go the way I hope, she'll want to move in with me sometime. I care about her, plan on taking care of her, and I'm gonna protect her."

"But who is going to protect her from you?" Suzanne asked softly.

Shane couldn't help but smile, "Darlin', Annie soothes this savage and I assure you, she doesn't need protectin' from me. I may be a wildcard, but that woman knows how to tame."

A sudden movement from the back hall had the three of them turning to see Annie standing there, her eyebrow raised in question.

"I feel like a teenager whose parents are questioning my date," she said as she glided into the room.

Shane stared at the vision in front of him, his breath catching in his throat. His eyes scanned her from the coppery waves falling over her shoulders down to the black dress that somehow covered more than the hooker skanks he had been around and yet seemed to scream 'here I am" at the same time. The dress showed a hint of cleavage that he couldn't wait to get his hands on again and flared around her hips that hid the sweetness he couldn't wait to taste. Her toned legs went on forever, and her tiny feet were encased in heels that he decided he wanted left on when he stripped her tonight. His eyes made their way back up to her green ones that he smugly noticed were taking him all in as well.

Annie totally forgot that Suzanne and Leon were still in the room. Wanting to jump in Shane's arms, she stood dumbly staring at the wall of masculinity in front of her. His blue eyes moving over her body stood out starkly in his tanned face. His strong jaw, that had just a hint of sexy stubble, had her thinking of burying her face in his neck as he took her. He was dressed in a blue button-up shirt with rolled sleeves, straining to contain his muscles. Wearing khaki pants, she realized that she had never seen him in anything other than t-shirts and jeans. Looking good in both, she couldn't decide which she liked better.

The silent perusing was interrupted by Leon clearing his throat.

Startled, Annie blushed and Shane just grinned, holding out his hand toward her. "Ready to go, baby?"

"We'll lock up after you, doc," Leon announced. "Now don't be late kids," he joked.

Suzanne gave Annie a quick hug, whispering, "You

look beautiful, doc. I do want you to be happy."

With that, Annie took Shane's hand and headed out for their first real date.

SHANE LIFTED HER up into his truck that looked almost new. As he swung himself into the driver's seat, she couldn't help but ask.

Smiling, he looked over as he answered. "Not new, but definitely not very used." Seeing the questioning look on her face along with the cute crinkle above her brow, he explained. "Bought it a couple of months before going undercover. Friend of mine has been keeping it safe for me."

"That must have been so hard," she said softly. Her words hung gently in the cab of the truck as they headed toward the restaurant. The silence made her nervous. "I'm sorry. I shouldn't have said anything about it."

Looking back over quickly he just shook his head. "Nah, baby. Don't apologize. I'm just trying to get used to being back out. That's almost as hard as havin' gone in."

Curious, she prodded, "What do you mean?"

Struggling with sharing too much and frightening her, he sat silent for a moment gathering his thoughts. "It was hard givin' up my life here to go in. But I was convinced it was needed and I was the man to do it. Just never realized how much I would give up to do it and I'm not just talkin' about my truck."

Annie twisted in the seat so that she could focus on him, wanting to know more.

He continued, "Baby, let's just leave it at this. To survive that world, I did shit I'm not proud of, not happy with. But it became my way of life. A man pissed me off, he got hit. I needed information from someone reluctant to give it to me, I got physical to make sure I got it. I kept my mouth shut and my emotions shut down. The women in the gang were there for a purpose and I had a cover to maintain."

At this, Annie winced and it did not go unnoticed by him. *Fuck.* He reached his hand across the seat and linked his fingers with her.

"Is that hard to give up?" she asked, pain laced her words.

Pulling into the restaurant parking lot he brought the truck to a stop. He also twisted his body to face hers. "Baby, that's not what I meant. I wasn't talkin' about the women when I said it was hard to get used to being out. That's got nothin' to do with us." Using his fingers to lift her head so that he could peer into her eyes, he asked, "You understand that, right?"

Nodding, she looking into his blue eyes, feeling as though she were the only woman in the world to him and hoping what she was reading was right.

"I just meant it's hard for me to make small talk or hold conversations."

Laughing, Annie reminded him of their lack of conversation when she was operating on Sarge. "You wouldn't talk so I just jabbered enough for both of us."

"Darlin', you were pure, fuckin' sunshine. Brightest light I had seen in a long time."

Looking down at their clasped hands, she said, "You don't seem to have too much trouble talking to me now."

"You're easy to talk to," was the simply reply. "But others...even Leon and Suzanne, well...I find myself not wanting to explain anything because for several years, I never explained my actions to anyone."

She just nodded, then her stomach growled loudly, protesting the meal of a protein bar that she had earlier in the day.

Laughing, Shane swung out of the truck, walked over to her side, and plucked her out of the cab. "Let's get you fed, baby. And then let's get you back to your place where I can peel this fuckin' gorgeous dress off your fuckin' gorgeous body!"

THE RESTAURANT WAS right on the river and their table overlooked the water. The lighting was soft, the food was delicious, and the wine was delectable. Annie looked over the candlelight to Shane and realized it was the nicest date she had ever been on. Then thinking of the night ahead, she clenched her thighs to ease the dull ache that had begun.

Shane, noticing everything, smiled at the small movement she had made then realized that the tightness in his pants was a result of the same line of thinking.

"You ready to get out of here?" he asked, his low voice flowing over her.

Smiling while nodding was the only answer he needed. Grabbing her hand, he escorted her back to his truck.

Entering the apartment, he rounded on her as he pressed her against the door, dying to taste her lips.

She flung her arms around his neck, pulling him down to her waiting mouth. She latched her lips onto his, immediately tangling her tongue with his.

His mouth captured her moans, and he felt his resolve to take things slowly crumble. Picking her up, he strode into the bedroom letting her slide back down his front.

Annie immediately leaned down to remove her heels, but he stopped her.

"Leave 'em on. Everything else off but I want to fuck you with those shoes on."

Instantly wet, she knew that he wanted to be in charge, but she had a few tricks of her own. Turning him around so that his back was to the bed, she placed her hands on his chest and gave a little push. He went backwards, a surprised look on his face that quickly changed to lust as he realized what she was doing.

She slowly unzipped the dress, letting each the sound of the zipper echo through the room. Sliding one strap off and then the other, she allowed the dress material to just hang on her breasts, tantalizing close to her nipples. She saw his pupils dilate as he feasted upon the strip tease in front of him. With a small movement she allowed the material to fall over her breasts and past her hips to puddle on the floor, leaving her in a strapless black, lacy bra and matching panties.

Shane started to sit up on the bed with his arms reaching out, but she held up a finger waving it back and forth. "Oh no, big boy. This part of the show is all mine."

Reaching behind her, she undid the clasp to the bra letting it join the dress on the floor. Hooking her thumbs in her black, silky panties, she slowly began to peel them down her legs, using her heels to kick them off to the side.

Finally standing in nothing but her heels, she leaned forward and began to crawl on the bed toward him.

She had only gotten both legs on the bed before she was grabbed and whirled around so that she was under him.

Jesus, fuck. She's killin' me. Knowing he would come in his pants if he didn't take over the show, he grabbed her and pulled her under him. He latched his mouth over one of her engorged nipples, sucking deeply. Immediately he felt her writhe under him, instinctively trying to ease the pressure in her pussy by rubbing it on his swollen cock.

Pushing himself off the bed, he stood and quickly divested himself of his shirt and pants. Shoving his boxers over his impressive cock, he noticed her staring at him, her green eyes shining with lust and...something he couldn't define.

Leaning over, he kissed her as though she were the last breath to be had. Their tongues tangled in an age-old dance as he explored every crevice of her mouth.

Annie loved the taste of him. She craved him, angling her head so he could take the kiss deeper. Wetter. Harder. She latched onto his tongue, sucking it into her mouth as she swallowed his groan. For a man as wild as Shane, she loved taking him over the edge.

Shane left her lips only to slide down her body until his mouth came to the prize between her legs. Using his hands to push her knees apart, he then used his fingers to mimic the action with her pussy folds. Licking her fully before circling his tongue on her clit had her hips jerking off of the mattress.

Smiling to himself as he relished the taste of her, he pushed his tongue inside over and over until she was screaming his name as she came.

Annie felt boneless as she lay panting on the bed. *What that man can do with his tongue!* She was aware of him moving back up over her body, but it was his talented tongue that was bringing her back to consciousness. She felt him latch onto one nipple while his hand fondled the other breast. The tingling sensation from her nipple went straight to her pussy that was still recovering from the last assault. Spreading her legs wider for him, she welcomed his hard cock into her willing body, feeling it stretching to accommodate his girth.

Plunging in to the hilt, Shane felt connected to her in more ways than just sex. Realizing he had been drowning in his former life, she was the lifeline that pulled him in, rescued him. Looking down at her flushed face, eyes closed, smile playing on her kiss swollen lips, her copper hair flowing on the pillow below – *My pure, fuckin' sunshine.*

His strokes increased in pace as he worshiped her body. He slid his hand down to her clit, fingering the swollen nub as he continued to plunge in and out of her tight pussy. Feeling her inner walls beginning to clench he knew her second orgasm was near. "Come on, baby. Come for me."

Annie felt the flames grow higher and higher until she gave over to the blaze of her release. Screaming his name once again as her pussy grabbed onto his cock, she raked her fingernails down his back, trying to pull him closer to her. Her breasts rising and falling rapidly as her heartbeat pounded, she could feel him as his breathing changed.

Opening her eyes, wanting to see him come, she watched as he plunged over and over until he threw his head back and roared out his release. His eyes were closed, his neck strained as the veins bulged and she leaned up to lick the spot where she saw his heart pulse.

His eyes opened as he crashed down on her, floored by the force of his orgasm. *Never, Jesus, never have I felt like that.* Knowing that he must be crushing her, he moved to the side, taking her with him so that she was partially on top.

They lay in silence, allowing their pounding hearts to slow and their breathing to even out. She continued to kiss his neck gently, loving the feel and taste of him just like she knew she would. With his arms wrapped around her, she felt cocooned in warmth and safety.

When he could finally think again, he opened his eyes and stared at the beauty in front of him. Tiny. Delicate. She fit perfectly tucked into his embrace. He raised up just long enough to lean over, grabbing the covers to pull on top of them. He saw his semen on her thigh.

"Fuck!" he shouted, looking down at her.

"What?" she screamed, scrambling to get out of his arms and out of the bed. Eyes wide with fright, she stood looking over at him, fear on her face. "What is it?"

"Jesus Annie, I am so sorry!"

Her fear was replaced by confusion as she wondered what was wrong.

Shane looked at her, standing naked next to the bed, her flight response strong. "I didn't use a condom, baby. I am so fuckin' sorry. But I swear, I have always used one. I have never, never gone without one. And I'm checked. I'm clean."

"Shane, you scared the piss out of me! I thought there was a spider or something in the bed!"

Looking at the expression on his face, she felt the giggle rising up out of her and was unable to stop. The more she giggled, the more ferocious he looked. She watched him stalk around the bed until he was standing right in front of her and she tilted her head back so that she could peer into his eyes.

"Baby, this isn't funny. You gotta know I would never put you in harm's way. If anything happens…"

His voice was stopped by her fingers on his lips. "Shane, it's okay. I'm on the pill to regulate my periods. And…I trust you. I'm clean too so we're good."

He pulled her into his embrace, wrapping his arms around her small frame. *I'm supposed to protect her and here I fuck up at the first opportunity.* Tightening his grip, he held her close, feeling her naked breasts press up against him. His cock began to stir which only seem to make her giggle more.

"Baby, giggling at a man's cock is not cool," he tried to admonish but found his own voice crack with laughter. "You seriously thought there was a bug in the bed?"

"Well, this place is old and it wouldn't be the first time there had been a bug here." Her giggles finally subsided. "I don't know. Somehow when you yelled out, it was the first thing I thought of."

Placing a kiss on her coppery head, he led her into the bathroom. "Let's get you cleaned up, baby."

Several minutes later they were back in bed, the covers pulled up, and she found herself pulled against his hard body. He had slung one of his legs over hers as though afraid that she would disappear in the night.

"Goodnight baby," he whispered.

"Welcome home, Shane," came the response.

Both smiling, they fell asleep.

Chapter 18

"**M**EOW," CAME THE cry in her ear along with a wet nose. Annie slowly opened her eyes feeling weighted down. *Boo must be getting really heavy.* She then realized that the cat was off to the side of her head and not on her chest. Awakening more, she smiled as she realized that during the night Shane had thrown his arm over her chest, pinning her to him in sleep.

"Meow."

Knowing that the cats would not leave them alone, she slid out from the bed and quickly fed the cats in the kitchen. Hurrying back to the bathroom, she quietly took care of her business, brushed her teeth, and brushed her hair before pulling it up on her head.

Opening the door she looked over to the bed and her heart skipped a beat. Leaning back on the headboard was Shane, looking incredibly sexy, petting all three cats.

"Hi," she said, suddenly shy, not knowing what to do.

He lifted his arm in a silent invitation and she scrambled into the bed, snuggling up close.

"You okay, baby?" he asked in his gravely sleepy voice.

"Perfect," she answered, leaning up to kiss him.

He took advantage and deepened the kiss, just starting to turn it into a deep, wet kiss when Boo's head moved between theirs, wanting attention.

"I had no idea cats were so demanding," he grunted.

Laughing, she moved out of the bed and went to the closet to pull out her clothes. Shyly looking over, she said, "I made some room for you." Pushing the door of the closet open wide, she showed him the space.

Shane looked in the tiny closet and could see where she made room for his belongings by pushing her things to the side. It did not escape his notice that the only clothes in the closet were clothes for work and the one evening dress that was still crumpled on the floor.

"You don't have a lot of clothes for a woman," he noted out loud.

Shrugging, she replied, "I don't need them. I need clothes for work and clothes for running and a few things just for comfort. Other than that, my needs are simple."

"Well, get dressed for comfortable 'cause we've got to hit the road."

"Shane, about that. I really think you should meet your family by yourself today. We're so new and I just can't imagine they would want me intruding."

Stalking over to her, he placed his hands on her shoulders, leaned down, and held her eyes as he spoke. "Baby, we went over this. We may be new, but we're not fuck-buddies. You mean somethin' to me, that means you mean somethin' to my family. I'm not spending the day without you. Annie, your sunshine got me out of my hell and my family knows that. I've already told them about you and they're expecting you. So get your sweet ass dressed 'cause if you keep standing there in your underwear, I'm gonna throw you back on the bed, fuck you silly, and then tell my mom why we were late."

"You would not!" she exclaimed, eyes going wide.

"Well, I'd probably not tell mom, but everything else would happen." Turning her to face the closet, he gave her a tiny push as he entered the bathroom.

Smiling to herself, she realized that the roller coaster had started.

THE DRIVE TO the suburbs outside of Richland was relaxing. Leaving the city behind, it was nice to see trees and neatly maintained neighborhoods.

"I miss this," she said wistfully.

Shane looked over to her. "Didn't you grow up in Richland?"

"No," she replied. "I grew up in Jefferstown. It's between here and Fairfield, where you said you had some friends."

"You never told me that," Shane said, realizing how little he knew about her background.

"You never asked."

She's right. The only thing I was ever thinkin' about

was gettin' that sunshine on me and then fuckin'.

"Sunshine, you're right. I never did, but we can rectify that right now while driving."

"Well, my dad works in construction. He loves to build with his hands. He started out just building houses, but then found that his passion was woodwork, so he has his own business where he designs and makes specialty wood finishes for houses. You know, things like the spindles on old porches, curved wooden window arches, things like that. He's really good at it and travels around the state working on projects like reconstruction of old homes."

Shane spared a glance over as she was talking. Her face was lit as she waved her hands around animatedly while talking. It was obvious that her family was important to her. *Now I know where that sunshine comes from.*

"My mom works as a secretary for an accountant. We're really close, but she can be a bit of a nuisance." Seeing his questioning face, she explained. "Mom loves me being a vet and is proud of me, but I know she'd like to see me in a relationship. She feels like I'm missing out when my evenings are spent with my cats."

Smiling, Shane said, "Well, I've already told you that my mom will start wedding plannin' when she meets you." Then he quickly added, "Don't let that throw you. I'll keep her in check."

"It's okay. It sounds like she's a lot like my mom."

"So who else? Any siblings?"

"I have one sister, still in college. I am about eight years older so we weren't very close growing up, but now we are."

They drove into a neighborhood of unique, older but quaint homes, unlike the modern neighborhoods where all of the houses are cookie-cutter copies of each other. They pulled into a driveway of a white, two-story home framed by a huge front porch. Shane had just gotten out of the driver's side when a scream pierced the air.

Annie looked up, seeing a woman running across the yard, her arms opened wide. The look on the woman's face as she threw her arms around Shane burned itself on Annie's mind. *A mother who hasn't seen her son in over two years. A mother who didn't know if he was coming home.*

As she watched the reunion of mother and son, she felt the raw emotion pouring out of Shane's mother. Tears slid down her cheeks witnessing the affection war with grief over two years lost on his mother's face. Pressing her fingers to her lips, she tried to choke down a sob. Shane's eyes were closed, but she could see the elation on his face. *Pure, unadulterated joy.* It was one thing to talk about his mother not seeing him for over two years, but to see the agony mixed with joy in person was overwhelming.

Noticing movement on the porch, her eyes swung over to see a young woman and man run down the steps following their mother into the family embrace. Another man, holding a small child with a pre-schooler by his side, stayed on the porch watching the scene in front of them evolve. Not wanting to disturb the reunion, she decided to stay in the truck, still trying to choke back the tears.

Finally, Shane lowered his mother back to the ground as she continued to hold his face in her hands. He wiped his mother's tears, leaning down to speak softly to her. Pulling her in again, he smiled at his brother and sister over their mother's head.

Glancing around, he realized that Annie was not there. Twisting his head, he saw her still seated in the truck, tears shining in her eyes. He knew she was giving them their moment. Smiling, he caught her eyes and watched her smile back at him. *Sunshine.*

"Mom, you've got to let go for a moment. I've got to get Annie."

At those word, Shane's mother jumped back looking into the truck. "Oh my goodness. I'm so sorry," she exclaimed as she let go of Shane.

He assisted Annie from the truck, then he tucked her tightly into his side as they walked over to the group in the yard. Shane's mother rushed up to hug Annie just as tightly as she was hugging her son.

"Oh my dear, you must think me to be an emotional fool!"

"Not at all, Mrs. Douglas," Annie quickly assured her. "I can't imagine what you have gone through. I just hope it's all right for me to be here."

"Please call me Mona and you are more than welcome here. My son has spoken of you on the phone and I know how important you are to him."

Shane pulled Annie back into his embrace and began the introductions. She assumed correctly that the younger woman and man were his sister, Megan, and brother, Rick. As they made their way onto the porch, she also met Megan's husband, David. Megan took the smaller child from her husband's arms so that David could pick up the shy four year old trying to hide.

"Megan, you just had this one when I left," Shane said in awe as he looked at his nephew in her arms.

"And you, little man. You must be Kenny," he said to the child peering back at him with big eyes.

Mona ushered them into the house, all settling into the family room. Annie couldn't help but notice the similarity between the home she grew up in and Shane's. Warm rooms comfortably furnished and decorated in what her mother called 'early family', meaning family pictures covered the walls.

Allowing Shane and his family to have more time to catch up, she looked at the family photos displayed. One in particular caught her eye. An older version of Shane stood with one arm holding a little girl and his other hand resting on the shoulder of a young boy, while smiling at Mona, who was holding a baby. The father was big, muscular, and very handsome. And Shane looked just like him. Her eyes went down to little Shane, seeing the blue of his eyes just as intent that that age.

"Annie," she heard Shane say. Turning around, she noticed him sitting on the sofa, an empty space next to him. "Come here, baby."

Smiling as she walked over, she glanced at Mona, who was beaming. "I love your pictures, Mona. My parents have family pictures all over their house too." Laughing, she admitted, "Even though I only have a small apartment, I decorate in 'family' also."

"No fancy painting adorning any wall is as meaning-ful as the family pictures in a home," Mona declared.

"Oh my goodness, Mona, you'll have to meet my mom. She says the exact same thing."

As soon as the words were out of her mouth, Annie blushed. "I mean…if you ever…I just meant…"

Shane pulled her into his embrace, kissing the top of her head while smiling at his family. "It's okay, baby. They know we're serious, so it makes perfect sense for the families to meet sometime."

The Douglas' had planned a cookout so the assem-bly moved to the back yard. Shane and his brother fired up the grill while Megan and Mona got things ready in the kitchen. Turning down Annie's offer to help, she sat in the yard with David watching the children play.

After making small talk, David turned to her saying, "I gotta tell you that I was worried about Shane coming back. Mona has had a rough couple of years with him gone."

Annie turned her attention to him, listening attentively.

"She hated for Shane to go into police work after their father was killed. I had only met him a couple of times, but he seemed to be a great husband and dad. Megan and I had just gotten together. I think Mona knew all along that Shane was too much like his dad to not follow in his footsteps. But going undercover? That nearly killed her, wondering if he would come home and if so, in what shape."

Annie continued to listen, realizing that David had stepped in to fulfill the older son and brother roll when Shane left.

"We made the mistake one night of watching a documentary on some policemen who went undercover in a motorcycle gang." He shook his head. "Big mistake. It was rough – the life they lived and what they had to do to fit in, and how messed up they were when they came back out." He picked up the ball that had rolled over to them and tossed it back to his son. "Mona is tough, having been a policeman's wife, but she jumped up and turned off the TV running out of the room. Megan went and talked to her, but she just kept saying that she was afraid of what was going to come back from that."

"He was a little...hard, when I first met him," Annie admitted.

"I have a feeling that being with you has tamed a lot of the wild that had grown in him," David said, smiling at her as he looked over to where Shane and Rick were laughing with Mona and Megan.

On cue, Shane's eyes searched for hers, his face smiling widely when they met. Annie smiled back, feeling his happiness from across the yard.

"Yeah," David agreed. "I'd say you have a lot to do with that taming. Now, just get ready as Mona starts her wedding planning!"

Shane looked over at Annie laughing with David as the children played all around her. His attention was so focused on how her copper hair glistened in the sunlight as her head was thrown back in laughter that he completely missed the look that passed between his mother and siblings.

Mona walked to him, encircling his waist with her arms as she lay her head on his chest, listening to his heartbeat. "She seems wonderful, son. I really like her." Leaning her head back so that she could look into the eyes that seemed so much like his father's, she asked, "So how serious is this relationship?"

"It's serious, mom. It's new so we're still learning about each other, but meetin' her was what made me decide that it was time to stop screwin' around and bring the cover and the case to a close. It had already gone on too long, but she was the light at the end of a long, dark tunnel."

Mona smiled into her son's face as another tear slid from her eye. "Then that's all I need to know. Any woman who brought my wild son back to me will have my eternal gratitude."

The rest of the day passed with pleasant conversation, including lots of stories of Shane as a boy, good food, good company, and even games of hide and seek with the nephews. As the evening drew to a close, Shane was saying goodbye to his siblings so Mona took the opportunity to slide over to Annie.

Annie smiled at Mona knowing that the day had been an emotional one. "Thank you so much for allowing me to crash your reunion with your son."

"Oh my dear, I wouldn't have it any other way. I just wanted to let you know how much I appreciate all that you have done for him. I don't know what shape my son would have returned to me in if he hadn't met you."

Hugging Mona tightly feeling the familiar sting of tears in her eyes, Annie just said, "I'm glad we found each other."

Shane walked over then and Annie stepped back to allow them some privacy to say goodbye. As they walked to the truck Shane pulled her in for a kiss before helping her up. The kiss was simple, almost chaste, knowing his family was on the porch watching, but for Shane it meant everything. The continuation of family. Dad, *you woulda loved her.*

To Annie it meant nearly the same thing. *Future. I want to spend the rest of my life with this man.*

Arriving back home, they retired for the evening, making love long into the night, each filled with dreams of forever, feeling as though the roller coaster was finally coming to a halt.

Chapter 19

ON SUNDAY, THEY spent the day getting Shane and Sarge moved in. Sarge had been staying with Matt for the past two weeks and as Annie was sorting out the closet space, Matt and Shane moved a few boxes in.

"Doesn't look like you have much here," Matt observed.

"I've got more stuff in storage, but I don't want to overfill Annie's place."

Matt looked around at the quaint, but tiny, apartment. "Yeah, it doesn't look like it can hold much more."

Shane offered him a seat as he flopped down on the sofa. "It's small but it came with the clinic, so she doesn't have to pay rent. I'm gonna start looking for a place, but now…well, I kind of have different needs now."

Matt looked over at his friend, raising his eyebrow in question.

"Before Annie, I would have just found a one bedroom apartment big enough for me and Sarge. Now, I'd like to find something nice with a couple of bedrooms."

"Things movin' along that well?"

Shane just nodded toward the bedroom where Annie was still sorting their clothes and said, "That woman in there changed me, Matt. Gave me her trust and had that sunshine beamin' down on me. Not gonna let that go. Gonna hang onto it and take care of it."

Just then Annie walked into the room, seeing the two friends talking. Smiling at them both, she walked over to the refrigerator and grabbed a couple of beers. Moving to the living area she handed one to Matt then sat next to Shane while handing him his. "What are you going to take care of?" she asked, indicating that she had overheard the last of their conversation.

Throwing his arm around her and pulling her in tight, Shane answered, "You, sunshine."

Matt laughed as he announced, "And that is my cue to leave."

Annie protested as she walked him to the door. Matt leaned over and kissed the top of her head. "Thanks, Annie, for taking care of him."

After Matt left, Shane moved off the couch and said, "Babe, you've worked all day. I'll order some pizza and we'll have a night in. How does that sound?"

"Sounds amazing," she said with a thoughtful look on her face.

Shane wrapped his arms around her as he asked, "What are you thinking about, sunshine?"

"Matt."

"Should I be jealous or maybe go pound that sorry-ass friend for makin' my woman spend her time thinkin' about him?"

Swatting him on the chest, she replied, "No. I was just wondering what his story is. I mean, he's nice looking and seems really loyal and a good friend, but...I don't know. I guess I just think everyone should have someone they love."

"Don't start matchmaking with my friends," Shane warned jokingly.

"Honey, before I can matchmake anyone I would have to have friends! Other than Leon and Suzanne, if it doesn't have four legs, I don't know them!"

Shane ordered the pizza and they sat on the floor using the coffee table as their dining table. Annie's question about Matt had Shane thinking about his friend. Before he went undercover, he and Matt had spent weekend days enjoying sporting events and their nights would often find them enjoying some of the nightlife around Richland. Neither one of them were looking for love, but lust was another matter.

"Now what are you thinking about so hard," Annie's voice interrupted his thoughts.

"Hell, woman, now you have me thinkin' about Matt."

"So, what's his story?"

"Don't know, baby. Before I went under he was a player, enjoying the nightlife and never with the same woman more than a time or two at the most." Sheepishly Shane admitted, "Since I've been back the last couple of weeks, I haven't really thought much about him other than that we get to be partners again. But you're right. He doesn't quite seem the same."

"Well, talk to him about it," came the logical reply from Annie as she wiped the pizza sauce from her lips with a quick flit of her tongue.

For a moment, he forgot what they were talking about as he watched her tongue slide across her lips. *We gotta finish the pizza so those lips can slide around my ...*

"Shane, where'd you go?"

Startled away from his thoughts about her luscious lips, he looked backed into her eyes.

"Sorry, baby. What did you say?"

Rolling her eyes, she repeated, "Talk to Matt. Find out what has been going on with him over the past couple of years."

"Babe. I've got a dick."

Looking at him with a confused expression, she cocked her head to the side. "What does that mean?"

"It means I don't go asking my partner about what is making him sad."

"Oh Jesus, Shane. You don't have to lose your man-card just to ask a friend what all has been happening in his life!"

Tired of talking about Matt when he really wanted to be buried in her, he moved to her side of the coffee table, crawling over her body as she lay back on the floor. "Want to know more about my man-card?" he asked, effectively pinning her underneath him.

Giggling, she admitted, "Oh yeah. You can show me

your man-card anytime you want."

THE NEXT MORNING Shane was gone when Annie awoke, but by the time she was out of the shower he was back in the kitchen with pastries from Mrs. Greenwald. And he brought plenty for Leon and Suzanne as well.

Kissing him goodbye, she watched as he headed out of the door to work as she walked down to the clinic. Smiling to herself, she could not help but think how right this felt. *It's as though he belongs here. With me. In my life.*

As soon as she walked through the door of the clinic she was immediately surrounded. Leon took the pastries out of her hand while Suzanne grabbed her other hand and pulled her into the room.

"So spill, chickie. How was meeting the family?" Leon asked while shoving a bear claw into his mouth.

Annie laughed, "Well, it was interesting. They hadn't seen him in a long time, so it was pretty emotional. But other than that, they were really nice." She noticed Suzanne's sharp eyes focused on her intently. "Honestly, Suzanne. It was good. His family is very much like mine. Speaking of mine, I need to call my mom."

"Of Lordy, I can hear the wedding bells already once Momma Donavan gets hold of this information," Leon joked.

"That's why I have been putting it off. But when she

finds out that I've met his family, she'll have a fit!"

The front door chimed signaling the start of another day as the three hustled to get ready.

SHANE LOOKED OVER at Matt where he was talking on the phone and taking notes in one of the many files they had strewn across their desks. As he hung up the phone, Shane said, "Let's get out of here man and have some lunch."

Once in the diner down the road, Matt looked over at Shane and said, "Okay, go for it."

Surprised, Shane asked, "What do you mean?"

"You've been lookin' at me like you've wanted to ask me somethin' all morning. Stop screwing around and just ask."

Chuckling as he shook his head, he admitted, "You've always known me. Guess that's what made us good partners." Pausing for a moment to think about what he wanted to ask, he finally just went for honesty.

"Look, last night Annie wondered about you and I had to admit that we haven't really had a chance to catch up. I realized that while I was dealing with my own shit, you were back here with a life that I don't know about. And...you seem quieter. You were always up for a good time and now ...I don't know...like you've got a lot on your mind."

Matt sat for a few minutes and Shane let the comfortable silence flow between them. Their food was delivered and they began to eat. As their lunch was almost finished, Matt began to talk.

"It was hard when you went under, but I knew you. I knew after the rescue of your friend's woman, you were determined to do anything to shut down that pipeline. Had a couple of partners while you were under. They were good. Not you, but good enough. I just kept thinkin' that I had not only lost my partner but my friend as well, so I kind of shut down. Stopped going out as much."

Shane sat listening as he got the feeling that there was so much more to the story than what Matt was saying.

"I met someone."

That got Shane's attention. He was about to ask to hear more, but realized that it must have ended badly for Matt's reaction to be what it is. So he let the silence speak for him once again.

"Met her at a bar mixer one night, but she wasn't a bar troll. Nice girl. Hell, drop-dead gorgeous. Real smart...a lawyer in the city. We got together and stayed together. Dated for six months."

"I had no idea, bro." Shane hung his head for a moment. "Fuck. I missed so much!"

"Yeah, well, some things are better missed," Matt said ruefully. "Met each other's families. Even talked about marriage, although looking back, it was more of a one-sided conversation. My side." He self-consciously rubbed the scar on his face.

Again the silence at the table spoke volumes. Shane knew that whatever was coming was not going to be good.

"I got the cut on my face when I was off duty and having to break up a bar fight. A drunk asshole broke a bottle and took a swipe at me like he thought he was in some goddamn wild-west movie. For a while, it looked really bad – stitches, all red and swollen. She didn't handle it well. Wanted me to quit the force. Said the scar upset her to look at it. I figured when it healed, she'd be fine. Then the typical started happening. She had to work late. Missed our dates. Said she had too much goin' on.

"Then I find out she's sleepin' with one of the law-yers in her firm. I won't go into details about how I found that out, but it wasn't pretty. We had a fight and she told me that since my face was no longer handsome, she just couldn't see herself with me."

Shane reared back as though slapped. "What the fuck?"

Matt just nodded. "Yeah. That was a year ago, so it's not like it was recent, but since then I don't socialize as much."

"That's fucked up man. I am sorry as hell I wasn't here."

"Nah. It's all good now. I focus on the job and find a bar chick to bang when I need to. Just not lookin' for anything like your sunshine."

Shane smiled at the thought of his copper-headed

spitfire. "You'll find it one day. The real deal, not some two-bit skank who wouldn't know a good man if it bit her in the ass!"

The conversation turned over to the cases on hand. "You did good work while under, Shane. We got convictions on most of those mother-fuckers that you sent our way."

"Yeah, but I never made it to the top. I knew about the prostitution angle that we helped shut down but the dog trade, well that was something that I was just getting' into when to prove loyalty I had to sacrifice Sarge and that led me to Annie...and the rest is history. But honest to god, Matt, I couldn't have taken much more without losing my soul."

"Don't beat yourself up. We may not have shut them down completely, but we hurt 'em bad. We may even be able to keep diggin' to find out where they house the dogs."

Walking out of the diner to go back to the station, Shane said, "I'm meeting Annie's parents this weekend."

Matt kept walking although his dour look was replaced by a grin. "Looks like one of us just might be gettin' married."

Shane clapped him on the back but couldn't help but smile as well.

Chapter 20

THE FOLLOWING SATURDAY morning found Shane, Annie, and Sarge in his truck heading to Jefferstown. The trip would take a little over an hour so he spent the time filling her in on his conversation with Matt.

"Oh Shane. That is horrible. I can't imagine having to live with knowing that you gave your heart to someone so shallow. And he is still so handsome. The scar doesn't take away anything from the man inside!"

Shane laced his fingers with hers as he glanced at the beautiful woman sitting in his truck. *Pure, fuckin' sunshine. All the time.* He brought her fingers to his lips, kissing them lightly.

As they drove into the driveway of the suburban home that was so similar to Shane's parents' home, they saw several cars already parked.

"Who all is going to be here, babe?"

Sighing deeply, she answered, "I have no idea."

The door flung open before they were able to get to the front porch. "Annie," her mother yelled as she hugged her daughter tightly. The tiny, red-headed woman then turned to Shane with a huge grin on her face. Grabbing him in a hug as well, she said, "You must be Shane. How nice to meet you!"

Shane and Annie smiled over her mother's head before being interrupted by a booming voice. "Ruth, let the man breathe."

Annie's mother let go of Shane, then turned, yelling loudly into the house. "Well, if you'd get out here to greet guests, I wouldn't have to drag them in to get a welcome."

A large man came onto the porch catching Annie as she jumped into his arms. Shane watched as father and daughter hugged, finding himself thinking of his own father. Mr. Donavan then turned to shake Shane's hand and the two men sized each other up. Shane figured he must have passed the test when Mr. Donavan suddenly grinned and said, "You can call me Harvey and this woman who's been huggin' on you is Ruth. Come on in son and have a beer." Shane winked at Annie before disappearing into the house.

Once inside, they were met with several members of Annie's family including grandparents and a few aunts, uncles, and cousins. As soon as she could get her mother alone she rounded on her.

"Mom, did you have to invite so many people? I wanted this to just be about us."

"Oh darling, you don't get to come home that often and everyone wanted to see you."

"You're not fooling me. The minute you found out I was bringing Shane with me, you were on the phone.

Mom, this is embarrassing."

"Nonsense dear." Her mother walked over to envelope her in a hug once more. "Honey, I know you think I just want to plan for a wedding and grandchildren, but it's not just that. You work so hard. You always have. You're driven, goal oriented, and you never stopped until you became a vet with your own practice. But honey, there's more to life and I want you to have that too."

Returning her mom's hug, she could feel the sting of tears threatening to fall. "I love you mom. He may just be the one."

Straightening to her full height, which was only the same five foot two inches that Annie was, she announced, "Well, then let's go feed our men!"

The afternoon was spent in a similar fashion to the weekend before at Shane's house with the exception of Harvey stealing Shane away to his workshop for a while.

Shane looked on with interest at the intricate woodwork that Harvey created. "These are amazing, sir. I've admired this type of work on houses that I drive by but confess to not having ever thought of who made them and how they were made."

"It's kinda like your children. You do the best you can but never quite know how they'll turn out. Now take my Annie. She's a hard worker. Decided years ago to be a vet and she's never strayed from that path. I worry about her though."

Harvey rubbed his hands over a few of the wood

pieces that he had made, allowing his rough hands to smooth along the curves. "Without sounding like a cliché, can you tell me about what you do, Shane? I know you're a detective and Annie indicated that you were undercover for a while. But son, all I really know is that shortly after meeting you, my daughter got shot at in her own clinic."

Shane nodded, knowing this conversation was going to be coming at some time. "Sir, my father was a policeman. Worked vice for a number of years in Richland and was killed in the line of duty before I could join him on the force. It'd been a dream of mine to work beside him. Instead, I had to bury him before I had that chance."

He paused and noticed that Harvey had leaned against the workbench heavily, as though that information weighed on him.

"I worked the streets before becoming a detective and moved into vice as soon as I could. I had one goal, and that was to take down as many drug dealers as I possibly could."

Harvey nodded but said nothing, so Shane continued.

"An old friend of mine had his fiancé kidnapped by some dealers and we barely got her out alive. I decided then that it was time. I went undercover, but honestly I thought it would last six months to a year at the most. Two years later, I was dug in deep but still not at the top. Then it got personal with Sarge here," he said as he rubbed Sarge's ears, "And that's when I met your daughter.

"Never meant for her to be involved. Never meant for any harm to come to her. Truthfully, never meant to see her again after she helped me the first time with Sarge. But I couldn't stay away."

Harvey nodded again and said, "That's real admirable, son. And I'm sorry about your dad. I bet he woulda been real proud of you. I gotta say though, that you still being in vice makes me nervous about Annie's safety. She told us you got her apartment and clinic wired but is she safe?"

Shane wasn't offended by Harvey's questions. *Hell, if I had a daughter who'd been shot at because of her boyfriend, I'd be pissed.* "While I won't make promises I can't keep, I can tell you that the ones we went after are now behind bars. My involvement is over in that case, but I am still not takin' her safety for granted."

Harvey sighed heavily as he raised back to a standing position, holding out his hand again. "Well, son, that's all I can ask. Welcome to the family."

Just then, Annie appeared at the door to the workshop to call the men to lunch. "Everything okay in here?" she asked, her eyes going back and forth between the two men she loved.

Her father slung his arm around her shoulders kissing the top of her head. "Everything's fine, doll-baby. Let's go eat your mother's good cooking!"

He walked on ahead of them and Shane took the

opportunity to steal a kiss. Looking at her questioning gaze, he said, "It's all good. We had the father 'what are your intentions with my daughter talk' and we're fine."

She rolled her eyes saying, "Oh lordy."

THAT NIGHT, AFTER Shane had come in from taking Sarge outside to do his business, he broached the subject of their living arrangements.

"Baby, you know Sarge needs more room to run and something that your dad said today got me thinkin' about findin' another place to live.

She tried not to let the hurt show on her face when she said, "But you just moved in. I kind of thought you would stay a little bit longer."

Shane caught the look in her eyes that she was trying so hard to hide. "Baby, you got me wrong. I'm talkin' about us findin' a place. Us. You and me. Well...and Sarge, Boo, Rags, and Tiddles."

At that, she burst into laughter. "You'd take all of us?"

Shane looked the floor of the tiny apartment, where his dog and her three cats were all angling for the best sun-spot on the carpet. "Babe, I'll start looking tomorrow."

She maneuvered over to straddle his lap, her laughter slowing to a sly grin.

Raising his eyebrow, he asked, "You got somethin' on your mind, sunshine?" sliding his arms around her back.

"Maaaaybe," she replied, rolling her eyes to the ceiling as though having to think about her answer.

His hands found their way to the bottom of her shirt and he began to slowly slide them upwards, dragging the material with them higher and higher until he had to lift it over her breasts.

Feeling adventurous, she unsnapped her bra and flung it to the floor as well. Then she slid her hands to her breasts, cupping them, pushing them together as though to present them to him for his attention. "Need a snack?" she asked seductively.

Growling his response he leaned forward latching onto one nipple while his other hand began to massage the other breast. Sucking deeply, he moved his mouth from one nipple to the other, hearing her moans echoing in his ears. Sliding his teeth to the pointed nub, he nipped, then lapped with his tongue to soothe the sting. His cock was painfully pressing on his jean's zipper, but he wanted to make this last.

"Babe, gotta take this to the bedroom," he said while trying to stand up.

Moaning, "Why?" was the only response she could think of.

"Too much company," he said against her breast, still sucking between words. With that, he stood up quickly as she wrapped her legs around his waist. Stalking to the bedroom he lay her down but before he could make a move she scampered off the bed.

She quickly divested him of his clothes as well as her pants and panties. She slid down on her knees surprising him when she took his swollen cock deep into her mouth.

"Oh Jesus, fuck," he moaned, placing his hands in her hair, trying not to grab her head and face fuck her. He threw his head back against the wall and felt his world tilt. How many woman had he let suck him off, especially in the last couple of years where that was preferable to stickin' his dick somewhere nasty, even with a condom. For an instant, he was back there – in the dark, dirty rooms that the gang used to hole up in, waiting on orders. The women would circle around the men, sucking them off or fucking them in a corner. No privacy. No way to avoid that shit if your life depended on fitting in.

Coming back to reality, he looked down at his woman, on her knees as though she were worshipping his body. Her eyes were looking up at him strangely and she slowly slid her mouth off of his aching cock.

Running her tongue over her lips she stared up at him, knowing that his mind was not with her. *Maybe I'm not doing this right. Maybe he doesn't like it.*

"Are you okay?" she asked tentatively, insecurity stealing over her.

Shane looked down as the doubt crossed her expression. *Fuck. How do I fix this?* "Baby, you're fine. I just…I didn't…"

"If I'm not doing it right, just tell me. I'll try to do

better," she said, trying to fight back the tears that threatened.

He dropped to his knees in front of her, gathering her up in his arms. "Oh baby, you were doin' everything right. It was perfect. You're perfect. I'm so fuckin' sorry I made you feel that way."

Biting her lip in uncertainty, she asked, "So what happened?"

Shaking his head, he pulled her tight against his body, relishing the feel of her flesh next to his. One large hand cupped the back of her head as he cradled her closely. "I just sometimes have…flashbacks."

He felt her stiffen immediately. *Oh fuck.*

"Flashbacks?" She pulled back to stare into his face. "Flashback like your nightmares? What kind of flashbacks?"

He was silent as his eyes implored her to just move on.

Her eyes widened in understanding as she jerked to a standing position. "Oh my God. You mean you were remembering others doing…on their knees…doing…oh my God," she said, turning from him with her hand clasped over her mouth.

"Baby," he began.

"No, no, don't baby me," she said with tears in her eyes. "I knew there were other women, you told me about it. I just had no idea that you thought of them when we were…oh my God." With that, she grabbed her panties off the floor, pulling them up.

Shane, desperate to stop her actions grabbed her arms, holding her firmly without hurting her. "Baby don't do this. I was not thinkin' of other women. Yes, my mind flashed back to a darker time, but there has never been anyone who has had my heart."

Annie crossed her arms over her chest in a protective action before walking to the dresser to pull out a t-shirt. With her back to him, she finally let the tears fall. "I can't do this now. I can't be with you and let myself go knowing you're *possibly* thinking of others." Dashing her tears from her cheeks she turned around to face him but the sad look in his blue eyes nearly undid her.

"Annie, there has never been another woman in my life that I've loved. No one. You are the only one to have held my heart. The only one I have ever spent the night with. The only one that I have held all through the night. The only one I want to hold. Baby, I am so sorry. I don't know what to do. I don't know what to say to make this right."

Hanging her head, she just nodded. "I don't know either. I know I love you and your past is part of you. But somehow your past has always seemed like just that...the past. I've never once felt like that part of who you were crept into who we are now."

Encouraged that she was still talking to him, he slowly moved forward until he was standing directly in front of her, without touching. He placed his fingers under her chin to lift her face up so that he could see her green eyes, bright with tears. "You are my sunshine. You are the reason I came out of the dark. You are the reason I have the desire to actually greet the real sun each morning and I know when the sun sets every evening, as long as you are with me, I'll still have the sun shining on my face. Baby, I can't change the past. I'll work on controlling the flashbacks and memories. But the bottom line is this…I love you. I only love you. I have never loved anyone until you."

As her tears slid silently down her cheeks, she felt the rough pads of his thumbs sweep them away. Taking a shaky breath that hitched painfully, she leaned her face into his chest. Listening to his heartbeat, she realized that he couldn't change his past. Remembering all that he had given up over the past two years, she knew he needed acceptance, not her recrimination.

Shane held her head against his chest, his heart pounding in both fear that she was going to leave him, and love for this tiny woman. Kissing the top of her head, he whispered, "I'm so sorry, baby."

She turned her face up to his and shook her head. "I'm sorry too. I know you can't change the past and I know you can't help when things flash back." Taking another shaky breath, she said, "We'll just have to find our way."

Breathing easy for the first time since they entered the bedroom, he held her tightly a few more minutes. "Let's go to bed, baby. Why don't you use the bathroom first and I'll make sure the apartment is secure, okay?"

Crawling into bed several minutes later, they looked

at each other awkwardly. Shane, taking charge said, "Come on, baby," as he pulled her body in tightly to his. "We'll sleep tonight. As long as we're together, everything is gonna be fine."

Annie felt the familiar warmth of his body surrounding hers and she drifted off to sleep quickly, the emotion of the evening having exhausted her.

Shane lay awake holding her for a long time. *I promised to protect her. But what about protecting her from myself?* Before dropping off to sleep, he decided to call the department shrink tomorrow. *I may have come in from the dark, but it still has a hold on me. No more. That shit stops.* Kissing her head one more time as he listened to her slow, rhythmic breathing, he finally slept.

Chapter 21

THE NEXT SEVERAL weeks flew by as Shane and Annie found themselves busier than ever. As the holidays approached, the clinic was packed with animals that ate things they shouldn't have eaten and worried owners. Annie's schedule did not allow any breaks and Shane was equally busy with trying to tie up the loose ends in several cases, keep an eye out to make sure none of the major players were making bail, and trying to find an apartment. Plus talk to the department shrink.

Matt looked over at his partner, studying files on his desk. "Is it helpin'?" he asked.

Shane looked up, knowing instinctively what Matt was talking about. He had confided about the incident with Annie to him. Taking a deep breath, he let it out slowly. "Only met him a couple of times, so I don't really know yet." Looking away for a moment in thought, he continued, "But yeah, I guess it's not so bad talkin' about it."

"How's Annie doin'?"

Shane's piercing glance came back to Matt's. "In general or with my shit?"

Matt shrugged. "Both, I suppose."

"In general, fine. Busy. She's been puttin' in long hours 'cause it seems the holidays are when everyone's pets get fuckin' stupid, eatin' shit they shouldn't. I asked her about takin' on another vet, maybe even part time, and she's thinkin' about it."

The silence stretched out between the two partners. "And my shit? Better. It was a little rough the first time...well, after that night when...you know."

"She loves you, man. She'll deal."

Shane swore, "That's the problem. She shouldn't have to fuckin' deal." Blowing out his breath, he rubbed his hand over his face in frustration. "I mean, we got over that hump, but I feel like I've been walking on eggshells ever since. I hesitate to initiate anything 'cause I'm worried that she's worried."

"Annie's smart, Shane. Give her more time and you keep gettin' help. It'll sort itself out. How's the apartment hunting going?"

At this Shane grinned for the first time. Matt looked at him curiously.

"I'm startin' to look at buyin' a house, not an apartment."

"No shit?"

"Matt, I'm wanting to take this to forever. She's the one and it doesn't make any goddamn sense to beat around the bush. I've got a big-ass dog that needs a yard to run in. She's got three cats that need their space too. I didn't spend hardly any of my money for two years, plus the danger-pay I got. I banked it all and have more than enough for a down payment."

"What does Annie think of this?"

"Well…"

"You haven't told her? Don't fuck this up, man."

"I wanted to see what was out there first, then bring her on board."

Matt smiled at his friend, nodding. "Good luck, man."

Shane looked at his friend for a moment, his mind sliding back to what Annie had said. *Matt is such a great guy, I hope he finds his happily ever after too.* His sunshine was right.

ANNIE AND SUZANNE were in the back doing surgery while Leon was handling the patients up front. Annie stretched her aching back, trying to get the kinks out of it.

Suzanne looked over at her with concern in her eyes. "You okay, doc?"

"Yeah, just tired of leaning over this table. These damn dogs will eat anything."

She had started her day with a neuter, then they were on their third foreign body surgery of the day. "One ball of ribbon, a golf ball and the winner now is…a sock!" she said as she pulled the sock from the stomach of the puppy.

Suzanne had to laugh at the mangled, wet sock dangling from Annie's fingers.

"Lordy, it makes me glad I have cats," Annie said as she began stitching up the dog.

"Do you and Shane have plans for the holidays? Are you going to split your time between your folks and his family?"

"Honestly, we haven't gotten that far in our planning. I know he needs to spend it with his family since they lost the last couple of holidays with him, but my mom will have a fit if I don't get into Jefferstown. I don't know. It's one of those things every couple has to figure out, but we've had so much other stuff to deal with, it just hasn't come up."

"What other stuff, if you don't mind me asking?"

"I'm working all the time, he's working late on cases and says for me not to worry, but I see him constantly checking to make sure the security system is on. He's been seeing a police counselor to help with some flashbacks, but due to the nature of them he can't really talk about it." Annie sighed deeply. "My apartment is too small for all of us."

"This is the hard part, isn't it?" Suzanne asked quietly.

Looking over at her as she finished the puppy, she asked, "What do you mean?"

Shrugging her shoulders, she replied, "The hard part of a relationship. The easy part is falling in love. The hard part is keeping that love."

In the time that Annie had been around Suzanne she had noticed that Suzanne never talked about dating or a boyfriend at all. In fact, she always seem to shy away from personal questions.

"So you know about the hard part?" Annie asked softly.

Suzanne turned her brilliant blue eyes on her boss and friend. "Yeah. I know. I was in love. I thought it would be forever."

"What happened?" Annie found herself asking, even though she was afraid of the answer.

"We just didn't have enough in us to make it last through the hard part. He needed ... to become himself, and I needed...well, I didn't get to keep what I needed."

Annie knew that Suzanne had shared all that she was going to share and so she picked up the still sleeping puppy and followed her out of the operating room. Once the dog was settled in recovery and they had cleaned up, Annie turned to Suzanne and hugged her.

"What was that for?" Suzanne asked with a smile on her beautiful face.

"I just thought that we both needed it."

Leon's voice broke through their moment, calling for Doc to come to the front. Walking into the reception area, Annie saw a man in his early thirties dressed in a nice suit waiting to be seen. Looking over at Leon, she waited for an explanation.

"Doc," Leon said. "This is Dr. Carl Ogden. He's here looking for a job."

Annie was shocked but recovered to walk forward and shake his hand. "Dr. Ogden. I'm Dr. Annie Donavan. It's nice to meet you, but I haven't advertised for a partner."

"Please call me Carl and I know you haven't advertised. I was hoping that we could talk for a few minutes if you have time. If not, I will be glad to come back at a more convenient time."

"Well, the clinic is closed now so I have some time. Would you like to come back to the office? It's small, but we'll be able to talk privately there."

Leon and Suzanne shot her a dirty look as she turned and led Carl toward the back. Annie almost giggled, knowing they wanted to see what the doctor had to say.

Once settled, she turned to him. "So Carl, what did you want to discuss?"

"I am looking for a job, but my situation is unusual," he began. "I don't normally live in the area but my mother fell and broke her hip. I've moved in with her temporarily to assist. She has some home care so I'm not needed twenty-four-seven. I worked in a clinic in North Carolina but had to take a leave of absence. I would like to practice, just part time, while I'm here. I was passing by the other day and noticed your clinic. I was hoping that perhaps during the holiday time you might be so busy that you could use an extra pair of hands."

Annie responded, "I'm actually very interested in someone helping out. I can't give you a lot of hours, but if your credentials check out, then I would consider having you on a part time basis. I'm finding that my surgery schedule is so packed that I have a hard time getting through the appointments. If you could work maybe three mornings a week, would that suffice?"

Carl smiled broadly, thanking her profusely. "Dr. Donavan, that schedule would be perfect." He stood and reached out his hand again.

"Leave your information with Leon and I will let you know as soon as I call your references."

She led him out to the front to meet with Leon and was surprised to see Shane standing there scowling. "Hi sweetie. I didn't expect you so early." She walked over to give him a hug wondering about his sour expression. She notice his eyes had not left Dr. Odgen's.

"I'd like you to meet a potential part-time vet who may be able to take some of the load off of me," she said. "This is Dr. Carl Ogden and this is Detective Shane Douglas."

The men shook hands but seem to be sizing each other up. Shane gave a head jerk then turned his attention back to Annie. "You ready to go, babe. Got somethin' I want to show you."

"Sure honey, but I need to finish up here."

"Doc, you go on. Leon and I will get things ready for tomorrow. You need a rest break anyway," Suzanne offered.

After making sure that Leon would be getting Carl's information and giving a quick hug to Suzanne, she and Shane headed up to her apartment so she could change.

"So do you want to explain to me why you looked

like you wanted to get into a pissing contest with Dr. Ogden downstairs?" she called from the bedroom as she quickly changed. "And where are we going so I will know what to put on?"

"We're going to check out a place for us to move to so just wear something comfortable. And I wasn't in a pissing contest." Before he could ask more about the other veterinarian, Annie came running out of the bedroom jumping into his arms, wrapping her legs around his waist.

"You found a place?" she screamed. "You found an apartment for all of us?"

Laughing, he grabbed hold and swung her around, kissing her soundly. "I did but we've got to get going if we want to see it tonight."

They headed out of town a few minutes later, Annie anxious to see the apartment that Shane had found. They continued to drive out of the urban center of the city to the north side, passing a large park and turning into an older residential area of town. The lawns were large and well maintained with huge trees lining the roads and filling the back yards.

Annie looked around curiously, wondering where an apartment building would be in this neighborhood. "Are you cutting through the neighborhood to get to another area?" she asked.

Before Shane could answer, he turned into a drive-way of one of the houses with a 'For Sale' sign outside. The white, two story colonial sported black shutters and a front porch that spread the width of the home. The large front yard held trees and flower beds and was surrounded by a rustic wooden fence.

Annie whipped her head around to look at Shane, seeing the smile on his face. "What are we doing here? Are you looking at this? When did you..."

Before she could fire out another question, he leaned over capturing her mouth. The kiss was gentle. Slow. Soft. Pulling back slightly, he whispered, "Welcome home, sunshine. That is, if you like it."

Her eyes widened as she turned her head back to the visage out of the front of the truck. "You bought a house? For us?"

"Come on, baby. Let's take a look," he said as he slid out of the truck, gently pulling her out of his side. "Sarge," he called and the dog jumped out of the cab as well, running through the yard.

Another car was in the driveway and a pleasant-looking lady emerged, briefcase in hand as she approached. Introductions were made and she led them up the porch steps where she proceeded to let them enter.

Shane had seen the house before, but found himself nervous over Annie's reaction. He held her hand but kept his eyes trained on hers to see what she thought.

She was stunned. She had no idea that he was looking at houses. *I thought he just wanted to get a bigger apartment. Not a house. But oh my God, this is amazing.* Wandering through the downstairs, she discovered the living room was on the left of the entrance hall and was flooded with natural sunlight from a large picture window facing the front side window as well. A brick fireplace stood on the wall opposite of the picture window, and she immediately noted the mantel was large enough for decorating in 'family'. To the right of the entrance hall, was the dining room, with the same wooden floors that extended from the living room.

Walking into the dining area, she tried to stifle a giggle. The realtor looked over quizzically and Annie explained that where she lived, she ate on the sofa with the coffee table. The realtor smiled indulgently and began pointing out the attributes of the house and neighborhood. Annie was in her own little world by that time, wandering from the dining room into the kitchen. Sucking in her breath, she looked around at the fully equipped kitchen filled with oak cabinets with decorative knobs, granite countertops, and new appliances.

Shane walked up behind her, wrapping his arms around her tiny frame, and whispered, "What do you think, baby?"

"It's amazing, Shane. It's gorgeous."

"Come on, let's look at the rest of it," he prodded. Leading her by the hand, they continued from the kitchen to the family room in the back of the house where the windows overlooked the back yard, complete with stone patio. Up the wooden staircase, they discovered a large master bedroom with a bathroom that made Annie stop in her tracks.

Shane watched as she gingerly leaned over and ran

her hand along the edge of the soaker tub. *She deserves this. She deserves all of this.*

They explored the two other larger bedrooms and the one smaller one that would be perfect for a study. *Or a nursery* he thought as he watched his beautiful woman take it all in. *I could see her. Standing by the window, the sun shining on her coppery hair, holding their child.*

"Shane, are you all right?"

Jolted out of his musings he smiled as he walked back over. "Yeah, baby. I'm perfect."

They finished the tour standing in the back yard enjoying the view. The realtor, knowing she had a sure sale, began pulling papers out of her briefcase. "Shall we go in to the kitchen where we will be able to use the counter for signing?" she suggested.

Annie's eyes cut sharply over to Shane's. "Sign? You're going to buy it now? But I don't even know how much it is? Shane I can't afford much. I can't..."

Once again, Shane shut her up with a kiss. Looking over to the realtor, he said, "Will you excuse us a minute."

She nodded and went inside.

Annie turned to him, ready to cut loose with her million questions and concerns, but before she could say anything, he placed his fingers gently over her lips.

"Sunshine, I need you to stop and just listen for a minute. Can you give me that?" She nodded against his fingers so he released them.

"We both grew up in a neighborhood like this. Old homes. Big yards. Lots of room for kids and pets to play. I always knew that at some point in my future I would like the same thing. I never looked before 'cause I never had a reason to. But baby, we're an *us* now. And this *us* is going to keep going. You with me so far?"

Her green eyes never leaving his beautiful blue ones, she nodded once again as her heart began to pound.

"Money is not a question here." He noticed her brow immediately furrowed, but he continued. "Baby, my pay's not shit and I've saved most of it over the years. The two years I was under, I didn't have to use hardly any, and on top of that I received extra for hazard pay. I invested and I've got a decent nest-egg. We'll have about a twenty-minute commute, but you can start looking for vet practices out this way if you want. I'll stay with the force for a while more then I may decide to take Tony up on his offer of security work. Haven't made up my mind yet, but his office is on this side of town so that would be good too.

"Do you get what I'm tryin' to say? I want you in my life. In my future. Not wastin' any more time getting to the life I want. I've been wild, but you've been the one to tame this beast. I want you, this house, our pets, and eventually our kids."

At that declaration, Annie's wide eyes filled with tears as she grabbed his face and pulled him down for a kiss. He let her take charge of the kiss for just a moment before he angled his head and took the kiss right where he wanted it to go. Wild, passionate, breathing her in and giving it back.

Slowly pulling away, she glanced over, seeing the realtor peeking through the window. "Shane, we have an observer."

"Don't worry about it, sunshine. That kiss just got her a sale!"

Laughing, the two of them went inside where Shane signed on the numerous dotted lines. Shaking hands with the realtor, they were assured that the sale should go through quickly since the previous owners had already moved and were anxious to sell. "You should be owners in about a month," the realtor announced proudly as she led them back outside.

Corralling Sarge back into the truck, they headed back into the city talking about the future.

Chapter 22

"DR. OGDEN, YOU have a client in room one," Leon's voice called from the back.

Carl looked over at Annie in the lab and laughed. "Does he always yell like that?"

Smiling, she answered, "Well, without a speaker on the phone or a PA system, yelling is the most effective, although not necessarily the most professional."

"Hey, whatever works. By the way, I overheard Suzanne talking about you moving into a nice new house in the suburbs."

"It is amazing! I've been cramped into that tiny apartment over the clinic for a couple of years now so to be able to move into a real house will be a dream come true."

"You must have done all right on your student loans to be able to afford a house now."

"Oh, I still have student loans, but I've been able to save a little." Uncomfortable with discussing finances with a stranger, she didn't elaborate that Shane was buying the house and that they had finally agreed that she would pay a portion of the mortgage. After a lengthy argument, of course.

"Well, it certainly gives me hope that I can afford a nice house sooner than I thought. You never know when a windfall will just drop in your lap though, do you?"

Annie was already walking back into the surgery room to get prepped for the next dental coming in so Carl had to hustle to get to his exam room client.

SHANE LISTENED IN as Matt took a phone call from an informant that they had been cultivating for a long time. Matt hung up with a smile on his face.

"We might just be gettin' a break. It seems that we've been chasin' down the wrong path, lookin' for an animal pound bringin' in the dogs. This guy thinks they may be brought in by a breeder."

Shane leaned back in his seat, rubbing the back of his neck with his hand. "That doesn't make any fuckin' sense. Breeders get top dollar for their dogs. They're not gonna sell them to drug dealers for nothin'. This guy's got to be shittin' you."

"Not certified breeders, but puppy-mill kind of out-fits. You know, those shit-holes where someone just breeds whatever the fuck they can and then tries to sell them. If the dealers have someone who is cheaply breeding dogs for them then they've got a ready supply. No records, never even been in a pound, so there is no tracing the dogs at all."

Shane looked over to the side for a minute, his mind

running over the new information.

Matt watched him carefully. Since Shane had talked to the department shrink and was firmly in relationship he seemed much calmer, but Matt could see the clouds pass across Shane's intense gaze at times and he knew that Shane was remembering the darkness. "You okay, man?"

Shane's eyes cut back to his partner's. Sighing deeply, he said, "Yeah. When I was livin' in the darkness, I swear I would almost start thinkin' like them. Then I get out and realized how fucked up it all is."

Shane had been to several appointments with the police psychiatrist and while he resisted at first, he actually found the man to be easy to talk to. He found that being able to talk about what all he had done while he was under, things that he could never have shared with Annie, helped alleviate the nightmares and flash-backs.

Shaking his head to clear his mind, he and Matt went back to work trying to find all of the information on the illegal puppy-mills in the area.

"DOC, YOU'VE GOT a consultation in room three," Suzanne said as she walked back to the lab area.

"What's the animal?"

"The lady didn't have an animal with her. She just said she needed a consultation with you. Oh, and she asked for you by name so I couldn't even send Dr.

Ogden in."

"That's odd. In this neighborhood we don't get too many clients wanting to check us out first," she laughed. "I guess I had better make sure I make a good impression."

Entering the examination room, she stuck out her hand as she said, "Hello, I'm Dr. Dona..." She stopped mid-sentence, staring at Rochelle. *Rocky. Shane's Rocky.* Tall, blonde, lots of tits and ass, rocking a pair of jeans and a t-shirt. Even casual she looked elegant.

The beautiful woman's gaze roved quickly over Annie and she smiled tentatively as she approached her. "Dr. Donavan. Yes, I know who you are. I'm Roche..."

This time it was Annie that interrupted. "Rochelle. Rocky. Yes, I also know who you are."

Rochelle glanced sideways for a second before bringing her eyes back to Annie's. "I see."

The two women stood staring at each other, the silence stretching between them as uncomfortable as an itchy sweater. Annie found herself wanting to shed the silence. "I don't mean to be rude, but I have other patients to see."

Rochelle seemed embarrassed as she said, "Yes, of course. Forgive me. I can't contact Stoney...I mean Shane, anymore. I'm still trying to work on things. I wanted to tell you though that I think you may be in some danger. I don't have anything concrete, just murmurings about a vet operating on a couple of the dogs."

"I'm in danger?" Annie repeated, fear crawling from her stomach to her throat. "But I thought the drug dealers were all in jail."

"Most of the group we were targeting are, but Dr. Donavan, there will always be others to take their place. And a few of the ones that were higher up are still free." Shrugging Rochelle added, "That's why I'll always have a job, I suppose."

"But I don't know anything. I'm nobody."

"I don't have any facts for sure," Rochelle added. "I just wanted to warn you to be careful." Looking speculatively, she continued, "And I wouldn't say you're nobody. I always wondered if any woman could tame the wild Stoney."

Licking her lips, Annie drew herself up and stared into Rochelle's eyes. "I won't discuss Shane with you."

Rochelle's eyes softened. "Oh, Dr. Donavan, you misunderstand me. I know he's yours. I knew that the night you saw us together. He was torn up about what you saw and what you thought. I've never seen him like that. I knew then that he loved you." Sighing while picking her purse up from the counter, she slung it over her shoulder as she prepared to leave. "Please be safe, Dr. Donavan. And thank you."

She passed Annie as she opened the examination room door, turning only to say, "Thank you for loving him."

Rochelle walked briskly out of the room and collided into Carl. He reached out to grab her arms so that she would not fall.

"I'm so sorry," he exclaimed as he steadied her, scanning her from head to toe, staring intently.

"I'm fine. Actually it was my fault for not checking the hall first," she said staring at him intently.

Flashing his smile, he couldn't help but add, "Well, if I have to run over a client, I am certainly glad it was one so beautiful."

Laughing, Rochelle glanced back at Annie before heading out of the door. Annie, still in shock over the visit, didn't hear Carl when he first asked about the client.

"Annie," he repeated. "Who is she? She didn't have a pet with her."

"Oh, just a potential client. I think she just wanted to check me out," she answered cryptically.

"Well, if she does choose us, make sure I get her next appointment!"

"YOU HAVE GOT to be shittin' me!" Shane growled.

Annie, giving him a minute to control himself, held her phone against her shoulder while she gave the cats a treat. Knowing that she needed to let Shane know about Rochelle's visit, she had excused herself from the clinic and ran back up to the apartment. Stepping over Sarge and his food bowl, she managed to get the cats fed.

"Of all the goddamn, fuckin' moves she coulda made, that one really rips it!"

"Honey, I know you're mad, but you haven't let me tell you what all she said. She didn't come by to start trouble between us. She came to warn me."

She could hear him speaking to someone in the background. "Yeah, goddamn Rocky came by the clinic to visit Annie. Got no fuckin' clue but that shit doesn't fly." *He must be talking to Matt.*

"Babe, what was she warning you about?"

"She said that she thought I might not be safe. She said she just heard rumblings about a vet who had operated on some dogs and she thought of me."

"Goddamn it! If she's got intel, she sure the fuck knows she shouldn't be bringin' that shit to your doorstep. Babe, listen to me. I'm sending some cruisers to go by the clinic and I'm calling Tony to make sure they have you on their radar. That other shit, I'm shuttin' it down right now."

Annie started to tell him not to do anything rash, but she knew he was going to do whatever he had to do. "Shane, please be safe. For me, please."

His angry voice softened. "Sunshine don't worry. I'll see you tonight. And baby?"

"Yeah?"

"Just one more week and we can be in our house. Keep thinkin' of that."

Smiling for the first time since her meeting with Rochelle, Annie relaxed. "I know, honey. I can't wait."

THE BAR WAS dingy, beer spills on the table from the night before were still sticky. The lighting was dim, so only the most sober of patrons would have even noticed the condition of the tables. Shane sat on one side of the booth looking at the woman on the other side, pissed at what she had done and yet pleased that he felt no residual attraction to her at all.

Rochelle held up her hand, "I know what you're going to say. I didn't think you'd want a meeting so I did the next best thing and went straight to the person I thought needed warning."

"You didn't think I'd want to know? You didn't think I'd need to get things set up to protect her? You didn't think that showin' up at the clinic in broad daylight was a problem? You just didn't fuckin' think and now you've brought all this shit right to my woman's doorstep!"

Rochelle sat in silence for a moment staring at him. Sighing while shaking her head, she agreed. "You're right. I'm sorry, Stoney."

"I'm not Stoney, Rochelle. You gotta get it through your head. My fuckin' name is Shane."

Jerking back, she pursed her lips before going on. "I get it, but for a year you were Stoney to me. And I was your Rocky. Yeah, that's right Shane. I was yours. I just made the mistake of thinking you were mine also." Taking a big breath she continued, "And I was wrong today. I should have called it in or reported to my contact. Hell, I could have even called you. I don't know…I just…wanted to see her. I wanted to the see the woman that finally tamed you. And when I did, I realized that I had nothing against her. I could see it in her eyes that she was yours."

"No more, Rochelle. You gotta get that. No more Rocky and Stoney. It was a play that helped pass some time and set up cover. But that was it. You're smart and you're driven. You wanna go places in the DEA so you gotta learn to play the game. But no more talkin' to Annie. No more bringin' this shit to her doorstep."

The beautiful woman across from him nodded as she gave a weak smile. "You're right. I fucked up. I'm not sorry I got a chance to meet her, but I fucked up. It won't happen again."

Without saying another word, Shane got up from the booth and gave her a head nod before turning and walking out of the bar.

Rochelle sat for a minute more at the table before moving over to the bar to order another beer.

LYING IN BED, Shane waited for Annie to emerge from the bathroom. The tension of the day had drained away when he got home and saw the packing boxes neatly stacked in the corner of the living area.

Annie had explained that if they were moving in a week she wanted to be ready, so she had packed up her books, CDs, out-of-season clothes, and some kitchen items and had them in neatly labeled boxes. Just seeing them made the move to their own home seem that much more real. During dinner she let him explain what had happened when he met with Rochelle, and then after dinner they snuggled on the sofa with the pets for a while watching TV. Heading to the bathroom, she told him to get ready for bed and she would be out shortly.

So now he waited, keeping his eyes trained on the bathroom door. He didn't have to wait long.

Annie walked out into the dim lighting of the bedroom wearing a smile on her face and little else. The sheer nightgown was fitted over her breasts, allowing the darkness of her nipples to be seen, before flowing down around her knees. She smoothed her hands down the gown looking nervous. "Do you like it? I've never had anything like this, but it was on sale so I just…"

"Come here, baby," Shane ordered gently, his eyes taking in all of her beauty. Her copper hair glistening in the soft lamp light, porcelain skin with pink tinged cheeks, green eyes searching his for approval. His cock was already standing at full mast, its approval evident.

She walked over to her side of the bed, crawling toward him, glancing down at the tented covers at his lap. "So," she said smiling, "You do approve."

Shane grabbed her, rolling them over so that he was pressing her down into the mattress. Gently grinding his erection into her body he said, "Yeah, baby. I approve." He took her mouth in a hard, wet kiss, delving his tongue deep as he breathed her in. Rolling so that she was on top, he slid his hands up the silky material until he was palming her breasts.

Annie threw her head back as the sparks ran from her nipples to her core. She began to rub her aching pussy on his dick, wanting to increase the sensation of friction that she knew would take her over the edge.

Her actions had him growling, "Love this nightie, baby, so I don't want to tear it. But I need to get you the fuck out of it now!"

Annie grasped the bottom and pulled it over her head freeing her breasts, which went immediately into his greedy mouth. She ran her hands through his hair as he feasted on first one nipple and then the other.

He slid one hand down to her pussy feeling the moisture pooled there. "You're soaked, baby. Fuckin' soaked for me."

She didn't want to wait any longer so she lifted herself up, placing his cock directly at her opening. Holding his eyes, she seated herself to the hilt, feeling him fill her completely. Screaming his name, she began to ride him as hard as she could, desperate for the orgasm that she knew would rock her world.

"You shoulda let me take care of you first," he said, watching her breasts bounce rhythmically as she moved up and down with the help of his hands on her hips.

"I couldn't wait," she panted.

Smiling at the most beautiful woman he had ever seen as she rode his cock telling him she couldn't wait to be on his dick, he slid his finger to her clit. That was all it took and she was screaming his name again as her pussy walls clenched him tightly. *Jesus, best sight in the world. My woman screaming my name as she is coming.*

As soon as she crashed down on his chest he rolled them again so that she was underneath him. Still seated inside of her he began to move in and out, her orgasm creating more moisture so that he slid easily.

He kissed her while thrusting until neither of them could tell where one ended and the other began. Feeling his release imminent, he ordered, "Come on baby, one more time."

She knew she was close so she pinched her nipples as he continued to thrust hard and fast. The sensations exploded as she came again right as he grimaced and pounded the last few thrusts. He roared her name as he came deep inside of her, filling her with his seed as her small hands grabbed at his back.

Shane panted as he fell on top, barely aware that he was crushing her. *It just keeps gettin' better and better. I've never come like that before. Pure, fuckin' sunshine.* The harshness of the past couple of years no longer invaded his thoughts, and never came to mind when he was with Annie. His mind was completely filled with just her.

She didn't seem to mind being crushed as she kept her hands on his back, gently moving them between his shoulders and his ass. She felt him slide out of her body and roll to the side, but she hated losing that part of him.

He tucked her in tightly for a few minutes before getting up to get a warm washcloth to take care of her. As he walked back to bed, he scooped up the nightie from the floor, folding it gently on the dresser.

"That needs to make it to the new house, baby."

"I don't know why Shane. It didn't stay on long enough to be appreciated," she pretend pouted.

"Sunshine, that is proof of how much it was appreciated. The quicker it comes off, the more it was appreciated."

Laughing, she rolled to him as he turned out the light. She cupped her hand around his strong jaw, peering into his blue eyes that shone in the light from the street corner. "I love you, Shane Douglas."

Kissing her gently, he replied, "Love you too, Annie Donavan. Can't wait to have a home with you, sunshine."

Smiling, in each other's arms, they fell asleep.

THE SOUND OF SHANE'S cell phone jarred them awake. He reached out and saw the display, **Matt**. "Yeah, man, what's up?" he asked in a sleep-gravelly voice.

He was silent for a moment so Annie turned on the lamp on the night stand to see him more clearly. His face was hard. Angry. Her heart began to pound as she wondered what was happening.

"Fuck. Yeah, I'll be there. I want someone on Annie immediately. Yeah, I know. Be there in about twenty minutes."

"Shane?" she said softly. "What's wrong?"

He looked at her and for the first time she saw fear in his eyes. "Rochelle. She's dead."

Chapter 23

THE LAST OF the furniture had been delivered and placed in the new home and all that remained was to unpack the boxes. The furniture they had been buying for the past month had been held by the stores and it was nice to see the house finally come together as they had planned.

Tony Alverez was outside of the house with Shane. Annie stood at the large window in the living room watching them as they talked while they looked at the house then pointed to the roof. Sighing she turned away walking back over to another box. She had tried to talk to Shane about Rochelle, but he gave her very little information. She knew that Rochelle had been killed, but he had not shared any details. Rochelle had been flown back to Texas where her parent's lived, and given a full burial with honors. But other than that, Shane had shut her out of his feelings about Rochelle's death.

He had Tony put someone on her so that she constantly felt as though she had a shadow. Right now, they were outside discussing the best security system for the house, leaving her inside to place family pictures on the mantel.

"You okay, baby?"

Startled, she turned around almost dropping the picture frame in her hand. "Jesus, you scared me!" Looking around, she asked, "Where's Tony?"

"He's got what he needs so he and his crew will be back tomorrow to get things set up."

Nodding, she looked at him, desperate for him to talk about what he was feeling. "Are you hungry?"

"No, babe. We can order something in a little while. You don't need to cook."

Walking over to Shane, she put her hands gently on his chest. "Honey, I wish you'd talk to me. Please. I know you're upset over Rochelle. I get that. She meant something to you and ..."

"What are you talkin' about?" he asked harshly, holding her hands still from rubbing on his chest.

"You. This closed off, not talking very much, brooding YOU. I know you cared about her and it's okay if you need to talk about it. I get that you can't be very happy now over our new house. I get that, Shane. But I'm not used to you closing me out. My untamed man will shout, curse, and get angry but at least I know what he's thinking." Her voice hitched as she tried to hold back her tears. "This man," she moved her hand back to his chest, "I don't know how to help."

Shane dropped his head for a moment before lifting it back up to hers. Taking a deep breath, he clutched her hands to his. *She's worried about me. Pure, fuckin' sunshine.*

"Baby, you got it wrong, but that's on me 'cause in tryin' to protect you, I've kept you in the dark. And that's got you mulling things over in your head and comin' up with the wrong idea."

"How can I know how to deal with this Shane if you don't tell me? I didn't know Rochelle, but she came to warn me and now she is dead. You're exactly right if you think I've been mulling things over in my head."

"I don't want you to worry about anything, Annie. That's my job."

She looked at him incredulously. "You're kidding, right? I'm supposed to just go about my job and this move and act like everything is normal because you're going to worry about it all? Newsflash Shane, it doesn't work that way. You worry therefore I worry!"

He lifted his hand to cup her face, rubbing his thumb over her cheeks. "I got this, baby."

Annie just looked at him, not having an idea of what he meant. She allowed him to lead her to the new sofa and was pulled down onto his lap.

Wrapping his arms around her small frame, he tucked her in tightly, one hand stroking her back and the other hand cupping her head. "Baby, I'm sorry. I was shocked by Rochelle's death, but my quietness on the subject wasn't due to my grieving over a lost love. I can't even say we were friends. We were both in a dark situation and took advantage of it. That was all. So I hate like hell that a fellow officer has fallen. And yes, I hate that a young woman was killed. But she knew the risks and knew what she was doin'. When I saw her, she admitted that she could have sent her intel to her contact or to me, but she broke cover when she went to the clinic. And she did that just so she could see you, meet you. She broke cover for somethin' that didn't matter. That was fucked. She risked her cover and she's now put you back in the light. That doesn't make me harsh, just real."

Allowing his words to have a chance to slowly sink in, he continued to rub her back in silence. After a moment, she leaned up and looked into his eyes and he gently moved his fingers over her cheeks.

"So if you haven't been grieving over someone, what has you brooding?"

"Baby, it's you I am worried about. I wanna make sure you're safe. I wanna make sure that nothin' happens to you."

She sat on his lap staring into the blue eyes that reached inside her, his love wrapping around her as tightly as his arms wrapped around her body.

"Sunshine, those family pictures you're puttin' up on the mantel – Baby, that's what I want you thinkin' about. Decorating in family. I don't want you worryin' about all this. That's the man I am. I wanna take this away so you can focus on just being sunshine."

Bringing both hands up to his face, she kissed him softly. "What bothers you, bothers me. What concerns you, concerns me. Shane, I can't be sunshine if I am worried about you."

She leaned in to kiss him again but soon found that he took over the kiss. Even so, it was slow. Soft. Full of promise. Full of love. Full of light.

SHANE AND MATT were driving to one of the animal shelters on the outskirts of the city, checking more leads about puppy-mills in the area. So far their efforts were coming to dead-ends. The registered breeders went into great detail about their disgust of the amateur breeders and especially the cruel treatment of the people running puppy-mills. And while they were able to get some names to follow up on, they still had not found what they were looking for. So now they were checking out the animal shelters, both registered and some that were a lot less reputable.

"Somebody at one of these places has got to know something. How can you have a facility that has a shit-ton of dogs running around and no one knows about it?" Shane growled in frustration.

Matt looked over, "How are you and Annie doin'?"

Shane grunted in response. "House is great. Timing is shit."

Matt said nothing, letting Shane have some space.

Sighing, Shane continued, "Love the new house. It's got room for Sarge and her cats. With the holidays coming on, Annie is already planning on decoratin'. We've got the furniture in and I should be fuckin' happy but with everything that has been goin' on, I feel like somethin' is always draggin' me down.

"We had an argument the other day about it all. She thought I was broodin' over Rochelle when all I can think about is makin' sure she is safe."

Matt asked, "Have you been able to find out more about why Rocky thought Annie was in danger?"

"Nah. Said she'd overheard someone talkin' about a vet who had worked on a couple of the dogs and she made the assumption they were talkin' about Annie. But there was no overt threat. Problem is, when Rochelle came to the clinic just because she was fuckin' curious about who I was with, she brought that shit right back to Annie's door."

"What did you tell Annie about Rocky?"

"Told her the truth. She knew Rocky was in my past, was nothin' more than a way to pass the time to hold up our cover. Makes me sound like a dick, but Rocky and I were up front with each other. There were no promises of anything other than physical. And she was fuckin' married at the time. I had no idea she'd gotten it in her mind that we coulda been more." Rubbing his hand through his hair, he shook his head. "We were fuckin' livin' wild then just to survive. I got out and glad of it."

They pulled up to the animal shelter, seeing the concrete buildings holding the dogs' runs. A middle-age woman walked up to them smiling. "Howdy! How can I help you?"

Introducing themselves to Maude, they began to

question her about her facilities and what she may know about any other facilities in the area.

"Well, I run this facility with mostly funds I get through charity work. Lots of people like to give, but my books are clean. Lordy, with all the red tape I have to jump through with the county to keep this kennel going, believe me, every penny is accounted for!"

They wandered through the area looking at the dogs running in the clean area. "What we are really lookin' for is any information you may know, or even have heard of, about non-reputable facilities. Like puppy-mills."

"Come on in detectives and I'll get us something cold to drink and we can talk."

Following her into a crowded but neat office, they settled into folding chairs next to her desk as she handed them sodas.

"I've been doing this for years. My late husband and I started our first rescue kennel about thirty-five years ago. It didn't take long for us to grow, but we realized that we needed the backing from the county. We became licensed and took care of the animals that came to us the best we could. Herbert died four years ago, but I keep going." She looked out of the window for a moment before bringing her gaze back to them. "I'll never get rich doing this, but these dogs are my family."

"What do you hear in the community about other facilities? Ones that perhaps do breeding in massive amounts with no regulations?"

"I've never heard of anything specific. But there would have to be some clues to where they are." she said.

"These dogs eat and they eat a lot. Now, I get a lot of my food from volunteers and donations, but someone who has a large number of dogs would have to be getting a lot of food. Also, these dogs make noise. That's why I'm out here where I have a couple of acres. Even with this space I got a few neighbors that complain about the barking. Facility like what you are talking about, especially if they are trying to fly under the radar, is going to need a lot more space. Lots of acres to make sure no one is bothered by the barking."

Shane finished up taking notes and then he and Matt took their leave after thanking her.

While Matt drove them back into the city, Shane pulled out a map. Richland was bordered by farmland and forests leading toward the mountains. "Jesus," he said looking at the area around the city. "This is like lookin' for a fuckin' needle in a haystack."

PULLING INTO THE driveway that evening, Shane sat for a moment looking around. The yard was neat, flower beds dormant in the winter, the light in the front windows sending out a warm glow. A wreath on the front door. *Home. Our home.* Sarge must have heard his truck pull up because he saw him jump up and look out of the window, followed closely by Annie peeking out as well. *Beautiful. Six months ago I would have never thought this was possible. A woman I love who lights up the fuckin' world. A house. A home.* Right then Boo jumped up in the window too. *A cat.* Laughing as he swung out of his truck, he jogged up the front porch steps.

Sweeping Annie up in his arms, he twirled her around the front foyer, carrying her toward the living room where the fire was roaring.

"Hey honey, what's up?" she asked as he set her down.

"Just glad to be home. Glad to have a home. Glad you're the one waitin' when I get home."

"Wow, what brought that on?" she asked, smiling up into the blue eyes that held her captive.

Shane walked over and sat down on the rug in front of the fireplace, pulling her down with him. Holding her close, he breathed her in. Her hair shown like a new penny in the firelight, her green eyes soft and warm.

"Baby, I've been a dick for a couple of weeks, and that stops now."

Seeing the confusion on her face made him love her more. *I've been a dick and she's already forgiven me.*

"I've been pissed about this case for a long time. I met you and decided to wrap things up and thought the case was over." He paused for a moment. "I've been so pissed about Rochelle bringin' this to your doorstep, but the reality is that I've been at war with myself. I'm the one who brought this to your doorstep to begin with, so it doesn't make a lot of sense to be pissed at her."

Annie cupped his face as she spoke, "Shane Douglas you listen to me. If you had never brought Sarge to me we wouldn't have this. I wouldn't have this house with the man I love. It's been a couple of weeks and nothing bad has happened. You're making sure I am safe. I'm being careful, so stop worrying. I want you here with me, body and soul."

They lay back on the rug, kissing gently as he slowly ran his fingers though her hair. The fire crackled in the background and for the first time Shane found himself relaxing. Truly relaxing. *I could fuckin' lay here forever with her in my arms.*

Just then her stomach growled and she giggled. "Come on honey, I've got dinner ready."

Pulling him up, she led him into the kitchen where she set dinner on the table. Looking over at him, she wanted to ask him a question, but hesitated.

"What's on your mind, baby"

"How did you know I had something on my mind?" she asked.

"Sunshine, I've had my pulse on you since the first night we met. You got somethin' to talk about, we talk."

"Well, I was wondering about the case. I know you can't tell me much, but I was just curious how it was going?"

Shane looked over at her, seated at *their* table in *their* house. *Smiling back at him. Wantin' to share in his life.*

"We're still tryin' to find the dog connection, baby.

Lookin' at puppy-mills now."

Annie screwed up her face in distaste. "Oh honey, those places can be really awful. Crowded, dirty, no room to run. And that doesn't even begin to describe the diseases."

"We talked to a lady at a shelter that said they would need a lotta room so that no one notices the barkin'."

"Or the smell."

Shane halted the progress of his fork to his mouth as he looked at her, still eating.

She continued, "I mean they don't always clean up after the animals so the smell of feces would be over-whelming I would think. Who knows what they feed them, so they would have diarrhea. The flies would be awful too. Without medical care, they would have open sores as well." Looking up, she noticed that Shane had stopped eating.

"Do you not like the dinner?" she asked.

"Baby, you just talked about a whole lot nasty stuff. Do you vets always do that?"

Blushing, she just laughed. "I'm sorry honey, I'm so used to talking about animals and what is going on with them that I don't even realize it isn't appropriate."

Shaking his head, he laughed too. "Well, I asked." Looking thoughtful for a moment, he said, "So, if you wanted to have this kind of operation and have it fly under the radar, what would you do?"

She pondered his question then replied, "The lady at the shelter was right. You would need some acreage.

Out somewhere private. Preferably with woods around."

"Why woods?"

"The trees would act as a natural sound barrier so the barking of the dogs would be heard less. Also, near a possible water source would be good, so that you could use that to at least have water and do whatever cleaning you are going to do. Or well water. Just not city water or the bill would be too high. They probably order the food. There are cheap discount online food stores they could get it from."

Impressed, Shane stood to clear the dishes bending to kiss her lips. He watched her lick her lips and he dove in for another. Deeper, wetter. The dishes clattered to the table as he arms circled around her, pulling her up. Leaning back, he stared into her face overwhelmed with the emotion he was feeling. *This untamed man was home.* "Love you, sunshine."

That night he showed her just how much he loved his home with her.

Chapter 24

ANNIE SAT IN the lab area of the clinic working on computer searches during a break between clients, trying to find more information.

Leon looked over her shoulder, then exclaimed, "What the hell are you looking up puppy-mills for?"

Suzanne and Carl came from the front at that moment and circled the computer as well.

Annie glanced over her shoulder at her staff with a grimace on her face. "These places are disgusting."

Suzanne echoed Leon's question, "Why are you looking them up?"

"I'm just trying to find out more information to see if I can help Shane."

Carl chimed in, "Help Shane with what?"

"Just a case he is working. It may involve dogs that come from a puppy-mill in the area so I thought I would see what I can find."

"Now don't you think he should do the detective work since that is his job, doc?" Leon said as he and Suzanne took an older cat over to the table to draw blood.

Carl, still staring at the horrible conditions on the

computer screen, asked, "Are you finding anything? I mean, wouldn't Shane have the same info, if not more, than you can get?"

Smiling at the group, Annie said, "Well that's where I think I have an advantage. I know a couple of vets in the rural areas outside of the city and in the state. I'm sending out messages to see if they have heard anything. I'm also looking into some of my professional sites to see where there may have been some extra or unusual requests for dogs in this area. I might be able to find something that I can offer to Shane."

Carl smiled at Leon over Annie's head as he exclaimed, "We've got our own personal Nancy Drew right here in this office!"

Suzanne, finished with the blood draw, ended the group discussion when she announced, "By the way, the Richardson family is bringing in their snake today. They think it may have eaten their hamster."

Annie just hung her head and shook it as the other laughed.

"Never a dull moment," Carl said as he headed out front to the next appointment.

Later, Annie called Shane to tell him of her latest findings. His response was similar to Leon's.

"Baby, what the fuck are you doin'? I don't want you anywhere nearer to this case then you already are!"

"Honey, I'm just checking on some things."

"Well, stop. You vet and I'll detect. Got it?"

Huffing, she agreed, then hung up.

"Clinic is ready for tomorrow, chief," Carl reported as he and Suzanne walked into the room. Leon was checking the stock in the lab cabinets finishing up the clinic's orders.

"So," Suzanne said, plopping down in one of the chairs, "What did Shane say about your research?"

"You can probably guess what he said!" was the reply.

"Look Annie, I know you want to help but if you were my girlfriend, I wouldn't want you anywhere near this kind of detective work," Carl added. "I mean, these guys sound dangerous. Crazy. Jesus, who does that to dogs?" He shook his head in disgust, then looking over to Suzanne said, "You ready to leave? I'll walk you to your car."

Leon looked over and nodded to him. "Thanks Carl. I've got a few minutes left here to finish the order."

"Well, I'm going to check my emails from earlier," Annie said. "I had one from a county vet that sounded promising."

Carl and Suzanne turned back to her with concern on their faces as they were walking out. "You aren't going to try to investigate, are you doc?" she asked.

"No! I promise guys, I won't do anything on my own. But if it looks like one of my county colleagues has any ideas, I'll let Shane know."

Satisfied, Carl walked Suzanne out to her car and then headed home himself.

"I've got the ordering finished for the month," Leon stated, shutting down the computer in the office. "Anything special you need me to do before I head home?"

"No, you're good to go."

"You still checking things out?"

"Yeah. Read this email from this veterinarian in the county next to Jefferstown."

Leon leaned over her shoulder reading.

Hi Annie. Haven't seen you in a long time. Still got the practice in the city? Got your email. While I don't know any specifics about puppy mills in our area, I have my suspicions. I've had some clients bring in dogs they said they bought from breeders, but when I questioned them, it definitely wasn't a breeder. The dogs were just in crates at one of the farmer's markets that the county has during the summer months. Dogs have parasites and some signs of malnutrition. I report it when it comes in and animal control goes by the markets but nothing so far. One of our clients has hunting dogs and he mentioned that he has heard dogs barking out in the woods near the old Truman farm but he just assumed it was someone raising more hunting hounds. Other than that I can't say that I have anything for you. Take care and if you ever get out of the city, look us up. I got married last year and we'd love to have you over. Malcolm Bursten, DMV

Leon was quiet for a moment as he finished reading. Looking down at her, he asked, "So do you think it's worth telling Shane?"

"It can't hurt to tell him. The dealers aren't keeping dogs in the city or the police would have found them by now. And the counties surrounding the city are just too big and rural for them to comb through." Shrugging, she continued, "I'll let him know and then he can decide what to do."

"All right, doc. I'm outta here. Shirley's going to have dinner waiting and if I want to get a little somethin' tonight, I best not be late!"

Laughing, she agreed, "Get home before both your dinner and Shirley get cold!"

THAT EVENING ANNIE shared her findings with Shane. When she had pulled her emails up on her laptop, she actually had three more from colleagues that all had some possible clues.

He looked over at her face, excited with the idea that she was helping him. Her green eyes shone with delight as her face scrunched in concentration. His concentration was diverted by the copper hair piled on top of her head and the sweet scent of honeysuckle from her bath wash. *Pure fuckin' sunshine.*

Glancing over, she quickly moved her hand over her face with a look of concern. "Do I have something on my face?" she asked blushing.

Leaning over, he placed a soft kiss on her lips. "No, baby. I was just admiring the view." He was leaning back in to take the kiss deeper when she suddenly spoke.

"Can we go this weekend and see if we can find some of these places?"

Shane jerked back, brow furrowed and ice blue eyes snapping. "What the hell are you talkin' about? We? Baby, there is no *we* when it comes to this investigation. You've already been attacked and there is no way in hell you are getting anywhere close to this."

Rolling her eyes, Annie turned to face him. "Shane, I'm not talking about going in, guns blazing, to break up a drug dealer's den. I'm talking about visiting some of these places that may be puppy-mills. If they're there and as poorly run as most, then as a vet I can get them shut down."

He rocked back in his seat and looked at her incredulously. "Annie, the answer is no. Even if there is no drug activity, these places are dumps, and the people who run them don't want to be found. They also don't mind protecting their interests. They sell dogs that are poorly bred and sell them as pure-breds and make a lot of money doing it."

"Shane, I know that. I know what they are. That's why I want to find some."

"Babe, you're still not getting the picture here. These people may shoot visitors *before* they find out why you're there and they sure as hell won't be friendly once they realize your purpose."

Annie turned her wide-eyed gaze back to him. "Honey, people don't shoot other people like that!"

He just stared at the innocent beauty in front of him and rubbed his hand over his face. *How do I let her know the dangers without taking away that sunshine?*

"Baby, you've got no idea of the world I have been in and I don't want you to. If I could keep you wrapped up in a bubble, swear to God I would. You've already been terrorized once by part of that world," he added, noticing her wince. "And I want to keep that world from you."

Staring at his pale blue eyes that held love and concern for her, she leaned back in her chair. "You're serious, aren't you? You're not just doing some caveman act on me."

"Yeah, Annie girl. I'm serious. You leave the investigation to me. You do your job, the job that you love, and leave the rest to me."

"I WAS GOING back over some files and came across the injuries due to a dog attack. Did you ever call the emergency vet?" Suzanne asked.

Annie thought for a moment before remembering the details. "Oh yeah. I got hold of Dr. Ketchum and he said he never saw a dog that evening, but that they had a new receptionist working there so there may have been an error or oversight."

Suzanne looked concerned. "Error? Mr. Charleston was very sure about what occurred. Why would the emergency vet not remember or have records?"

"I don't know. His explanation made sense to me at the time, but to be honest with everything going on, I really didn't follow up any more."

"Do you mind if I do some digging? Mr. Charleston seemed so sweet and he is so protective over his dog since his wife passed away."

Smiling at her assistant, Annie agreed. "Sure. Check back with him and then with the vet if you want."

They turned toward the hall as the yowling of an angry cat was heard. Leon walked in with a cat attempting to rip him to shreds, but he had the animal in a firm grip.

"Could use a little help here Suzanne, if you two are tired of playing detective vet!"

She was already walking toward him, ready to assist. "What a whiner, Leon. It's just a little kitty!"

Later, Annie came out of an examination room and saw Carl at the front desk. "Hey, I didn't think you were working today."

"I needed to get away from my mom for a little bit while the therapist was there so I thought I'd stop by and check on some of my files. I was curious about your consultation from that gorgeous woman a while back. Did Rocky ever come back and bring her animal?" Wiggling his eyebrows, he said, "I was kind of hoping to find out if she was single."

Annie hesitated, not knowing what to say. It seemed wrong to lie to Carl, and yet, the situation surrounding Rochelle's visit was so personal. "Um, I haven't heard from her since she was here." *At least that's not a lie.*

"Too bad. Hey, I'm meeting some friends after work for drinks. Do you want to join us? You can bring your boyfriend."

"Thanks, but he's working late and I'll be here catching up on work as well. But have fun."

After Leon and Suzanne left for the day, Annie finally finished her reports and shut down her computer. Leaning back in her chair, she closed her eyes and rubbed her temples. Thoughts had been swirling around her mind for hours and she just wished she could turn them off. *Shane. Their house. The clinic. Suzanne finishing her program. Leon taking on more responsibility. Matt. The puppy-mills. Shane's case. Carl. Rocky.*

"Auggggh!" she yelled out loud. *This is why Shane is the detective and I am the vet. Animals I understand. I assess their condition and then systematically begin to find the causes. Dogs don't have ulterior motives. Cats may want to scratch you if they are scared, but they're not trying to kill you.*

Standing up from the office chair she tried to roll it back under the counter, but the wheels were stuck on something. Bending down to see what was the obstruction she saw a man's wallet. Grabbing it, she stood up as she opened it to see who it belonged to. The driver's license showed it was Carl's. *He's out with friends and won't have his ID for bars.* Looking at her watch, she wondered if she had enough time to get it to his mother's apartment before he left with his friends.

Snatching up her purse, she locked the clinic and headed down the street, having written down the address from his employee file. Four blocks down the road, she saw him jogging toward her.

"Annie! I was just trying to get back into the clinic. I think I may have dropped my wallet."

"I've got it. I found it under the desk and was trying to get it to your mom's place before you left to meet up with your friends. I would hate for you to get carded and not have ID," she laughed.

He looked concerned. "You were going to my mom's apartment?"

"Well, yes. I thought that was where you lived."

"It is, but I...well, I don't think you should ever drop in on her," he said looking embarrassed. Rubbing the back of his neck, he looked up at her and explained, "She's...kind of...cantankerous."

"Cantankerous?" Annie asked.

"I know she's in pain so for the most part I just ignore it. But, well...she can sometimes not be very polite to people."

"I see. Well, I'll remember that. I'm just glad we caught up with each other," she said handing him the wallet. "Have a good evening."

Thanking her, Carl turned and headed back down the street. Annie turned back toward the clinic where her car was parked and began walking down the street again, this time noticing how much darker it was. Stopping under a street light, she realized that there were quite a few street lights out in the neighborhood, making the sidewalks eerie.

"Dr. Donavan," a male voice sounded as a man materialized from the shadows. He was not as tall as Shane but was bulky, as though he spent a great deal of time in a weight room.

She instinctively took a step back, clutching her purse. *Damn, I should have my mace in my hands!*

The man noticed her defensive posture and stepped into the light so that she could easily see his face, while keeping his hands in plain view at the same time. "Doctor, my name is Jobe, from Alverez Security, and have been assigned to make sure you get home from the clinic each night. I saw you walking away from your car and meet with the other doctor, so I wanted to make sure you were all right."

Annie stood still, wide-eyed, the adrenaline rush was still pounding through her.

"Doctor, may I show you my identification?"

She nodded and replied, "Yes, please."

She noticed that he smiled just a little. "Why are you smiling?"

He handed her his Alverez Security photo identification giving her a chance to scan it and his face. "I'm smilin' because you're so polite even before knowing if I am who I say I am."

"Why haven't I seen you before?"

"Ma'am...I'm sorry...Dr. Donavan. It's my job to go unnoticed. I'm here so that you don't have to worry about your safety, but to also stay in the background. Now, may I escort you to your car?"

Smiling at Jobe, she agreed, "Yes, thank you. It was getting dark and I was concerned."

"Doctor, may I suggest that you not attempt to walk the city streets unescorted again?"

She wanted to protest, but knew that if Shane was aware that she had been out in the dark, alone on the streets, he would not be happy. Nodding, she reached her car and unlocked it. Turning, she stuck out her hand. "Thank you, Jobe. I appreciate you assisting me. I'm sure that watching me and the clinic must be a very boring job for a man like you."

"Dr. Donavan, I assure you that no job is too small, and watching your clinic is certainly not boring. But even if it was, I would still do it to the best of my ability. Your safety is paramount. Shane's a good friend and that makes you important."

Smiling her goodbye, she got in the car and drove home. Pulling into the driveway, she noticed the lights in the house were on. So was the front porch light. So were the security lights. And Shane's truck was in the driveway. And his silhouette was in the window.

By the time she was getting out of the car, he was already off the porch and stalking toward her. Before she could get out her greeting he was upon her.

"You want to tell me what the fuck you were doing walkin' alone on a city street in the dark with hardly any street lights working?"

Annie's mouth dropped open in surprise. *Jobe.*
Damn, he called Shane. The first flush of emotion was
surprise. Then embarrassment. Then anger. Green eyes
widening, she looked up at his angry face. The face that
smiled at her over the breakfast table and stared at her
intently when she was screaming his name in passion.
And right now that angry face was pissing her off.

"Oh no you don't. You do not get in my face when
I am just getting out of the car after a long day at work
and start yelling at me."

"Baby, this is not yelling. This is me wanting to
know what the hell got in my woman's head that made
her go out looking for an apartment building on a dimly
lit street in the dark?"

Annie darted around him and stomped up the stairs,
yelling over her shoulder, "Why don't you just ask my
shadow, Jobe? He can tell you what I was doing. Oh
yeah, that's right. He already did!"

Shane was coming up the stairs behind her when the
door almost slammed in his face. Barely catching it with
his hand he shoved it open, making sure she wasn't
standing in the way.

"Babe, we are not through discussin' this," he said
following her into the kitchen.

"Shane. Hello? This isn't a discussion. This is you
yelling at me like some kind of wild man and I don't
like it. I also don't like the feeling that you have someone tattling on me! If you want to have a discussion,
then let's discuss. You know... 'Hi honey, how was your

day? Anything interesting happen?' Not getting in my face in the driveway!"

Shane stood in the doorway of the kitchen watching Annie stalk around, grabbing pots and pans and slamming cabinet doors. Her eyes snapping, cheeks flushed. Her copper hair had escaped the pony-tail and was waving about her face as she marched from one side of the kitchen to the other.

He dropped his head and stared at his feet for a moment, rubbing the back of his neck with his hand. *Wild man. If she only knew how wild I used to be. I gave orders and men jumped. Sometimes I only had to give a look and people would follow. I did things…not going there. That wild life is over. Done.*

He looked back up, his chest tight with emotions. "Sunshine," he said gently.

At that endearment Annie stopped her mini-tantrum at the sink and slowly turned toward him. Her green eyes met his pale blue ones and her anger faded. In front of her was not the beast from a few minutes ago, but her man. Calm. Tame.

"I'm tryin' here, Annie. Yeah, Jobe called and told me what had happened and I lost it, babe. All I could see was innocent you wandering down a dark city street, few street lights, gettin' ready to go into an apartment building that you didn't know anything about." As he spoke, he slowly walked over to her until her could wrap his arms around, pulling her in to his chest.

"Honey, it was not dark when I started out. Carl's

apartment that he shares with his mom right now is only about four blocks from the clinic. I was just going to run there and leave his forgotten wallet. He met me coming down the street, heading back to the clinic because he realized he left it. We chatted a few minutes and then I was going to walk back to the clinic."

He stood and held her tightly, one hand wrapped around her middle and the other holding the back of her head protectively. *Of course, she had been doin' something nice for someone. Pure, fuckin' sunshine.*

"I confess," she added, "that it got dark very quickly and I didn't realize how many street lights were not working. I was scared when Jobe approached…"

"He scared you? He didn't identify himself?" Shane's voice raised again.

Leaning her head back, she raised her eyebrows as she looked into his face. "Shane, don't be silly. Of course he identified himself."

Sighing, he pulled her back. "You're right. Jobe knows how to handle his job. And babe, his job right now is you when I can't be there."

Snuggling in tighter, she said, "Isn't this better? Discussing this?"

"Baby, you gotta cut me some slack. I'm workin' on it…tryin' to pull back. Tryin' to learn how to take care of what is mine in a way that is tamer than I am used to. But Sunshine, don't ever forget, you are my woman. And. I. Take. Care. Of. What. Is. Mine."

He leaned down and captured her mouth in his, the

kiss immediately hard and wet. He breathed her in as though his life depended on it.

Dinner forgotten, they barely made it to the bedroom before they began stripping their clothes off. Falling onto the bed Annie opened herself up to him as he knelt between her legs, kissing the inside of her thighs until she was squirming in want.

Pressing her down with one hand on her stomach, he smiled up at her as he dove in to the hidden treasure, lapping her slick folds. Sliding his hand up toward her breast, he rolled her nipple between his thumb and finger while thrusting his tongue inside. Feeling her lose control he sucked on her clit, eliciting a scream from her as her orgasm pulsated throughout. Lapping the juices, he then slowly kissed his way up her stomach, over her breasts giving each one attention, until he finally made it to her lips.

She could taste herself on him as she pulled his tongue in deep. She felt his cock at her entrance and she pushed up, impaling him deep inside her pussy. "Harder," she panted.

He leaned up, looking at her smiling face. "Yes, ma'am," he said as he began pounding in and out, feeling the friction increase against her tight inner walls. *Jesus, best I've ever had.* And he knew it wasn't just her beauty and innocence, but what he felt for her.

He grabbed her hands and pulled them over her head. "Hold the headboard, baby. Don't let go." She quickly obliged, smiling. He leaned down and pulled her nipple deeply into his mouth, swirling the hard bud around with his tongue.

She reached one hand down to caress his back, but was quickly ordered to hold on to the headboard again. She complied knowing it was going to be amazing for her, and her lips curving into a delicious smile.

Shane continued to pull out almost all the way before plunging deeply back in, over and over, until he had her screaming his name again.

Annie felt the orgasm slam through her, taking her over the edge and leaving her floating back down as he continued to thrust. She looked at his face with lazy eyes as he leaned his head back, neck tensing, as he poured himself into her waiting body.

He continued to thrust gently until he was spent, then fell to her side pulling her with him. Still connected, they lay as their hearts pounded before slowing to beat in unison.

Having let go of the headboard, she smoothed her hands over his back, feeling the muscles ripple underneath her fingertips.

He held her close, rubbing her back from her neck to her ass and back again.

Annie smiled against his strong chest, his heartbeat strong and solid against her cheek. It wasn't easy taming her wild man, but it was worth it.

Chapter 25

MATT LOOKED OVER at Shane, who was clearly agitated. Leaning back in his chair, he tossed the files down on his desk. "You wanna tell me what's got you so uptight?"

Shane turned his icy glare on his partner, saying nothing for a moment.

Matt just grinned. "Got all the time in the world, man."

"Fuck," Shane growled, shaking his head.

Matt leaned forward putting his hands on the files piled up. "You and Annie okay?"

Shane let out the breath he had been holding. "Yeah," was the only answer forth-coming. Matt stayed silent so Shane continued. "We had a pretty big fight last night." Sighing again, he looked down at his hands as he cracked his knuckles. "It's hard, you know?"

"What's hard? You got an amazing woman who loves you. You're not about to fuck that up are you?"

"No," came the vehement answer.

"So what was the fight about?"

"She's been doin' some investigating on this case. Talked to some vets in the counties surrounding

Richland and came up with some possibilities. Now she want to go out and actually visit to try to shut down the puppy mills, especially since we are thinking that is where the gangs are getting their dogs."

Matt jerked back. "You gotta be kiddin' me? She's thinking about playing detective and putting herself right back in the line of fire?"

"Yeah, I know, right? I shut that shit down quick, but not without a fight."

"Well, she knows you love her so you just tell her how it's gonna be."

"She's got other ideas." Shane looked up, rubbing the back of his neck. "Sometimes relationships were easier before. At work, we have a chain of command and we know where we stand. Even when I was under and I got in the gang, we had a chain. You knew who you could command." He paused for a moment, looking directly at Matt. "I can't change who I am. It's too ingrained to want to take care of her. But damn, she was mad."

"So how'd the argument end?"

"We discussed it," Shane said with a smirk.

Matt raised his eyebrow, "Discussed? You discussed it?"

"Yeah," Shane said, dragging out the word. "I calmed down, she told me what she thought, I told her what I thought, and then we started makin' out."

Matt leaned back in his chair, roaring with laughter. "You may call it discussing, but that lil' bit is taming you, brother, and you don't even know it!"

"Fuck you, man," Shane said as he grinned back. "You just wait until you find the right one."

Matt's laughter quieted, a look of pain flashed through his eyes before he turned his look back to Shane. "Well, maybe. But I haven't met her yet. So until I do, I'll just enjoy watching your beautiful woman bring you to heel."

Just then the chief walked over, a droll look on his face. "If you two are finished trying to figure out how to get a woman or keep a woman, perhaps you can bring me up to date on what you've dug up that I can give to the prosecutors."

Smirking, the men followed the chief into the conference room where they were met by others in the task force. Nodding their greetings, they began discussing the new evidence.

"When the local man, Cal Penski, was killed about two and a half years ago, we were able to shut down his end of the organization pushing the drugs through his strip clubs, which were nothin' more than fronts for prostitution. And often drugged prostitutes working against their will. Another group just moved right in, but weren't using the strip joints. This group was movin' drugs from one place to another inside of dogs. We were able to get most of the gang, except for some of the top people. It appears that Gerard Washington left the area to parts unknown, but Xavier Thomas stayed to try to recoup his losses. You all know I was never able to find out where the dogs were comin' from or where they were transporting them to. But we think that Rochelle and the DEA were getting close, and that's probably why she was killed. Someone figured out she was getting intelligence."

"So what have you found out about the dogs?"

"Suspicion is pointing to some possible groups breeding dogs that keep a steady supply to the gang. They are always big dogs, never very old, and not registered with anyone. We've looked at pounds and city shelters, but their adoption records don't indicate any connection at all. But puppy-mills are around, hard to find, and quite possibly the source of the dogs."

"All right. Keep working that angle," the chief said to Shane and Matt as the rest of the group began reporting their findings.

FRIDAY AFTERNOON COULD not come soon enough for Annie. Regardless of Shane's warnings, she could not help but look at the websites touting the horrors of the puppy-mills. Suzanne looked over her shoulder as Annie scrolled through pictures.

Shaking her head she said, "Doc, you've got to stop making yourself crazy over this. I know it's upsetting, but what can you do? You've talked to Shane and he is going to follow up on some of the rumors. Don't you think that might be enough?"

Annie tossed her copper hair over her shoulder as

she looked up at her friend. "I seem to remember you on the phone the other day with Dr. Ketchum arguing with him about a dog being attacked."

"That's different. That affected one of our clients and I swear that doctor is hiding something."

Annie raised her eyebrows in response and Suzanne hustled off to answer the phone. Leon was taking a rare day off to celebrate his anniversary with Shirley.

"So what's Dr. Nancy Drew up to this weekend?" Carl joked as he walked into the room.

"Shane is tied up with a case and is working tomorrow, so I thought I would take the opportunity to visit a couple of farmer's markets outside of town to see if I can find anyone selling pets that look ill."

Carl and Suzanne shot each other a look of concern over Annie's head. "Do you think that is wise?" Carl asked. "You going alone?"

Laughing, she turned in her seat to look at her friends. "Guys! What do you think I'm going to do? I just want to see for myself what is out there. I'm not going to attack anyone!"

"I wish I could go with you, but I am going to visit my parents this weekend. I'd go home on a different weekend if I could, but this is the only one that works for me."

Annie swung her gaze to Suzanne. "The only one?"

Her face hardening for a moment, a flash of pain sliced through Suzanne's eyes before being quickly replaced by a steely gaze. "I have someone from my hometown that I don't wish to run into so my parents let me know when it is safe to come visit."

Annie realized that Suzanne had just given more information about her personal life than she had ever in all the time that Annie had known her. She wanted to question further, find out what had Suzanne so closed off, especially about men, but knew that it wasn't the right time or place with Carl standing there.

Nodding, she agreed, "No, you go home. I don't need a babysitter."

Carl looked between the two women sighing loudly. "Look, I've got tomorrow morning off, I'll go with you Annie."

Beaming, she announced, "Perfect! I won't have to drive out there alone and you can make sure I don't go all bad-ass on some poor puppy-mill owner."

"You going to tell Shane what you are doing?" Carl asked.

Sucking her lips in, Annie averted her eyes. "Well, I think I will tell him that I am going shopping. There's no reason to worry him."

Carl and Suzanne shared another look over Annie's head and Carl just shook his head as Suzanne rolled her eyes.

SHANE LEFT THE next morning to go to the station and Annie was ready to leave as soon as he did. *Thank goodness he didn't think anything about me going shopping*

early on a Saturday morning. Feeling slightly guilty that she was doing some snooping without telling him, she knew that he would have had a fit if she had confessed her intent.

Within a half an hour she had picked up Carl and they were driving out of town.

"Where's our first stop?" he asked yawning loudly.

"I've got three I want to check out based on the emails from my vet friends in the county. The first one is on the north side of town and is the closest. Then we will hit two on the west side of the city, toward Jefferstown."

Arriving at the first market, they were greeted by a hive of activity. Colorful tents were set up, each filled with produce overflowing with locally grown vegetables, berries, and plants for sale. They started on one end of the market and wandered along the aisle. Carl couldn't help but stop and buy some produce as they were looking.

"Come on, Annie. Don't tell me you aren't tempted by these berries."

She had to admit that they looked scrumptious and found herself buying some as well. "You know I'm here for dogs and you are tempting me with food," she jokingly accused. By the time they finished walking the entire market, they finally found one older gentleman sitting on the tailgate of his ancient, beat-up pickup truck. He had a large, clean crate with four bloodhound puppies in it, all clambering for attention.

Annie immediately went over to the truck to look at the dogs. The puppies were clean and healthy, their coats shining and eyes bright.

"They are gorgeous," she exclaimed as the dogs immediately jumped and bayed for her attention. Carl had to laugh at the antics of the puppies as he examined them also.

"Did you breed them?" Annie asked.

The old farmer puffed up proudly as he answered, "Yep. My old gal, Sallie's their momma. Thought she was beyond breedin' years, but she went huntin' with my son and his dogs. All hounds, just like her." He chuckled in telling his story. "Didn't know Sallie could still have any more puppies, but this here is her last. As soon as I could, I got her spayed." Looking down in the crate, he gazed fondly at the last of his dog's brood.

"They are beautiful animals. I can see they are well kept," Annie said sincerely.

The old man's clear gaze met hers as he announced, "Young woman, I love my farm, I love my family." Smiling, he added, "I've loved one woman and she is still the light of my life. And I love my dog. I'm a lucky man."

Carl came up behind Annie as she stood smiling back. "Then I think they are very lucky as well."

Saying goodbye to the puppies and the old farmer, they made their way back to the car. Carl looked over to her as she was quietly pulling back onto the highway.

"What are you thinking?" he asked.

"I guess I had gotten it into my head that anyone who sold dogs out of a crate was some kind of a money-grubbing dog peddler."

"Do you still want to check out some others?" he asked while popping fresh berries in his mouth.

"Absolutely! Why? Are you tired already?"

"Nope. Drive on, doc. I may need refilling my berry basket by the time we get to the next one."

Smiling, she kept driving until they pulled into the next market. Their experience there was very similar to the first one they had visited. At this market, they found several dog owners with puppies for sale. The puppies looked healthy and she found nothing suspicious about the families that were selling.

Piling back into the car again, they drove to the next market, the one farthest from town. At the end of the produce section was a panel van with the sounds of barking coming from inside. Approaching cautiously, they walked toward the noise.

A young man stepped out of the first van, throwing open the back door to show a crate crowded with puppies. The puppies were skinny with runny eyes. The man eyed them as he said, "You interested in pure-bred dogs, lady?"

Annie could feel the hairs on the back of her neck rise as she realized that several other men got out of their van and had circled behind her and Carl as they looked at the dogs.

"Doc," Carl said under his breath, trying not to

move his lips as he whispered. "We need to get out of here."

Annie felt his fear as strongly as she felt hers. Turning quickly, she smiled broadly as she said in a sing-song voice, "Awww, these puppies are darling! What kind are they?"

She forced herself to make eye contact with the young man even though his very appearance made her fearful. From his shaved head to his tattoos that ran down his neck under his dirty t-shirt, he exuded danger. His eyes crinkled at the corners as he smiled at her blatantly, his gaze dropping to her breasts.

"They're pure-bred German Shepherds, lady. They got papers and everything."

Pure-bred, my ass. Jesus, these dogs look horrible. "Really? They look a little skinny to me. Do their papers include visits to the veterinarian and their immunizations? I am assuming that they have that included in their papers?"

The smile left the man's face as his eyes shot back up to hers and he stepped menacingly toward her.

Glancing backing at the young man, she forced herself to smile as she turned to Carl, noticing his uncomfortable stance. "Oh honey," she said brightly, "Do you want a puppy?"

"No," he choked out. "Come on, *dear*." He took her arm just as one of the puppies began to whimper.

Annie moved over closer and noticed how young the pups were. *There is no way they should be weaned by now.*

"Do you sell many puppies at these markets?" she asked, trying not looking at the men who had closed the circle around them. "I mean, you can't sell that many pure-bred dogs at a little market, can you?"

"We sell enough. Got people who always come buy our dogs," he said with a sneer.

"Marco!" barked out one of the other men. "Shut the fuck up!"

Chastised, the man closest to her scowled, but turned away.

"Lady, if you don't want a dog then move on. We've got other business to do," came a voice from right behind them, causing Carl to grab her arm.

"Come on, dear. These men don't need you playing with their dogs," Carl said, pulling her back through the men toward the market.

Without glancing back, they walked to the car and began driving away as quickly as possible. Not a word was spoken between them for a few minutes. Finally, Carl slumped down in his seat rubbing his hand over his face. "Oh, Jesus, Annie. That scared the fuck out of me!"

The adrenaline rush was still causing her hands to shake on the steering wheel, but she was trying to put on a brave face. "I'm sorry, Carl. That was not what I expected." She was silent for a moment. "I wanted to help the puppies so much."

Carl looked over at her, seeing tears in her eyes. "I know, doc. I did too, but no joke...I just wanted to get out alive. Promise me you won't try anything stupid. Shane's going to have a shit fit as it is." Turning back to her, he asked, "You are going to tell him aren't you?"

By this time they were a few miles down the road and she pulled over at a mom-and-pop gas station. Sighing deeply, she said, "Yeah. In fact I really need to call him now so that he can decide if he wants to come check them out himself."

Carl threw his head back on the seat in frustration. "Oh my god, I am going to get eaten alive by your boyfriend. He is going to kill both of us."

For once, Annie couldn't disagree.

"OKAY, THANKS," SHANE said, hanging up his phone. Matt looked over, waiting for his very angry partner to speak.

Shane looked up and said, "The county sheriff said that by the time they got to the market the vans were gone. They talked to some of the regulars at the market, but they said that when the vans come, they always stay off to the side. No one had any idea where they come from or when they show up."

Matt said nothing for a moment, letting Shane get a handle on his anger. "She coming here?"

Shane's eyes snapped back up. "Oh yeah. Oh, fuck yeah. And so is Carl. I can't believe that she went out after we *discussed* her not getting involved and that crazy-ass vet went with her instead of talking her out of it! Jesus, when I think of what could have happened! Well, she's going to be talking to one of the investigators here and I've made sure they know to put the fear of God into her."

Just then he saw her coming down the hall. As angry as he was, he couldn't help himself from jumping up and going over to her.

She immediately put her hand up and was going to tell him not to fuss, when he grabbed her in a bear hug. Wrapping her arms around him, she buried her face in his neck and found herself unable to hold back the tears.

"I know you're mad. I'm sorry," she hiccupped out. "I just wanted to see what these dogs might look like."

Shane held her tightly for a moment, not allowing his thoughts to travel to the what-ifs. He looked behind her, seeing Carl appearing discomfited. Setting Annie back down, he looked into her big green eyes, saying, "Sunshine, we are going to *discuss* this later. But for now, you've gotta talk to Detective Carter again." Looking up, she saw the detective that had interviewed her earlier. Sighing, she just nodded as she started to walk away with him.

"Carl," Shane bit out and Carl jumped. "You are going to talk to my partner Detective Dixon. And I'm going to be in there as well. And after you finish with him, you and me are going to have a little chat."

"Great," Carl moaned as he followed them down the hall.

Two hours later the detectives were finished, at least

happy that they had some possible descriptions, including tattoos, to go on. Shane and Carl had their talk, Carl looking decidedly unhappy. Annie walked over to him, giving him a quick hug. "I'm sorry I drug you into this," she said.

He nervously looked over her shoulder as he hugged her back, seeing Shane's glare. "It was my idea to go with you, doc." Letting go of her, he smiled as he said, "See you on Monday," before he turned and walked out of the door.

Annie slowly turned around to see Shane standing off to the side. Pulling her lips in, she walked over to him keeping her gaze on his. Reaching up, she placed her hands on his chest, feeling his heart beating underneath her fingertips. "Are you still mad?"

The anger and fear that had been at an all-time high several hours ago had waned. Taking a deep breath, he shook his head as he wrapped his arms around her and pulled her in close. Kissing the top of her head, he said, "No baby. But we do have things to discuss. Things like how can Jobe keep you safe when you are just supposed to be shopping, and we don't know where you are? We're supposed to have trust, sunshine, but you knew when you went out this morning that you were deceiving me. And Carl? You drug him along not understanding the dangers of this world I've been telling you about."

Annie just nodded her head against his chest, feeling the tears welling up again. "I was scared," her quiet voice said. "I don't understand how people can be so cruel to animals."

Closing his eyes, he pulled her in even tighter. *What would she think if she knew some people treat their children worse than those dogs?* Glad that his sunshine did not deal with those horrors, he just said, "Lots of shitty people in the world, baby. I gotta deal with them, but I don't want you to. So no more, right?" He gently pulled on her hair so that she raised her eyes up to his. "No more investigating? No more going out on your own? No more putting yourself in danger, right?"

Nodding, she agreed. "Yeah. Just doing my job from now on. I'll be the vet and you be the detective." Lifting her eyes back to his sky blue ones, she pleaded, "But Shane?"

He looked down into the green orbs that he swore held his soul. "Yeah, sunshine?"

"I can't sit by and do nothing if there is some way I can help."

"I get that, baby. But don't go off by yourself and don't drag your friends into it. Tell me. Let me step in and do what I need to do." He held her gaze for a moment. "Promise?"

"I promise," she said, and stood on her tiptoes to reach his lips. Kissing him lightly, she lowered back down. "I loaned my car to Carl to get home and he'll bring it to me on Monday. Can you take me home?"

Smiling as he tucked her into his side, throwing his arm over her shoulders. "Nowhere I'd rather be than with you, babe. Nowhere at all." Giving a head jerk to Matt, he took her home.

Chapter 26

WAKING UP SLOWLY the next morning, Annie couldn't help but smile. Last night, Shane had showed her just how much he loved her as he worshiped her body. Stretching, she felt sore in a few muscles that had gotten a workout. Before she could roll over a muscular arm snaked under her breasts and pulled her firmly back against his rock-hard chest. Immediately she felt his erection pressing into her ass and his lips raining soft kisses on her neck.

"Ummmm," she groaned as she felt herself get wet and her nipples harden as his hand cupped her breasts. "Morning," she said, twisting her head to capture his mouth.

He slid his tongue into her mouth, immediately turning the kiss into a hard, wet, possessive mating of tongues. He felt her meet him stroke for stroke, inflaming him more, and he slid his leg between hers separating them. He slid his fingers into her folds, noticing how wet she was. *That's my sunshine, always ready for me.* He pushed his swollen cock into her welcoming body, driving into the hilt.

Sliding in and out, he began with slow, deliberate

strokes before the sensations overtook and he started to thrust wildly. One hand held her hips, pulling her back to meet his strokes, and the other held her breast, tweaking her nipple. *Come on, baby. Come for me.*

Annie threw her head back as the friction sent electricity pulsing through her pussy to deep in her core. One final roll of his fingers on her nipple and the explosion had her screaming his name.

"That's it, sunshine." He buried his face in her silky hair as he felt his orgasm overtake and he emptied himself deep into her. Thrusting several more times as though to eke out every bit of him into her waiting body, he finally lay sated, panting as he pulled her back in closely once again.

Both lay side by side, letting their racing heartbeats slow and their breathing become less ragged.

Lifting his head so that he could see her face, he asked, "You okay, baby?"

"Um hmm," was the only reply.

Rolling her to face him, he asked again, "Baby, look at me. You okay?"

She opened her eyes and stared at his beautiful pale blue eyes, full of concern. "I am, honey. Why?"

Shane pushed her sweat-damp hair from her face and stared back into her beautiful eyes. "We've gone at it quite a bit since we got home. Just wanted to make sure you're okay."

"Oh, honey. I'm perfect," she said with a grin as she leaned in for a kiss.

"Yeah you are, sunshine."

The rest of the day was spent in a rare day of working around the house in the morning and piling up on the sofa watching baseball on TV in the afternoon. The house was beginning to really feel like home and Shane always said he liked her decorating *in family*. Looking around at the pictures on the mantle, she wondered when they would add more. *Marriage, children.* They hadn't talked about these things yet, so she wondered if he wanted them as much as she did. Looking over at his strong profile staring at the large screen, she realized that she wanted him in her life forever.

He looked over at her staring at him and lifted his brow in question. Wrapping his hand around her neck, he brought her gently over to him, tucking her tightly next to him. "What's on your mind, baby?"

"I was just wondering where you saw us going, Shane."

He smiled, knowing that her honest question showed exactly what he loved about her. No pretense. No making him try to guess what she was thinking or needing. He thought back to his two years of darkness. *All that time trying to guess what the hell everyone needed without letting them know who he was and I walk out to pure, fuckin' sunshine.*

"I see us gettin' married and having kids. Living in this house and raising our family here," he said honestly.

She twisted quickly in his arms to stare intently into his expressive eyes. All she saw looking back at her was love. Smiling, she grabbed his face and kissed him with all the love she had. "I hoped for that, but wasn't sure if it was what a beast like you wanted."

"Sunshine, don't you know? You've tamed this beast." With that, the baseball game was forgotten as he reminded her just how much he loved her.

MONDAY MORNING FOUND Annie hurrying down the street toward the clinic, her pastry bag in her hand. Smiling, she remembered Mrs. Greenwald sharing that she finally had a date with Mr. Machelli. "Hmm, love is in the air, so maybe I can do some work on Suzanne and Matt. They both need someone to love."

Running into the clinic, she found Leon in a panic. "Suzanne hasn't come in yet and Carl called to say that he won't be in either. So it looks like it is just you and me, doc. Thank goodness it's an easy morning. We don't have any early appointments."

"Suzanne texted me this morning to say that she was sick and couldn't come in, but I didn't know about Carl. Well, if we get anything major in we'll just have to refer them to the emergency vet."

Annie walked in to the back area to make sure they were ready while Leon manned the front desk. Hearing the jingle of the front door, she knew that Leon was greeting whoever was coming in so she made a quick trip to the office to store the pastries and fire up the computer. A loud thump came from the front and she walked out, not hearing anything else. *That's odd. Usually Leon talks non-stop to the clients.* She walked through the lab area to head to the front when suddenly she stopped in her tracks.

Her breath caught in her throat as she stared at the face of the young man from the van of puppies she had encountered a few days previously. In his hand he waved a black plastic device, but she didn't know what it was.

"Where's Leon?" she whispered, her eyes never leaving his hand.

"You don't know what this is, girlie? I got me a stun gun and your man out there is not gonna be botherin' us. Now you do just what I say and I won't have to use this on you."

A small dog came running over to the man's feet and he immediately kicked out, sending the dog whimpering away.

Annie's eyes, wide with fright, looked at him with her questions unspoken.

His smile curved his lips as his eyes roved over her body. "You wondering about the dog. Yeah, pretty smart, huh? I walk in with a dog and nobody thinks anything about it. How about you and me just take a little trip out the back door."

Annie's eyes glanced at the security cameras in the corner of the room, hoping someone at Tony's security company was watching. *Jobe! Jobe should be outside.*

The man's eyes followed hers and as he realized that they were on cameras, he shot into action. Whirling around, he grabbed her with one hand and held the taser against her with the other.

The shock was immediate and her muscles contracted before she went limp. He threw her over his shoulder in a fireman's hold and jogged to the alley door. Throwing it open, he was greeted with one of his buddies who grabbed her arms and tied them quickly behind her back before they threw her on the floor of the van.

"Go man! They got fuckin' security cameras!" she heard someone shout before they pulled out of the alley and onto the road behind her clinic.

Annie, stilled stunned, couldn't seem to get her body or mind to work properly. Not able to do anything but lay still, she hoped the security that Shane put in place was already in action. *Shane. Please find me.*

As the van was pulling away, Jobe received the signal from his earpiece that someone was in the clinic. "Fuck!" he yelled into his microphone. "A guy went in with a goddamn dog. I thought he was a client."

As Jobe charged in he saw Leon down on the floor of the reception area, starting to move. "He got her. I could hear them. He got her," Leon rasped.

Jobe was running to the alley, but all he could see was the back of the van as it turned onto the road opposite of where his SUV was. Knowing he could never catch them, he yelled into his mic. "Too far. Call the cameras up and get Tony."

"He's already on it. He's calling Shane right now," came the answer back.

Running back to Leon, he could hear the sirens coming closer as Leon pleaded for him to find Annie.

"Don't worry man. My boss is talking to Shane. Jesus, fuck. Those assholes don't know what they've done."

Leon looked into Jobe's face as he was assisted to stand. The question in his eyes went unspoken.

Jobe looked at him, his face tight with anger. "I'm pissed as hell and we're gonna get the doc back. But Shane? Fuck man. They've let loose the wild man and don't even know it."

SHANE LOOKED DOWN at his phone in the middle of a briefing, seeing Tony's number. "What's up?" he asked as he stepped outside the room. He was silent for just a few seconds before his legs gave out from under him.

Matt jumped up grabbing the phone from Shane, not knowing who he was talking to. "It's Dixon. Talk." The words coming back almost took him to his knees as well.

"Fuck." He immediately put his phone on speaker as others gathered around.

"Got everything on camera. Man came in with a dog, just as though he was a client. That's how he got past my man outside. He dropped the dog then tasered the man in the reception area. Went back, talked to Doctor Donavan for just a moment, and then tasered her. He carried her out and was met by another man who tied her up. They left in a white panel van. We got the plates and have called it in officially." Tony rattled all of this off quickly and efficiently.

"Is Shane still there?" Tony asked.

"Yeah," Matt answered.

"She didn't have her purse, but her cell is on her. We've got a trace on it. My men are rolling into the office now. We're sending you the coordinates."

A policewoman rushed into the room. "The officers that went to the clinic to assist were told to check on the young woman, Suzanne, that works there. He was afraid that she was in danger too since he can't get hold of her on her phone. I've got two officers going to her apartment now."

Shane looked at Matt, his mind racing. *Fuck, pull it together. Think it through.* "Carl. We gotta get someone to Carl's place as well. He was with her the other day so he may be in danger as well. Get Leon to get his address. He lives with his mother down the block. Hell, get Jobe on it. He knows the address."

Snagging his phone, he started to walk down the hall with Matt right on his heels.

"Shane," Matt said while grabbing his arm. "Where are you goin'? You've gotta stay here man."

Shane turned on his friend and partner, a look of pure white anger shooting from his ice blue eyes, growling, "Get your hands off, Matt."

"Shane, you can't go running outta here half-cocked. Right now, you don't know where she is. She needs you clear-headed, working the problem. She needs you to get all the intelligence we can gather. It's the only way to find her and keep her safe."

Matt looked into the eyes of his friend, seeing anguish war with the anger that was there.

"I've just got...," Shane's voice cracked and he dropped his eyes for a moment.

They both looked up as the chief came around the corner looking for them. "Got more. The girl Suzanne was found in her apartment. She's alive but had been tasered as well and tied up. That person must have used her phone to text in this morning so that no one would be looking for her."

"Jesus, fuck," Shane bit out, realizing how organized this operation had been.

"There's more," the chief said, causing Shane and Matt to focus their eyes on him again.

"Dr. Carl Odgen. His mother died a few months ago. There is no apartment that he shared with her. It's just his stuff and not much of it. He's missing too."

"So he's an imposter? Not even a vet?" Matt growled.

"No, he's a licensed veterinarian. We don't know at this time what his involvement is. We just know he doesn't live with his mother and he's missing."

Matt and Shane looked at each other, trying to fit the pieces together.

"If Carl was part of the gang, he had plenty of opportunity to hurt Annie. Hell, even at the markets the other day he could have helped take her. It doesn't add up."

"Men," the chief said, calling their attention back to him. "I don't usually agree with partnering with a security agency, but I want you two over at Alverez Security. We need everything we can get." With that, the chief turned and walked back into the briefing room while Matt and Shane charged out of the building.

ANNIE WAS LYING in the back of another panel van, bouncing on the hard metal floor, her arms and shoulders screaming with pain from being tied behind her back. Tape covered her mouth so that she couldn't make a sound. Her kidnappers had changed vans twice; each time the drivers had stayed the same. The young man who had tasered her kept looking back over his shoulder.

She lost all sense of direction, not having any idea where they were going. *Oh, please let Leon be all right. And let Shane get hold of the security tapes. But they've changed vans. The license plates will be different.*

Just then the van made a sharp turn and the road became very bumpy. She felt every jostle, every pothole, every movement of the van as her head banged against the metal floor once again. A movement to her side had her jerking her head around. The young man had crawled out of his seat and into the back of the van.

Heart pounding, she could feel bile rising, but tried

to force it down, knowing with her mouth taped shut she could choke.

"You're very pretty, doctor," he said, eyes glittering as they stared at her chest. He reached out a finger and traced her jaw down to her neck, then down further as he slid his hand over her breast and squeezed. "You and me, we could have a lot of fun," he said.

"Marco! Stop feeling up the girl and get your ass back up here," the driver yelled.

The one called Marco scowled as his gaze shot between the driver and Annie. His eyes drifted back down to her heaving breasts. Giving one final squeeze, he crawled back up to the front of the van and sat back down in his seat.

Silent tears slid down her face onto the cold metal floor as despair washed over her. She had no idea where the end of the road was going to be, but she began to realize that she was heading toward hell.

Chapter 27

SHANE AND MATT were ushered immediately into Alverez Security. The outside of the brick building located on the edge of the city was unassuming, belying the high-tech equipment on the inside. They entered through an ordinary door leading into what looked like the reception area of any business. A polite, professionally dressed woman sat at the reception desk, and as soon as they entered she pointed to the wooden doors behind her.

"Gentlemen, you may go through. You are expected."

They pushed open the doors and encountered a short hallway with offices on one side and a conference room on the other. Heavy steel doors were at the end of the hall. As soon as they entered the hall, a young man with wire-rim glasses met them.

"Shane, Matt. Follow me, please. Tony's waiting." He led them through the steel doors and they couldn't help but feel shocked at the difference. The side they came from was a normal business office. On this side, computer stations were all around a large room, with a few doors leading out from it. Electronic maps were on the walls with a group of men standing around one of them. Tony looked over and headed their way.

Reaching them, he grasped Shane by the shoulders, looking him directly in the eyes. "We'll find her man. We're on it. Your force is on it. We'll get her back."

The gaze that met his was ice. Cold. Deadly. Nodding in understanding, Tony led them to the back where a group of men were working. Two on computers, three on secure phones with one of them marking the maps.

"What have you got," Shane growled, recognizing Jobe at the map. Jobe met his gaze, regret in his eyes.

"Her cell phone was on her person. We've traced it to the western side of town, continuing to head west toward Jefferstown, and we're plotting the coordinates now. It matches the information we pulled from her clinic computer where she had been doing some research. We also have the information from the county vet emails she received."

Tony asked, "Where was your investigation?"

Matt took over answering, knowing that Shane was holding on by a thread. "We know that we have lost Gerard Washington. It appears that he was the top drug king in this area, but when we took down most of his organization he left town. Pissed, but he left. My guess is we are looking for Xavier Thomas. He was the one who was hurt the most in the dismantling. Gerard is high enough he can settle somewhere with his millions or start over. Xavier lost face when we grabbed everyone else and we know he's still in the area. He is trying to keep the drug running business going in hopes to recoup his money, and his prestige with the higher-ups, and using the dogs was lucrative for him."

One of the men hung up his phone as Tony looked his way. Shane noticed the silent communication among the men working for Tony's security business. Without any other direction, the man began reporting. "Secure emails are coming in from the veterinarians that Doctor Donavan had been in touch with. I've forwarded this on to Vinny," he said, as he nodded toward another man sitting at a computer. "He's feeding this into the map coordinates."

"Good to go, Gabe," Tony said as he turned his attention to the man called Vinny.

Shane, feeling overwhelmed by emotion, forced his racing mind to focus. His eyes swung from Gabe to Vinny, then back again.

Gabe noticed and acknowledged with a head nod. "Yeah, twins," was the only explanation necessary.

Vinny's fingers were quickly flying over the keyboard, his eyes occasionally glancing at the map displayed on the wall. As all of the men gathered closer, three red circles appeared. "That's the area we are looking at, based on the information we have from the possible puppy-mill sites."

The signal on the map indicating her cell phone location was not at any of those locations, although it was close to two of them.

"What about her cell?" Shane asked.

Neville, the young man that had escorted them in, spoke up. "She could have dropped it or it could have been found, or maybe they are holding her in a separate location."

"I've got that much," Shane growled. "I want to know what else you can tell me." By this time his patience was wearing thin when all he wanted to do was hit something. Someone.

"Well, if she still has her clothes, then it could still be with her, but out of signal range."

Matt and Tony barely grabbed Shane by the arms as the launched himself at Neville.

"You goddamn mother-fucker," Shane raged.

Neville gave a squeak before jumping back behind Gabe. "I...I didn't mean...I'm sure she still...um...has her...um...clothes."

Tony intervened. "Neville, out. Finish up in the office." Swinging around on Shane, he got in his face. "You gotta hold your shit together man. We have to look at all possibilities to make sure we go in smart. You can't handle this, you get locked down here in this building when we roll. You got me?"

Shane's arms were still held by Matt, but his icy glare was on Tony. "You try locking me down and I'll tear this place apart. You. Got. Me?"

The men in the room were silent as the battle of wills continued. Shane's rage was broken into by Matt's voice in his ear. "Man, you gotta hold on for her." At that, Shane jerked as if punched. Matt continued, "No matter what, she needs you. She needs you focused. She needs to know you'll not only find her, but take care of her no matter what has happened."

With those words, Shane slumped back, visibly shaken. Shaking his head to gain focus, he looked at Tony. "I got this," he said simply, looking from Tony to the other men in the room.

They nodded in return, and then the group went back to the map, plotting out their strategy as Matt coordinated their information with the chief.

THE BUMPING OF the van became worse and the sound of tree limbs hitting the sides of the van could be heard. The realization that they were going deeper and deeper into the woods dawned on Annie. *Oh, Jesus. Will Shane ever find me?* The sound of dogs barking in the distance interrupted her thoughts. The noise became louder and the van finally came to a jerking halt, rolling her body painfully onto her strained shoulder. Looking up, she saw Marco and the driver getting out. Just a few seconds later the side panel door slid open and Marco's leering face leaned in as he grabbed her feet and pulled her toward him.

She tried to kick out at him, but within seconds he flashed his knife at her.

"I can slit you like the dog bitches we got," he said, his eyes glittering.

Her eyes widened in fear and she stilled her legs. The desire to defend herself combatted with her desire to stay alive. Looking into his malice-filled eyes her breath caught in her throat and her bravado left. Fear wrapped its icy cold tentacles around her as he drug her the rest of the way out, the knife held closely to her chest.

"Not so tough are you bitch?" he said as his free hand drifted across her breast again. Pulling her to a standing position, he gave a sharp push between her shoulder blades, moving her away from the van.

She forced herself to take her eyes away from his face and glance around. The van was parked next to several identical vans in a clearing with thick woods all around. The tall trees created the perfect screen from prying eyes. Near the vans was an old barn and to her right was a small cabin. The sound of dogs barking could be heard much louder now that she was outside. Wooden and wire crates were stacked behind the barn toward the woods and the smell of feces was strong. She felt the bile rising again and forced herself to try to breathe deeply, but with her mouth taped shut each breath through her nose just brought the stench closer.

Men were moving around the compound, seemingly attending to unknown tasks, but eyeing her with undisguised interest. *They don't seem scared that I'm seeing them. Because they know I won't leave here alive.* That thought nearly brought her to her knees as she stumbled.

Her arm was roughly grabbed from behind. "Fuck bitch, get moving," Marco ordered as he shoved her along the path toward the cabin.

Annie's legs moved automatically as her mind raced with thoughts of escaping, staying alive, and wondering what was going to happen. The door to the cabin swung open as they arrived and she was given no choice but to keep walking.

"Oh, Jesus fuck. Annie, Jesus no!" came the expletive from the man standing at the entrance to the cabin.

Carl.

Her eyes sought out his as her mind raced to understand his presence in this place. He was forced to step to the side as Marco shoved her forward once more, propelling her through the cabin door.

Her eyes blinked as she entered the room, Marco's knife still pressed to her side. As her eyes became accustomed to the dimness of the front room, she saw a desk piled with papers, a laptop, and several cell phones. A man was sitting at the desk talking on one of the phones.

He turned toward her as she neared, his cold eyes scanning her from head to toe before coming back to land on her chest for a moment, then sliding back up to her face. "Gotta go. We have a guest," he said with no warmth. "Yeah. She's much prettier than the other vet we were using." A deep chest chuckle came from him as he clicked off the call.

A hard-back chair was placed in the center of the

room directly in front of the desk. Marco moved her around to the front and with a hand to her shoulder pushed her down into the chair. Annie wasn't sure her legs would have held her up anyway, but the pain in her shoulders reached an agonizing level.

The man sitting behind the desk stared intently at her before speaking. "Cut her."

Annie's eyes widened in fear but before she could react, she felt the ties on her hands being cut, and for the first time in a couple of hours she could move her hands from behind her back. The numbness in her arms was replaced with tingling as she gripped her hands and rubbed them together.

She brought her eyes back to the man at the desk again just in time to see him jerk his head to Marco. Not interpreting the head jerk, she was once again caught off guard when Marco's hand grabbed the end of the piece of tape over her mouth and ripped it off.

The pain was intense and her hands involuntarily flung up to hold her stinging lips. "Aughhh!" she yelled, unable to contain the utterance.

Carl moved toward her and covered her mouth with his hand. Pressing tightly against her lips, he mumbled, "The pressure will take out the sting."

She looked up into his face, still not understanding his presence. *Did they get him too?* Her eyes darted about, but the cabin's interior gave no answers.

"Allow me to introduce myself. I am Xavier Thomas. You, my dear Doctor Donavan, have caused a great deal of trouble for my organization."

Annie sat, trying to still the shaking she felt all over.

"We have had a nice business here until your cop boyfriend infiltrated to take us down. And then, my innocent Doctor, you have continued to make things difficult by your curiosity."

Carl spoke tentatively, "Xavier, you shouldn't have done this. You've kidnapped a cop's girlfriend. Jesus, you'll have them crawling all over the place."

Xavier's eyes cut upwards toward Carl's and his thin lips curved into a smile. "Exactly."

Annie glanced up at Carl but could tell he didn't understand Xavier's comment any more than she did.

Just then the driver of the van walked in and moved to the man behind the desk. Leaning down, he whispered in his ear. The cold look in the man's eyes became even frostier.

"It appears that Marco has not been as hospitable as I would have required. I have just been informed that he touched you. Is this correct?"

Annie sat still, not understanding anything that was transpiring, while Carl's hand stayed loosened against her mouth.

"Answer him," Carl whispered in her ear.

Glancing up to his eyes, she saw fear in his face as well.

"Don't keep him waiting," came the next whisper.

She turned her gaze back to the man behind the desk, her heart pounding so loudly she was sure they could all hear it.

Slowly nodding her head, she heard a croaked "Yes" before realizing it was her own voice.

Xavier growled, "When I give an order I expect it to be obeyed. I can't trust a man who can't control his baser urges."

She saw Marco move toward the door with his hands up in front of him. "What the fuck, man? She's just a piece of a…"

Annie's eyes grew large as she saw a man approach Marco from behind and with the flash of a long knife slit Marco's throat. He crumpled to the ground and twitched for just a moment before stilling with a pool of blood seeping from the open gash.

Jumping off the chair, she stared horrified at the vision in front of her. The sound of screaming, howling animals filled her ears as she dropped to her knees on the floor next to the chair. Carl rushed over, grabbing under her arms to haul her up against his body as he moved to shield her from the sight on the floor, gently making shushing sounds.

Gasping for breath she finally realized that the animal sounds filling the cabin were coming from her. Her body continued to shake as Carl tried to still her.

"Xavier, what the fuck? Jesus, did you have to do that right in front of her?" his voice bit out.

With a flick of his wrist, Xavier motioned for one of the other men who had quietly entered the cabin to remove the body. The sound of it being drug across the floor and outside had a new wave of tremors flooding Annie's body.

"Sit," came the order. Another hard-back chair appeared and Carl sat pulling Annie down next to him.

Forcing her eyes to look at the man who had so effortlessly ordered the killing of another man, she sucked in a breath to try to clear her head. *Focus. To stay alive. Focus.*

"As to why you were brought here, my dear Doctor, the answer is very clear. We need to move our operation. Or rather I should say we have to move our operation because of your boyfriend's and your interference."

"He's...a detective. It's...his job," she said with a shaky voice.

Xavier's look quieted her immediately. "I assure you, Doctor Donavan, that gives him no points in his favor with me."

Carl squeezed her leg as she licked her still stinging lips. She understood his silent message to be quiet, but anger was slowly taking over fear.

"You're...a criminal. A...drug...person."

At this definition, she noticed his eyebrows raise. "A drug person?" he asked with a hint of amusement in his voice. "Is that the best you can come up with?"

"You're...a murderer. You have dogs killed. People killed."

Xavier's head reared back as deep laughter emanated from him. He looked over to the men still standing just inside the cabin. "Do you hear that? I am a murderer of dogs?"

"Annie, shut up," Carl whispered.

Her head whipped around as she speared him with her glare. "And you. What the hell are you doing here?"

Xavier's mirth over, he speared her with his unwavering gaze again. "I'll tell you what he is doing here, Doctor Donavan."

She felt Carl stiffen next to her.

"I needed someone to make sure the dogs were healthy enough to travel. Someone who could assist with easier ways for them to ingest their...cargo. I needed a professional who, shall we say, could be persuaded to work for me and keep his mouth shut. And throw in one who would keep an eye on you at the same time, well Doctor Ogden fit the bill perfectly."

Annie suddenly felt as though all of the air had been sucked from the building and was aware of Carl throwing his arm around her shoulder to anchor her.

Breathing deeply, she pushed away from him. "Keep your hands off of me," she growled.

"It's not what you think," his voice pleaded. "It's not like what he said."

Xavier's voice cut into their stare-down. "It really doesn't matter why either of you did what you did. All that matters now is that I am moving forward." He paused as their attention came back to him. The smile that Annie now recognized as dangerous grew as he continued. "We are being forced to move our operation and I will be removing all obstacles. You two are obstacles.

"I will, of course, be leaving your bodies in plain sight here for the police to find." Hearing Annie gasp, his smile deepened. Leaning over his desk, malice twinkling in his eyes, he spoke, "Did you think for one second that his undercover infiltration would go unpunished? I took care of Rocky and your death will make sure that other such agents will be less willing to play the hero. He will eventually find his way here, and your body will serve as a reminder that no one fucks with me."

His eyes cut back over to Carl's horrified expression as he continued. "And you, Doctor Ogden, have served my purpose and I find that I do not want to chance having you with us in our new...location."

Moving around the desk, he ordered, "Lock them up for now."

Annie and Carl were roughly hauled up and propelled back outside, this time forced to walk to the barn that was located on the opposite end of the clearing. Maneuvered through a door, they were forced to climb a rickety ladder to the former hayloft and tied to a post near the back of the building. The cracks between the planks of the old barn loft allowed sunlight to filter in and afforded them a view of the activity below.

"Annie, I'm sorry," Carl started. His voice carried a pleading tone as he willed her to look at him.

Anger poured off of her as she kicked out at him.

"How could you? Jesus, you're a vet. You gave an oath. You're supposed to protect and heal. Not drug, maim, and kill. I can't believe you are a part of this."

"Let me explain. Please," his voice ragged.

The look on his face stilled her. "Why Carl? Why?" she asked, her voice quiet and full of pain.

Hanging his head for a moment, gathering his thoughts, he looked back into her face. "A year ago I was practicing in another state, but had been applying for jobs here in the area because my mom was sick." Seeing the doubt in her eyes, he continued, "Yes Annie. I did have a mom in the area and she was sick. I received a communication from what I thought was another vet and came in for an interview. When I met with Xavier for the first time, I had no idea who or what he was.

"He said he needed a veterinarian to help with dogs that were part of his business. He made it sound like they were guard dogs in training. He made it sound so legitimate." His voice trailed off as though his thoughts had moved into the past. Remembering.

"He offered a lot of money and I thought it would be a great transition. I could make decent money, help with mom, and keep practicing veterinary medicine in a private setting for a while." Shaking his head, "Jesus, I thought I'd found the perfect solution."

"When did you realize it wasn't what you thought?"

Sucking in a huge breath and letting it out slowly, "It only took a couple of weeks. At first they had me just seeing dogs they brought in. They made sure I got paid and they even took over mom's medical expenses which had drained her bank account dry and had almost drained mine dry as well. By the time I ever saw this place I was firmly in their control.

"Annie, you have to believe me when I say that the first time I was brought here I became physically sick. I barely made it to the woods before I lost my lunch."

"Why did you stay? You could have told the police. You could have done something."

"I did do something, Annie." He saw her angry glare but plunged on. "I needed the money. If I said anything, they would kill me, and then where would mom be? I had to play their game to keep things going. But I did the best I could. I inoculated these dogs, I treated their injuries, I made sure they had food and water. And I tried to get them to do surgery to remove the drugs without hacking them open."

At that, Annie's eyes filled with tears, all of the fight going out of her. *How can I judge him? Would I have done differently?* "How is your mom now?"

Looking her directly in the eyes, he confessed, "She died a few months back. I had money to pay off the creditors, pay for a funeral, and get her affairs settled."

The questioning look she gave him had him nodding in understanding. "You're wondering why I didn't stop then?"

He gave a rude snort before answering. "By then, they had me in your clinic. I had gotten close to you, Suzanne, and Leon. They manage to get people to do things they want by threatening things that matter."

"Oh my God. They threatened you by using us?" her voice shook.

Nodding, he looked sadder than she thought she had ever seen anyone look.

"Yeah. That kept me doing their dirty work while still trying to do the best I could for the animals."

Seeing her look of understanding, he quickly replied, "Oh Annie. I'm no hero. I'm probably just a huge coward, but I knew I was already damned. I might as well keep being damned to keep them away from you all."

Looking around, she began to wiggle seeing how tightly she was tied. "Can you move your arms at all?" Annie asked.

Eyebrows raised in question, he shook his head as he attempted to move. "Why?"

"I can feel the rough wood where my hands are tied to the beam. Maybe I can break through the ropes," she answered, as she began moving her arms in an awkward jerk, wincing as the pain in her shoulder increased.

The activity in the yard had increased as wooden crates were being taken from the barn and loaded into the back of the vans. They heard a shout, "Get this in the vans first and then we'll have a truck in to load the dogs in a couple of hours."

Looking at each other, the unspoken threat hung between them. *Would they still be alive in a couple of hours?*

Chapter 28

MATT WATCHED SHANE stand in front of the map projected onto the screen, his eyes staring, roving over the area. Silent. Steely. And Matt knew, in agony.

Walking over he placed his hand on Shane's shoulder. "The intel's comin' in man. Just a little bit longer."

"I keep thinkin' this fuckin' map is suddenly gonna have a huge star on it that'll just scream out and tell me where she is."

"I know, but Shane, you gotta keep your shit pulled together."

Shane swung his narrowed eyes around to Matt's, but before he could speak Matt jumped in.

"I know, man. I don't have what you and Annie have, but that doesn't mean I don't get this. What I'm telling you is that you've got to hold it together so that when we head out you don't go wild and make it worse for her."

At that, Shane dropped his head as he stared at his boots for a moment. "Lived that shit. Know that shit. She can't handle that. No fuckin' way."

Matt, quiet, let his friend get it out.

Lifting his gaze back to Matt's, Shane continued, "I

saw men killed for doin' something the wrong way. I saw women slapped just for lookin' at someone. And that was nothing." Pulling in a shaky breath, he said, "I saw women taken, mostly with their own will, gettin' fucked in some corner. But then after one had her, the others would join in, and it was obvious that wasn't what any woman wanted. Those animals didn't care. They took what they wanted and if you wanted to stay alive, you let them take."

His eyes went back to the map. "Jesus, fuck. I can't believe they've got her." This time his voice cracked and Matt put his hand on the back of Shane's neck and squeezed.

"Stay strong for her. We're gonna get her and she's gonna need you."

Matt and Shane turned around as the doors behind them opened and two men walked in. Shane felt his breath leave his body in a rush. Tom Rivers and Jake Campbell, old friends from his academy days and now detectives with a neighboring city's police force, came stalking in and straight to Shane. Tall and well-built, both men made an imposing sight – one that Shane was glad to see.

Tom stopped directly in front of Shane and wrapped his hand around his friend's neck keeping his eyes on Shane's agony-filled expression. "Tony called. Jake and I dropped everything and we're here. Unofficial. Just two friends visiting some old academy friends. But. We. Are. Here." Leaning in closely, he got right in

Shane's face and said, "I know, man. I know."

Shane greeted his Fairfield friends, staggered that they had come. He battled back the emotions that threatened to choke him as he held onto Tom before grabbing Jake in a bear hug as well.

Suddenly the room around them began to erupt in activity once again. Gabe shouted out, "The county sheriff's office just raided two of the puppy-mills in the area and came up with nothing on Doctor Donavan. The third one looks like it may be it. The sheriff is gatherin' his men and will wait for us."

Tony came in speaking, "Just got off the phone with your chief. Since it is in the county and not the city he has no jurisdiction, but DEA is heading out that way as well as FBI. Tom, Jake. Good to see you. You two are here visiting old friends and just helping out. Shane, you and Matt have no legal authority in this case now, which your chief wants to make sure you remember."

Shane's steely blue gaze met Tony's. "You think I give one fuck about jurisdiction?"

Tony put his hand up in defense. "Shane, we've been friends a long time. I'm just reminding you that if you go rogue, you could lose your job and your pension."

The room was full of testosterone on high alert as Shane leaned in closer to Tony. "Then I guess I'm gonna kiss my fuckin' pension away."

A tiny smile cracked the corners of Tony's lips as he said, "Well then. Welcome aboard to Alverez Security."

"Got the rendezvous coordinates," came the shout from Vinny, as a red circle appeared on the map. It looked to be deep in the woods, near the base of the Blue Ridge Mountains.

"Let's roll," Tony shouted as all of the men began suiting up and heading out. Kevlar vests, guns, revolvers, night goggles, stun guns, were all quickly grabbed and each man hefted up a large duffle bag. Tony looked at Shane and Matt then nodded toward two filled duffle bags on the floor. "Yours," he stated, and they grabbed them on their way out of the door.

The men piled into huge black SUVs with tinted windows. Pulling out of the security garage underneath the building, they headed west.

Finally. Shane felt better with his body active instead of just his mind going over and over all of the ways they could hurt Annie. *Lock it down. Lock that shit down. Focus. One goal, one reason to live. Get her out. Then get the mother-fuckers that took her.*

SEVERAL HOURS HAD passed and the activity in the compound had not decreased. As soon as one van was loaded with crates from the barn and driven away, another one would pull up and the loading would resume. As best as Annie could tell, five van-loads has already left.

The sun was beginning to set as it was just peeking over the trees, sending long, filtering rays through the barn-loft slats. Anne's eyes traveled back to the dog cages behind the barn, stacked four high, each barely allowing the dog to stand. Even from where she was at she could tell that many of them were sick, probably from the cramped and soiled conditions.

"I know what you're thinking," Carl's voice cut through her musings.

Annie's eyes darted back to his face as she raised her eyebrow in silent questioning.

"Honest to God, Annie. This place was worse when I first got here. At least I convinced them to spend some money on feeding and keeping the dogs in good condition."

"What for? So they would have an easier time ingesting drugs before traveling in horrible conditions only to be hacked up in the end?"

Grimacing, Carl just shook his head. "I didn't know what to do. Mom needed so much medical equipment and nursing care. Jesus, all I ever wanted to do was practice veterinary medicine, you know?"

Annie sighed. "Yeah, I know. Me too."

"It costs so fucking much money and no one ever thinks about that," he said, looking more dejected than she had ever seen. "I had so many bills and then mom's added on were overwhelming. God, I thought when I met Xavier I had hit the mother lode. A private vet job, money to pay off loans and mom's care." His voice cracked, "Jesus, how fucked can it all have gotten."

"Carl, we can't give up. I know Shane is tearing up

the countryside looking for us. He'll have the police and I know the DEA are involved and I'm sure his friend Tony has his security men on it as well."

He lifted his tired eyes to her face as she implored him to see the light at the end of the tunnel. "Annie, the odds of the cavalry coming are pretty slim. Why do you think no one has found this place before? It's hidden. Secret. Buried. Jesus, we'll be dead before they find us."

Annie tore her gaze away from his, focusing on the dog crates below. Chewing on her bottom lip, she said simply, "I may not be able to get out of here alive, but I'd love to set those dogs free before I go."

Continuing to rub the thin rope holding her hands behind her against one of the rough beams in the loft, the rope finally snapped and her hands were free.

He looked at her, wide eyed in surprise, his mouth working but nothing coming out. Her body achy and stiff, she winced silently as she moved over to his back to remove his rope as well.

"Annie, I want out of here as much as you, but how?"

"I don't know Carl," she hissed. "You think I'm used to planning something like this?" She managed to get his rope loosened enough for him to work his hands free. The activity below was still humming. "You've been here. You tell me how to get out of this. Together we should be able to figure out something."

They both sat silently for a moment, continuing to think as Carl drug his hand across his face, dejection pouring off of him. Looking back up at her, he said, "Don't you get it? I'm screwed."

"Not if we get away," she answered back in frustration. "What is wrong with you? Why are you giving up without a fight?"

"I'm a dead man," his voice broke as he pressed his fingers to his lips in an effort to still the shaking. "Either they kill me or I go to prison for assisting in drug trafficking. Either way, I'm dead."

A loud voice from below interrupted their thoughts. "Just two more loads and we're done."

Annie squatted next to him, thinking back to all of the fun they had had in the clinic with Suzanne and Leon. The animals he cared for. Walking Suzanne safely to her car. Taking her hands, she cupped his face. "You're a good person, Carl."

At this his eyes sought hers, the questions evident in their depths, so she continued. "You're a good person who got duped into a bad situation. The police will take that into consideration, I'm sure of it. Especially if we get away and you can provide evidence against them. You don't give up. Don't give up on me and don't give up on yourself."

She continued to hold his face before wrapping her arms around him, instinctively knowing that he had been holding this all in for a long time. She heard him sniffle, then clear his throat as he leaned back away from her.

"The woods around here are thick. That's one of the

reason's I heard them say they picked this place. If we can get out of the barn undetected and make it to the woods, we might be able to hide there."

Pulling back away from him she smiled. "It's almost completely dark and they are still occupied. Let's try now."

Silently crawling to the far side of the barn loft, they felt for rotten boards that could be removed easily. They found that most of the side slats were fairly loose, but pondered the noise that would be made when they tried to move them.

Carl quickly said, "When they finish loading a vans they start it up and that makes a lot of noise in the barn until the van pulls away. Sit like this and be ready to kick when I say so." He positioned himself so that he was laying on his back, propped up on his arms with his legs bent and feet against the old wood. Annie quickly mimicked his position.

In less than a moment they heard the sound of the next van's engine starting and Carl whispered, "Now." With the barn's interior reverberating with the sound of the van's engine as the van was pulling out, they both kicked several boards away from the wall of the loft's wall. The boards cracked and gave way, splintering into pieces. Scrambling up, they quickly pulled the pieces away, leaving a gap large enough for them to slip through.

Looking at each other, Annie couldn't help but grin while Carl shook his head.

"We're not clear yet," he reminded her.

"Yeah, well, we're not tied to a barn post waiting to be killed right now either," she whispered back, peeking through the hole in the wall.

The drop-off from the barn was about twelve feet down to the ground. "Let me go first and then I can try to break your fall," Carl said. Annie nodded and moved back from the hole. She watched as he disappeared through the broken slats and then quickly crawled back over to peer down. Sighing in relief, she saw that he was on his hands and knees but was quickly standing and turning back to her. Listening carefully to see if they had been detected, she quietly scooted to the edge of the hole, letting her legs dangle out of the barn loft. Glancing quickly down, she saw him raise his arms up toward her, nodding in her direction.

She slid out while twisting her body so that she was now completely dangling out of the loft, just holding on with her hands.

"Come on. I've got you," she heard Carl whisper. Letting go she dropped into his arms and they both fell backwards onto the ground. *Free! We did it!*

THE MEN FROM Tony's security team had joined forces with the local sheriff's office that had been greatly understaffed for this type of maneuver, as well as with the DEA agents. Not one for normally sharing, the DEA wanted this case wrapped up so tightly they were willing to get all the help they could as long as they retained jurisdiction.

The task force was spread out in the woods completely surrounding the compound. There were DEA agents several miles away capturing each van as they came down the road, quickly taking down the drivers and members and confiscating each van-load of drugs and equipment. Moving them swiftly away from the road, they set up to grab the next one that would be coming.

Shane was making his way toward the cabin, feeling certain that would be where Annie was being held. Crouching behind the cages of dogs, he stealthily maneuvered to the side when he saw several men come out and head toward the barn. Xavier Thomas. Shane's body became tight with even more anger, recognizing the man responsible for most of the drug trafficking in the area and more personally, what happened with Sarge. Xavier's cold, calculating orders had ended the life of several men as Shane had witnessed. And now he had Annie. *Tonight, mother fucker. You die.*

"Is this the last van?" Xavier called out to one of the men closest to him.

"Yes, sir. Just loading the last one now. Should pull out in about 10 minutes," came the reply.

Giving his next round of orders, Xavier spoke to the same man. "Get the prisoners out of the barn loft and bring them back here. I think a very public execution will be perfect for the police to find."

Shane's blood ran cold as Xavier chuckled. Glancing toward the barn, he shifted his stance behind the crates and began to move toward the barn, away from the cabin. "Moving toward the barn," he whispered into his mic. "Roger that," came Tony's reply.

He noticed that Matt, Jake, and Tom were maneuvering with him. They wanted the gang as much as anyone, but for them...it was all about Annie.

Staying in the woods as he crept around, Shane's heart nearly stopped, when peering through the night goggles, he saw two figures jumping from the upper level of the barn. The first was a man, but the second figure was definitely a woman. *Annie. Thank fuck, she's alive.* Feeling a touch on his shoulder, he glanced around to see that Matt, Jake, and Tom were focused on them as well. "Get her. I'm goin' after Xavier."

Tom simply nodded and began to edge his way around the perimeter. Shane knew that Tom, having had his woman kidnapped a couple of years before, understood. Although at that time, Tom just wanted his fiancé safe. Shane...wanted vengeance.

"Know what you're doing?" Matt whispered into his mic. A curt nod was all he received in answer from Shane.

Before either of them could move, a shout rang out across the compound. "Get out! Feds got the vans!"

The men on the compound immediately began to run to the remaining vehicles or toward the woods. Shots were fired, but Shane wasn't able to see where they were coming from. He had last seen Xavier moving back toward the cabin and was heading that way when, suddenly, the dogs in the crates next to the cabin began barking wildly. And he heard a voice. One he knew. Intimately.

"Go, get out. Go!" a woman's voice was screaming as a few barking dogs began running around the compound.

Annie! How the hell did she get back over here and not safely tucked in the woods?

Shane's goggles allowed him to see Xavier pounding out of the cabin, raising his arm toward Annie's back with a gun in his hand. *Fuck, I don't have the right angle!* He quickly came up from his crouching position, running toward her as he brought his gun up to aim at Xavier.

"Annie!" he yelled, hoping she could hear him over the chaotic noise all around the compound as task force agents rushed the gang members who were returning fire.

A shot rang out from Xavier at the same second a figure in the dark jumped up to push Annie down to the ground. Not knowing if Annie was hit Shane fired, hitting Xavier squarely in the chest.

Seeing Annie lying still on the ground with another body, blood pooling out from underneath her, he ran over to Xavier who also had blood pouring out of him as his eyes glittered. Compound lights were turned on and Shane jerked off his night goggles, aiming his gun directly at Xavier.

"You lose, Stoney. I was going to be a dead man anyway once Gerald left," Xavier said, blood bubbling out of his mouth. "I got your woman. Both of them. I got Rocky and now I got the pretty little doctor."

Matt approached Shane, carefully putting his hand on Shane's shoulder. "Don't do it, man. Don't fire on him now. You said she tamed you. Don't let that wild back out. Annie wouldn't want that."

Shane jerked at hearing Annie's name, his revolver still pointed directly at Xavier's head.

"Shane!" barked Tom, kneeling next to Annie and the unknown rescuer. "She's alive!"

At that, Shane whirled his body around seeing Tom pull Annie out from under the other man. Rushing over he threw his body on the ground, pulling her up against his chest. Pushing her hair away from her face, his breath caught in his throat as her wide, green eyes gazed into his face.

Her cheek was swollen and bruised and there was dried blood from a slash on her neck. She immediately reacted as she threw her arms around his neck, her whole body beginning to shake. "You came, you came," were the only words she could choke out.

To Shane, they were music. "You're safe, baby. I got you." Rubbing her back with one hand while cupping the back of her head with the other, pressing it tightly to his chest, he rocked her as he continually assured her that it was over.

"Shane," came a soft call from over to the side. He and Annie looked over at the same time, seeing what Matt was seeing. The unknown rescuer who had shoved Annie out of the way was Carl, his chest opened with a bullet wound directly to the heart.

"Nooooo!" screamed Annie as she lunged herself from Shane's lap to Carl's body before he could stop her. Wrapping her arms around Carl, trying to pull him up to her, she began to sob uncontrollably. "Nooo, nooo, nooo," she cried over and over.

Jake and Tom stood nearby, willing to be of assistance, but knowing that Shane needed to be the one to calm her.

Shane moved over to her, taking her by the shoulders and talking softly. "Baby, you've got to let him go. Come on, sweetheart." Even as he said the words, he knew she wasn't hearing them.

"It's not his fault. It's not his fault," she sobbed over and over, holding his bloody body close to hers.

Shane, recognizing that she was in shock, looked to Tom and Jake for help. They kneeled down, gently placing their hands on Carl, pulling him slowly away from Annie as Shane moved her back toward him. Her fingers tightened on Carl's shirt at the last second before she let him go, an agonizing cry coming from deep inside of her.

"Baby, let them take him. Let them see to him now," Shane whispered, then felt her let Carl slip from her grasp. He turned her in his arms, enveloping her as she sat in his lap on the compound ground. Holding her tightly, he allowed his eyes to roam around the area for the first time since seeing Xavier come out of the cabin.

The DEA agents had all of the gang members that were still alive on their knees with their hands on their heads. Guns trained on them, they were being searched and then handcuffed. Tony's men had gathered off to the side near Shane while Tony reported to the DEA agent in charge.

A DEA medic came over, kneeling first by Carl's body checking for a pulse, then moving over to Shane. "Sir, I'd like to check out Doctor Donavan." Shane shifted her slight weight and then stood with her still in his embrace with the assistance of Tom.

Annie's arms, still tightly wound around his neck, increased in their hold as they stood. "Baby, you need to let the medic check you out." The only response he received was her head shake while still plastered to his chest, her breathing hitching painfully as her sobs subsided.

A garbled whisper near Matt caught Shane's attention. Glancing down, he saw Xavier's mouth moving, gasping. "Looks like you won after all, Stoney," he uttered before the life finally left his eyes.

"Yeah, I did," he acknowledged, cocooning Annie from the two men on the ground. One who tried to take her life, and one who saved it.

Chapter 29

ANNIE SAT IN the back of the ambulance in Shane's lap while the medic cleaned her wounds and checked her out as the group of rescuers hovered nearby.

"Doctor Donavan, we will need your complete statement as soon as possible, but we understand that this has been a shock. I do need to ask you about Doctor Ogden and his level of involvement."

Her green eyes opened wide as she replied, "He wasn't involved. He was just as surprised as I was that this place was here."

The agent in charge looked at her doubtfully. "I understand, Dr. Donavan, that you may not have been aware of any involvement that he had, but we are investigating him as well. Anything you can tell us will aid us in that investigation."

Pulling away from Shane, she glared at the man in front of her. "He's dead. He died saving my life. I assure you he wasn't involved in this group at all."

"Well, he may not have mentioned anything to you. If you think of anything, please let us know."

"Don't hold your breath waiting. I'm telling you that he died a hero and that's how I will remember him.

You want someone to pin this all on, you take that piece of...of...man lying in his own blood," she choked out, putting the fingers of one hand to her lips to stop the quelling while pointing to Xavier lying in the dirt.

Suddenly, her eyes focused on the crates on the other side of the compound. Jumping out of Shane's lap, she ran toward them on shaky legs.

"Fuck! Come back, baby," Shane shouted as he took off running behind her. *The dogs. Jesus, she wants the dogs.* He grabbed her arm, gently slowing her down, but did not stop her completely. Keeping her steady on her legs, they walked together to the cages.

Her eyes took in the horrible conditions up close and the stench almost made her gag. As other agents gathered around, she took control shouting out orders.

"You need to call animal control. I let a couple of dogs out earlier, but I wasn't thinking clearly. Until the dogs can be safely handled, you need to keep your hands and fingers away from them."

Her eyes quickly scanned the cages, counting over twenty, each with more than one dog. "You need to call the SPCA of Richland as well as the surrounding counties to be able to have enough people and handlers."

Shane stood back, a smile on his face, as he watched her take charge of the animals, ordering around the agents and police. Matt, Jake, Tom, and Tony's men stood to the side watching her as well.

"You've got some woman there, Shane," Jake commented.

Tom clapped him on the back. "I see you've finally got what I discovered a couple of years ago."

Tony and his men continued to watch in amusement as her orders were being carried out. Only when the dogs were safely out of the crates and loaded into clean containers to be taken to a location for inspection could she calm down.

Annie turned to walk back over to Shane, a smile finally lighting her bruised face as she made her way to him, exhaustion taking over as she slid into his embrace.

He kissed the top of her head, holding her tight, then looked at the circle of men surrounding them and smiled. "Pure, fuckin' sunshine, boys. Pure, fuckin' sunshine."

The fight instantly left her body and she slumped back against Shane. Lifting her eyes to his, she pleaded, "Take me home, Shane. Please."

Touching his lips to hers, he replied, "You don't have to beg, baby. There's nowhere else I'd rather be." With that, he stood with her in his arms and they walked toward Tony's dark SUV with the rest of their group.

No one knew if she was telling the truth about what she knew about Carl's involvement. But as far as they were concerned, she told what she felt. That was all that mattered.

ANNIE DIDN'T REMEMBER the drive to their house. She didn't remember being carried to their bedroom. She didn't remember being undressed or being tucked in. What she did remember was waking up to the sight of Shane's massive chest pressed under her face, his arms around her protectively. She breathed him in. *My wild, untamed man. He came for me.*

The morning sun was streaming through the windows, illuminating the couple lying in the bed. She leaned her head back and saw that his eyes were taking her in, intently staring.

"Did you sleep, honey," she asked as her fingers lifted to smooth the small crinkles at the corners of his eyes.

"Not much," he confessed. "I just wanted to stay awake while I held you, makin' sure you were really here with me." He hesitated before continuing, "When I think of what could have happened..."

His eyes closed for a moment, and when they opened again, she could see pain lingering in their depths.

"Shane, I'm right here. You came for me. You got me. I'm safe because of you."

He grunted as he said, "Baby, you were escaping on your own. I'm so fuckin' proud of you."

She placed a gentle kiss on his lips, and he allowed her this emotion before taking it deeper. She moaned in his mouth, igniting his passion despite having no sleep the night before. Rolling over, he pressed her down into the mattress using his forearms to hold his upper body from crushing her. He held her head in his hands, relishing the feel of her lips against his as his cock nudged against her stomach. He felt her hips begin to move up and down, as though she were desperately seeking relief.

He slid his hand down to the bottom of her nightie while taking the kiss deeper and wetter. She had just sucked his tongue in her mouth when the sound of scratching on the door interrupted.

Their eyes flew open as they looked at each other for a moment, waiting to see if the noise would stop. The scratching continued, accompanied now by whimpers.

Shane dropped his head to her shoulder and sighed. "Gotta take Sarge out babe and you gotta feed the cats."

Unable to stifle her giggle, she kissed him quickly before he had a chance to roll off of her. "That's a promise of what will come later," she assured him as his eyes skimmed over her, his smile lighting his face.

Shane walked to the kitchen, letting Sarge out into the back yard while Annie fed the cats. Flipping on the coffee maker, she turned to see Shane already setting out the cups. They moved about the kitchen in perfect harmony, making breakfast as though they had been doing it for years together.

After a quick meal, they walked out on their patio with their second cups of coffee. Shane headed into the yard to toss a ball with Sarge while Annie settled onto the patio glider. She watched him smile as he tossed the ball and then wrestled on the grass with their dog. Her mind went back to the first time she was with them, months ago...the dark alley, Sarge needing surgery, Shane hiding who he really was. She, who never took risks, threw caution to the wind that night and now she had the love of a wonderful man. *Her tamed, wild-man.* She couldn't hold back the smile that lit her face as the memories poured over her.

At that moment, Shane stopped in his games with Sarge and looked over at Annie, sitting on the patio glider, one leg tucked under her and the other pushing the glider gently back and forth. Her beauty made his breath catch in his throat. *How the hell did I get so lucky?*

The morning sun peeked over the trees into the back yard and was now streaming down on her, catching her coppery hair in its beams, illuminating all around. Just then her face, seeming lost in a memory, broke into a smile. As her eyes lifted to meet his, the smile on her face became even larger, spearing him with her radiance.

Smiling back, he began to cross the yard heading toward her. *Pure, fuckin' sunshine,* he thought once more, knowing that he was going to hold that for the rest of his life. *Pure, fuckin' sunshine.*

Epilogue
(four years later)

Doctor Douglas – you have a client in room two.

THE PLEASANT RECEPTIONIST'S voice carried across the PA system and Annie stood up, stretching her back as she looked out of the window before leaving the lab area to move toward the front. The window faced the field next to the clinic, the wildflowers in the meadow in bloom. The grass around the clinic was trimmed neatly and she could see the edges of the dog kennels and runs in the back. She could also see the sign that hung near the kennels – **Cranston and Donavan**.

Leon passed her in the hall carrying a wiggling Daschund pup in his arms. He leaned over to kiss the top of her head saying, "You doing okay doc?"

"Thanks Leon, but I'm okay. Just getting a little twinge, that's all." She walked into the exam room where her vet tech Suzanne was already finished with her part of the exam and was ready to assist Annie.

The client was with her two children and their mama cat with its four kittens in a box. Annie and Suzanne worked quickly and efficiently, their years together aiding in their harmony, examining all of the cats while answering the children's many questions.

"Your clinic is very nice," the client said as she tried unsuccessfully to shush her children. "Have you been here long?"

Annie smiled with pride as she replied, "We opened about a year ago. I used to have a practice in the middle of downtown Richland, but this location is so much closer to my home. And besides that, it is just what I always wanted."

"Are you the only vet here? How can you take care of all the animals?" the little girl said.

"Well, I have two other vets who work with me and then I have four assistants."

The little girl's questions were endless, but Annie answered them all, remembering herself at that age wanting to know everything she could about animals.

After they left, it was near the end of the day and the others in the clinic surrounded her.

"Guys, it's not like I'll be gone forever," she laughed as they all hugged her. "Just a couple of months."

"We just want to wish you luck on your little *vacation*," Leon joked.

"Oh yeah, my *vacation* will be really relaxing, I'm sure."

Suzanne hugged her tightly saying, "Now call me the first minute you feel something, promise?"

Looking into the eyes of her beautiful friend she hugged back, promising.

"You 'bout ready to go, baby?" came the gravelly voice behind her.

Annie turned around smiling at the sound. Standing in the reception area looking every bit as handsome as the first time she ever laid eyes on him was Shane, holding Ross, their very sleepy two year old son. "Yeah, honey. Just saying goodbye."

He nodded benevolently, then waited as she quickly said goodbye to the rest of her staff as Leon and Suzanne cooed over Ross. As she walked toward him his eyes dropped down to her swollen belly and he felt the familiar pounding of his heart whenever he thought of what all she had brought into his life. A home decorated in *family*, a wife, a son, and a soon to be born child…sunshine in his dark world.

That evening, after Ross was settled in his bed, and as the sun was setting, they sat on the sofa together relishing the quiet time, knowing that in less than a week their house would be bursting with a new baby and family galore. She leaned her heavy body against his and he wrapped his arms around her, one across her chest and the other hand protectively on her stomach.

"It's going to get wild around here soon," she said, thinking of the coming weeks.

"You okay with all of that, baby?" he asked, pulling her in closely, lifting a hand to push her hair away from her shoulder so he could place a gentle kiss there.

"Sure, honey. It's the roller-coaster, remember?"

Shane laughed, remembering their conversation

from long ago in her tiny apartment. "I also seem to remember you telling me that you were scared of heights and falling off."

"And I remember you telling me that it was living. And being on the roller-coaster with someone you love makes the ride worth it." Twisting around in his arms so that she could peer into his eyes, she smiled as she cupped his strong jaw. "And honey, you were right. You and that little boy upstairs and this baby coming...make it all worth it."

Shane leaned in and took her mouth. The kiss was soft. Tender. Full of promise. Full of love. The kiss of a wild man who had been tamed by love...and pure, fuckin' sunshine.

The End

More by Maryann Jordan

The Fairfield Series – available

Emma's Home
Laurie's Time
Carol's Image

Coming soon

Love's Tempting
Love's Trusting

Some Author Suggestions

MJ Nightingale

Fire In His Eyes

Ex-army buck, Victor, teaches innocent sexy school teacher, Monica, all about sex, and not the old-fashioned variety your grandmother was used to either. Filled with gut wrenching emotional turmoil due to Victor's secrets, you can be sure one of them will melt and the other will burn.

Afraid to Love

Teddy is not your average bartender by no means. A cop on the mend from 9/11, he wants nothing but good times and to live each day to the fullest. When it comes to the bedroom, well, hmm, let's just say he is not your average Joe. Then, he meets a fiery red-head named Ana, and she can teach him a thing or two. He falls for her, but she pushes him away. Why? Because she has so many secrets, and they make her Afraid to Love.

Afraid to Hope

Jay and Louisa are both battle scarred, but ready to start anew. His scars are not just from the war in Iraq, and hers are not just from a teenage pregnancy that resulted in raising a child alone. The scars in them run deep, and the both have secrets. Can two people so deeply wounded learn to trust each other enough to share those secrets? And if they do, will those secrets make or break them?

Andrea Michelle

Escape the Doubt

Is taking a chance with your heart worth the escape, or was it better to have never loved at all? Can forgiveness really set you free?

After the unexpected death of her Dad, and the haunting manner in which he died, Riley Shaw built invisible walls around her heart. Barriers she created to protect her from splintering into broken pieces that couldn't be repaired. She was unable to move forward from her past, letting the guilt of her parent's mistakes dictate her own choices.

Dean Warren was safe. Being with him was innocent and peaceful because she didn't truly love him. His words held her captive in a false sense of security. His eyes were deceptive, and his promises of never pushing her beyond what she was willing to give were broken, leaving Riley in a state of regret and doubt.

Joshua Parker had the power to take what was left of Riley's splintered pieces and ruin her completely, or make her whole again. He was her best friend, her next-door neighbor—everything she wanted and settled on never having. Loving him was as easy as breathing air.

The fear of losing him forever was more real to her than the feelings she couldn't escape.

When faced with the very thing she feared the most, and in the arms she thought were safe, Riley finds herself questioning every decision she has made over the past two years. When she finally escapes the doubt in her head, and accepts the truth in her heart, is it too late?

*This is book one in a series and is not a standalone.

Warning: Not recommended for anyone under the age of 17 due to underage drinking, sexual content and adult language.

Embrace the Moment (Book 2 in the Shifting Series)

Torn apart by a tragedy, pushed together by fate. Nothing is coincidence.

Riley and Josh have been through it all together, first as best friends and now as a couple.

Faced with a decision that will test their relationship, these two learn to fight harder than ever before to keep their hearts intact. Once the decision is made, there is no going back. With the past creeping into their present, and miles between them, they learn nothing is easy. Every moment matters.

Can Riley and Josh survive the first year of college apart? Will their love remain strong enough to embrace every moment that belongs to them? Or will someone from the past interfere, take what he wants and ruin them forever?

"For each star in the sky, I have a reason why I love you. When you look up at night, never forget this truth."

—Josh Parker

Not recommended for anyone under the age of 17 due to underage drinking, sexual content and adult language.

Warning

This is book two in the series. To better understand the characters and the story line, I strongly encourage reading the books in order. These are not stand-alone novels.

Jen Andrews

The Reason Just Say Yes Series, book one

Zoey James is in a funk. She has been through more in her twenty-three years than most people have experienced in their entire lives. After her ex-husband tries to take everything she's worked so hard for, she makes one rule: *Never* date someone she works with.

When her father's newly hired mechanic moves into the apartment above their family-run business, Zoey's lonely life is flipped upside down.

As a teenager, New Zealand native, Andy Tate's family is tragically killed in an accident, and he is taken in by his aunt and uncle. Andy is pulled away from the only place he's ever known as home, and moved halfway around the world to Northern California.

Ten years and one failed marriage later, Andy finds himself living in a new city, with a new job at James

Racing, and living in an apartment next door to Zoey, his new boss's beautiful and damaged daughter.

After an interesting chain of events over one weekend, Andy and Zoey form an unexpected bond. Even though he's the only one who can get through to her, she will do all that she can to keep him at a distance and not break her one rule.

Will Andy be the reason for Zoey to start living her life again, or will she continue on her downward spiral, until she finally hits rock bottom?

M.L. Steinbrunn

Forgive Us Our Trespasses

How long would you wait to be with the one that you love? How much of yourself would you hide in order to keep them?

Brooks knows the moment he meets Vivian that he will do whatever it takes to protect her, even if it means leaving her. Running from his past, he spends the next decade trying to forget the shattered heart that he left behind.

Is there any betrayal worth the cost? Are there some sins that cannot be forgiven?

After a lifetime of rebuilding the walls guarding her heart, Vivian confronts the harsh reality that some fortresses are not meant to stand. Winding through a gray fog of disappointment and deceit, she must conquer her deepest fears to accept the love she believes she is too unworthy to have.

As the paths of these two battered hearts cross once more, together they seek redemption for their sins. However, when the secrets of their pasts come knocking on their door, forgiveness and love will be tested, and they will be forced to answer the question: "When the lies run out, will the truth finally set you free?"

Forgive Us Our Trespasses is an adult contemporary novel and is not intended for younger readers due to mature content. It is now available.

EJ Shorthall

Silver Lining

Amber Merchant had it all. Living with and engaged to her teenage sweetheart, nice house and the job of her dreams.

Not anymore!

Following a devastating revelation from her Fiancé, Amber finds herself moving on and vowing to never entrust her heart and soul to another.

During an evening out to celebrate her newly single life, a chance encounter with a tall, dark and handsome stranger leaves Amber's head reeling. Intrigued by her draw to him but scared for her heart she flees.

Craig Silver, twenty nine year old CEO, is the last person Amber needs in her life. Battling his own demons, Craig is content on a life of meaningless affairs, one night stands and no commitments.

At first it seems their attraction is mutual… until she runs.

When fate intervenes and their paths cross again, Craig refuses to take no for an answer. Encouraging Amber to take a chance on a single date he sets them on a path of love, lust, truth and deception.

Victoria Brock

Impulses

After a disastrous end to a far less than perfect relationship, twenty-four year old, Samantha Kennedy has traveled the path of promiscuity in order to strive for affirmation of her desirability. Unknown to her, Samantha's beliefs of the world of men, is about to chart a new course when she begins a new position at reputable law-firm, Wentworth and Associates, and sets her eyes on her boss, San Francisco's tall, dark and handsome, renowned lawyer, Hayden Wentworth.

After suffering the aftermath of his first love and having his heartbroken, thirty-one year old, Hayden Wentworth has lived the past year in black and white. Haunted by demons as a result of the torment he has endured, Hayden's bleak world is about to be revived by his attractive new secretary and sexual predator, Samantha Kennedy.

If they are to come together, Samantha and Hayden must relive their pasts in order to bury them for once and for all.

But what happens when you fall deeply and desperately in love with someone who has the traits of the one person who you strive every day to hate and resent?

Sometimes, indulging in your impulses is a way to stray from your fears. Sometimes, it's the only way to face them.

Seeking Nirvana (Dark Evoke #1)

They say that old habits die hard, and twenty-seven year old, Kady Jenson, is about to discover how true that statement actually is.

Waking up in a hospital room with a complete stranger at her bedside, should have caused panic and confusion, but for a reason unknown to her, Kady finds herself drawn, and calmed by the presence of the rugged, devastatingly handsome man with the pleasant Irish brogue.

It's when she discovers that she has just woken from a four day coma, with a three year void in her memory, which spawns confusion and panic.

Kady soon comes to realize that things change with time, and not only appearances.

Not only is the sexual chemistry she once shared with her long-term boyfriend, now a long-ago memory, but Kady also begins to unconsciously fall back into unremembered habits, and with each day, the increasing sense of foreboding, becomes increasingly harder to ignore.

Left on her own when her boyfriend goes on a business trip, Kady seeks help from the Irish stranger as they go on a quest together, in a race against time, to piece the puzzle together.

Kristine Raymond

Here To Stay

Sam Mackenzie rode into the town of Hidden Springs looking for a place to belong. He takes a job at Ryan's Ranch and is immediately attracted to the ranch's pretty, *female*, owner.

Kate Ryan is a woman determined to make it on her own. Chafing at the thought of having to hire help, she nonetheless falls for the handsome stranger who answers her ad.

When they meet, sparks fly and they are drawn to each other. But life in 1867 Arizona Territory isn't easy. When a secret from Kate's past comes to light, they are each faced with the challenge of making a difficult decision.

Will they turn and run or are they here to stay?

Hearts On Fire

Jack Tanner has never had a shortage of beautiful women on his arm...or in his bed. As the marshal of Hidden Springs, he has his pick of any eligible woman in town. So why is it that the only woman he wants is the one who won't even give him the time of day?

Landry Prescott has had a crush on Jack Tanner since the day she laid eyes on him. Feeling like she is unable to compete with the young, beautiful women that he surrounds himself with, she chooses to ignore him instead.

When Landry's life is threatened, Jack comes to her

rescue and the spark of interest that had been buried in each of them ignites into a blaze of passion. Is their newfound desire the result of circumstance? Will their love burn out quickly or will they forever have hearts on fire?

Abby's Heart

Abby Prescott is a proper young lady who has never ventured far from home. She travels west to attend her aunt's wedding and suddenly finds herself captivated by the beautiful, rugged landscape as well as the attention from not one, but two men.

Malcolm 'Boots' Dunn is a young man who is on top of the world. He has re-opened Cooper's Mine – a gold mine that has been closed up for more than twenty years. Fun-loving and easy-going, pretty Abby Prescott catches his eye and he knows that she is the one for him.

Simon Archer is a solemn, hard-working man who spends his days apprenticing as a blacksmith and his nights dreaming for a woman to share his life with. When he meets Abby, he knows that she is the woman of his dreams and he will stop at nothing to have her.

As both men vie for Abby's affections, she innocently encourages their advances with disastrous consequences. When the dust settles, which one will win Abby's heart?

A Chance on Love

Dr. Ben Kincaid is content to spend his days and nights treating the people of Hidden Springs. Not even his closest friends know the heartbreak that haunts him. Ten years earlier his wife left him, taking their only child with her. Ben vowed to never again trust anyone with his heart. Shiloh Bishop came to Hidden Springs looking for a fresh start. Having been forced into an arranged marriage with an older man, she's lived a life of misery. When she finds herself suddenly widowed and expecting her first child, she looks forward to starting a new life. Ben is captivated by Shiloh the first moment he sees her but he is unwilling to let go of the chains of mistrust that are wrapped around his heart. Shiloh is determined to rebuild her life and has no intention of ever becoming another man's wife. When a deadly illness strikes the town, they have no choice but to rely on each other. Admiration and respect soon turn to passion, but will it be enough for them to take a chance on love?

Sandra Love

Broken

Cordelia Rose has a horrible life. She gets bullied by students at school, beaten by her father, practically abandoned by her mother, and wants to end her life and the suffering. But when some strange things start to happen, she questions whether or not she has a purpose in this life. Then she meets a brother and sister that mean more to her than she even realizes. They are her protectors, and her kindred spirits. Just like her, they are bruised and broken, though for different reasons. When she finally discovers the truth of her existence, her mind is jumbled with everything she has to take in; not to mention the battle she has to fight, inside and out.

Broken Hearts: Kaleigh's Revenge

Kaleigh had her heart broken. And now she wants revenge. But that's hard amongst the battle raging around her in her home city of Ithaca. Add to that the fact that she's a fallen angel with a curse, and you've pretty much got the worst time of her life... But her new friend, Gabe, may just make it the best time, too.

A.d. Ellis

For Nicky, A Torey Hope Novel Book 1

Elizabeth Decker views herself as shy, totally average, and pretty much insignificant. She's nothing special, at least not compared to her little sister, Audrey. Elizabeth is content with her plain and lonely future; she's too insecure to contemplate a relationship thanks to her sister. Audrey is a bombshell and uses this to get what she wants. She's a girl who will stop at nothing to control anyone and everything around her. She craves power and doesn't care if she has to hurt Elizabeth to get it.

Nathaniel Morgan has spent his whole life fighting for his twin brother, Nicholas. Somewhere along the way, he lost himself. Now he's just getting by. He's devoted to his family, but emotionally detached from the women he burns through like wildfire. He has no plans of getting into something as complicated and committed as a "relationship".

Nicholas Morgan has placed the new librarian, Miss Elizabeth, on a pedestal and is begging her to meet his twin brother, Nathaniel. Elizabeth and Nathaniel agree to meet, for Nicky. Both are caught off-guard when unexpected sparks fly between them. This was not in their plans. Will Nathaniel and Elizabeth be able to escape a past that still plagues them? Or, will the past, suspicions, and insecurities come between them one too many times?

**This is a contemporary new adult romance. It should only be read by ages 18+ due to adult themes and situations. This book is a stand-alone but should be read before book 2 in the series.

Because of Beckett, A Torey Hope Novel Book 2

You met Audrey Decker through Nate and Libby's story in *For Nicky, A Torey Hope Novel Book 1*. This is Audrey's story. It is highly suggested that you read *For Nicky* before reading *Because of Beckett* so that you can be emotionally vested in Audrey's story.

Audrey Decker is a mean girl, a bitch, a bully. She has no plans to stop treating people badly and she's definitely not going to stop using sex as power. But when she ends up in therapy against her wishes, an ugly and painful repressed past is uncovered and Audrey's world is tipped on its axis. Everything she thought she knew, everything she thought she was, is all changing.

Jeremiah Jordan returns from serving two years

overseas with a detached and hardened heart. When his world is rocked with unexpected news and difficult challenges, Jeremiah faces them head on. He's comfortable with where he is right now; he has his parents close by and his son is his world. He definitely doesn't have time for the hassle that has always accompanied dating in the past. He doesn't have it in him to put effort into forming relationships that may just hurt him or his son again.

A chance encounter, second chances, and a little boy who believes in learning from mistakes is all it takes to bring Audrey and Jeremiah together. However, deserving a second chance and taking that second chance are two very different things. Learning from mistakes and letting go of the past may be easier said than done. Can Audrey and Jeremiah push through the pasts that are haunting both of them or will their romance wither and die under the weight of it all?

Because of Beckett *is a story of love, forgiveness, and second chances.*

***Because of Beckett* is recommended only for ages 18+ due to harsh language, adult situations, and mature themes. Certain pivotal points of Audrey's history may trigger unpleasant memories for some readers.**

Andrea Long

The Alphabet Game (Part One A-E)

Stella Mulroney is playing a game. It's taken her two years but she finally has an interview at Gregory & Sons, the top London law firm that looks after her stepfather's interests. She plans to discover what her Multi-millionaire Stepdaddy really invests in and bring him down.

Unwittingly, she's caught the attention of Gabriel 'Gabe' Gregory, son of her Stepfather's top Lawyer. He wants to know why Stella has such a need for revenge and would prefer her to channel that fury into a game of his own, 'The Alphabet Game'. After all, his is much more fun to play ...

The Alphabet Game (Part Two F–K)

Stella Mulroney had been getting an education, with Lawyer Gabe Gregory teaching her The Alphabet Game, a sexual exploration from A through to Z, so she could infiltrate the sex clubs owned by her stepfather. After the restaurant debacle, Stella now has more to learn. Can Gabe be trusted, or is her stepfather no longer the enemy? Stella hires a Private Investigator to help her track down her stepsister Isabel, who might hold some of the answers. Or then again, maybe Isabel has secrets of her own ...

The Alphabet Game (Part Three L–R)

As Stella starts work at The Rodeo, the New York sex club owned by her stepfather and Gabe's dad; Gabe himself reels from the secret his mother kept from him for years. The Alphabet Game continues, but is it still about the sex or are deeper feelings emerging? Stella finally uncovers a lead in her quest for revenge. However

Arnie Gregory isn't so keen for his secrets to be revealed and Stella is about to find out what happens when he's crossed ...

The Alphabet Game (Part Four S-X, Y, Z)

It's the end of the games. The sexual alphabet is coming to a close and Stella has a test to take. Arnie Gregory has been pushed too far and the revenge plan becomes a fight for survival that not everyone around Stella can win. Her stepfather, Mitch Daniels shows his true colours and there's someone else who hasn't been totally honest about who they are. With fame for some and infamy for others, The Alphabet Game ends with a kiss ...